Black eyes set in a long, foxlike face stared feverishly up at her. The creature bared its sharp yellow teeth in a grin that quickly turned into a wince of pain.

"You're a human."

"So?" said Emily. *You're talking to a faerie,* she thought.

"So this is the part where your kind usually screams and runs away," said the creature.

A faerie. A creature from the storybooks.

"I don't scream," said Emily distantly.

A creature that doesn't exist.

"How brave of you."

ALSO BY PAUL CRILLEY

The Invisible Order, Book Two: The Fire King

OTHER EGMONT USA BOOKS
YOU MAY ENJOY

Candle Man, Book One:
The Society of Unrelenting Vigilance
by Glenn Dakin

Candle Man, Book Two:
The Society of Dread
by Glenn Dakin

The Dragons of Noor
by Janet Lee Carey

Stealing Death
by Janet Lee Carey

Violet Wings
by Victoria Hanley

THE INVISIBLE ORDER

BOOK ONE

RISE OF THE DARKLINGS

PAUL CRILLEY

EGMONT
USA   NEW YORK

EGMONT

We bring stories to life

First published by Egmont USA, 2010
This paperback edition published by Egmont USA, 2011
443 Park Avenue South, Suite 806
New York, NY 10016

1 3 5 7 9 8 6 4 2

www.egmontusa.com
www.paulcrilley.com

THE LIBRARY OF CONGRESS HAS CATALOGED
THE HARDCOVER EDITION AS FOLLOWS:
Crilley, Paul.
Rise of the Darklings / Paul Crilley
p. cm. — (The Invisible Order ; bk. 1)
Summary: After saving a piskie's life, twelve-year-old Emily Snow
finds herself in the middle of a centuries-old war between rival fairy
factions and a secret society named The Invisible Order.
ISBN 978-1-60684-031-3 (hardcover) — ISBN 978-1-60684-238-6 (eBook)
[1. Secret societies—Fiction. 2. Fairies—Fiction.
3. London (England)—History—1800–1950—Fiction. 4. Great Britain—
History—Victoria, 1837–1901—Fiction. 5. Fantasy.] I. Title.
PZ7.C869276Ri 2010
[Fic]—dc22   2009025150

Paperback ISBN 978-1-60684-225-6

This novel is based on the short story "The Invisible Order," which originally
appeared in the anthology *Under Cover of Darkness*, published by DAW, 2007.

Printed in the United States of America

CPSIA tracking label information:
Printed in July 2011 at Berryville Graphics, Berryville, Virginia

For my family,
Caroline, Bella, and Caeleb.

It is not children only that one feeds with fairy tales.
—Ephraim Gotthold Lessing (1729–1781)

⊁ ⊰

Some day you will be old enough
to start reading fairy tales again.
—C. S. Lewis (1898–1963)

Contents

⊷ CHAPTER ONE ⊷

*In which Emily sees something she thought belonged in stories
and runs afoul of the villainous Mr. Ravenhill.*

FIVE O'CLOCK IN THE MORNING
ON THE FIRST DAY OF EMILY'S ADVENTURES.

O n the day she found out about the hidden war being fought in the dreary streets of London, Emily woke up praying for snow.

She knew it was selfish, but if it snowed she wouldn't have to work. She wouldn't have to trek to Farringdon in the freezing darkness and buy her penny's worth of watercress. Instead, she could simply crawl back into bed with her younger brother and sleep till sunup.

Emily lay shivering beneath the sheets, staring up at the shadowy black water stains on the ceiling and listening to William's steady breathing.

Please be snowing, she thought, closing her eyes tightly.

She repeated these words to herself a few more times,

then slipped out of bed and pushed aside the torn net curtain that covered the window. She wiped away the mist from her breath and stared out onto the street.

Frost winked and glittered in the moonlight, a thin layer of gleaming white that reminded her of the powdered icing on Mr. Warren's cakes. Disappointment welled up inside her, a heavy weight in her stomach. There was no snow.

She sighed and lifted her coat from the old rocking chair, pulling it around her shoulders as she stepped over the prone bodies of the new tenants. Emily didn't know who they were. She just knew they paid their money to Mrs. Hobbs yesterday, and the landlady had told them to sleep on the floor in the room she shared with William. That was the way of it in Cheapside. Her ma once said they were actually the lucky ones. Some landladies put fifteen people into a room. Emily had heard that when they did this, people sometimes died in their sleep. They sealed the windows to keep warm and breathed one another's air until there was nothing left to go around.

For days after she heard this, she used to wake up and listen to make sure William was still breathing.

Thinking of her brother made Emily glance at the bed. William was awake, watching her as she got ready.

"Why aren't you asleep?" she whispered.

"Had a dream," he mumbled.

Emily sat down on the edge of the thin mattress. She smoothed the blankets around his thin form, making sure there were no gaps. "A bad one?"

He shrugged beneath the covers. "I dreamt that Ma and Da were back. Ma was making us breakfast, and you and Da were reading stories like you used to. But then they started to fade away. They were shouting for help, but we didn't do anything."

Emily sighed. Their da had disappeared three years ago now. A year or so after that, their ma vanished as well. William had been having bad dreams ever since. Sometimes they weren't too bad, like this one, but other times they were truly frightening, causing him to wake up in the night, screaming in terror and bathed in sweat.

They'd never found out what had happened to their parents. Their da had been away on business when he went missing. The landlady at the lodging house where he'd been staying said he'd gone to bed and locked his door, and the next morning there was simply no sign of him. His door was still locked from the inside. It was as if he'd simply . . . vanished. Ma went to the police. They looked into the disappearance but gave up after a few days when they couldn't find any clues. They said this kind of thing happened all the time. People vanished.

Then the same thing happened with their ma. She just

disappeared. Didn't come home from the shops one day. This time Emily hadn't gone to the police. If they'd found out she and William were alone, they would have separated them and sent them to the workhouse.

Emily stroked his hair. "Doesn't sound too bad," she said. "You've had worse."

William mumbled in agreement and snuggled down under the blankets again. He closed his eyes, ready to go back to sleep.

"Hoy," whispered Emily. William opened his eyes a crack. "Don't get too comfy. You're to speak to Mrs. Derry about work in the shop, remember?"

William nodded sleepily. "I'll remember," he said with an enormous yawn.

Emily stood up. She took a last look around to make sure she hadn't forgotten anything, then left their small room and stepped into the dark corridor of the tenement building in which they lived. She pulled open the front door and felt the sharp bite of the cold against her cheeks, the last remnants of sleep leaving her as she breathed in the frigid air.

She stepped onto the deserted street, wondering if this was what all twelve-year-old girls had to go through every day of their lives.

Emily wanted to get to the market early that morning. Mrs. Eldridge had promised an extra bunch of watercress to whichever girl got there first and helped lay out her wares. An extra bunch wasn't much, but it meant a sweet pudding for William if she managed to sell it.

Emily walked briskly along the narrow streets of Cheapside, her hands thrust deep into her coat in a futile attempt to keep warm. She ducked through a tenement and onto a road that took her into Church Lane. Laundry lines crisscrossed high above between the buildings. Someone had left a sheet out overnight; it had frozen solid and hung heavy on the line, weighing it down so that the rope looked about ready to snap.

A broken railing between two buildings gave Emily access to the labyrinth of backstreets that wove around and behind the main thoroughfares of London. The dingy pathways were thin and suffocating, the buildings leaning in on her. Emily had been warned not to travel through the alleys, but she always did. If she had to choose between a scolding and walking extra miles in the freezing cold, it wasn't a choice at all.

Emily was halfway to the market when she heard the noise up ahead. She came to an abrupt stop, almost slipping on the icy cobblestones.

She waited. There it was again: a scuffling sound coming from around the corner. And . . . something else. She frowned. It sounded like pieces of metal clacking together.

Emily looked around, wondering what to do. She could head back onto the main streets, but that would add another half hour to her journey, time she couldn't afford to lose. Victoria Ashdown had said she planned on getting to Mrs. Eldridge before Emily did, and Emily couldn't let that happen. Victoria thought she knew everything just because she was fourteen. There was no way Emily was letting Victoria get that extra bunch of cress.

She crept forward until she stood near the mouth of the adjoining alleyway, leaning against the exposed redbrick of a grocery shop. She listened for a moment but still couldn't place the sounds. *Only one way to find out*, she thought, slowly peering around the corner.

She had expected something simple. Maybe some tramps fighting over some food. Or some cutpurses divvying up their ill-gotten gain after a night of thieving.

But what she saw made her freeze with shock, her eyes going wide with amazement as she tried to take in the scene before her.

An almost silent battle was being fought in the shadows of the lane. But there was nothing ordinary about the battle being fought before her.

Because not one of the participants stood any higher than Emily's knee.

About half of the fighters wore dark furs and old, tatty leathers. Their bodies were covered in black spiral tattoos, clustered so thickly that it was difficult to see the skin underneath, causing the creatures' yellow eyes and sharp teeth to stand out in contrast. Those they were fighting wore more natural-colored attire—brown leathers and earth-colored clothes. They also had spirals on their skin, but nowhere near as many as their enemies. Their markings had been applied in a pale blue ink, making them harder to see.

Dark blood covered the fighters as they battled in the tight confines of the alley, the only sound the frantic scraping and scuffling of feet on the wet cobblestones and the fierce clattering of bronze swords and daggers.

As Emily watched, one of the injured creatures broke away. An arrow caught him in the back and he collapsed, twitching, not five feet from where she stood. He lay there for a second, then melted into the cobbles, his skin liquefying into a bloody puddle that gave off the stench of bad meat.

Emily stood transfixed, her heart thudding fearfully in her chest. She should run away. She knew that. What if they saw her? But she couldn't seem to get her legs to work.

Suddenly, a piercing whistle shrilled in the distance. Emily jumped, clamping a hand over her mouth. That sounded like a crusher's whistle. Were the police coming to investigate? A moment later the first whistle was joined by another, this one farther away but growing steadily closer.

The fighting in the alley stopped abruptly, as if the whistles were some kind of prearranged signal. The creatures froze in place and cocked their heads, listening as they drew in ragged breaths. Then the creatures sheathed their weapons and stepped away from one another. The black-painted ones closed their eyes and faded into the shadows. Emily strained to catch a glimpse of them, but it was as if they had simply disappeared. The others slipped between gaps in the walls or into the gutters. Emily saw a few of them climbing the dirty facade of the building that faced the alley, pulling themselves up onto the roof and vanishing from sight.

In five seconds the creatures were gone. Emily stepped reluctantly into the lane and waited a moment to make sure nothing was about to jump out of the shadows. The buildings seemed to stretch higher here. The sky was a thin slit of black pinpointed with brittle stars.

What had she just witnessed? Were they *goblins*? Gnomes? Faeries? They couldn't be, surely? Those kinds of things didn't exist. They belonged in storybooks, like the ones her da used to read to her. Not out here in the real world.

But what else could they be? She certainly hadn't imagined seeing them. Emily hurried through the alley, wanting to be as far away as possible before the owners of the whistles arrived. The passage turned sharply left here, and Emily could see a faint orange glow coming from where the alley fed back into the streets. She ran toward the light.

She didn't get far. A silhouette rose slowly out of the shadows that pooled at the bottom of a wall. Emily staggered to a halt. She couldn't move, could only watch in numb horror as the shape revealed itself to be that of a tall, thin man, his spindly arms and legs unfolding like the limbs of a spider. Emily looked over her shoulder, thinking she could run back the way she had come, but there was another shape approaching, this one round and fat. He had a whistle in his mouth, which shrilled with every puffing breath he took. There was nowhere for her to go.

The man in front of Emily walked toward her, brushing his hands together, as if to dislodge any loose dirt he might have picked up. He was so tall and thin, his clothes so tightly fitting, that the impression she got was that of a skeleton in a velvet suit. His elbows stuck out to either side, and she could see the low orange glow of the dawn through the triangular gaps.

She stared up at the man. The early-morning sky framed the dark silhouette of his head and top hat. She couldn't see much of his actual features, just the tiny pinprick of light glinting in his black eyes.

He stopped in front of her and sighed, expelling a cloud of white breath into the cold air, and lifted the hat from his head. He lowered it against his stomach, then drummed his long fingers on the top.

Barump.

Barump.

Barump.

Emily swallowed. She wanted to say something, anything, to break the spell, but the muffled noise of his fingers seemed to drown out her thoughts.

"And what, pray tell, do we have here?" asked the man.

He bent forward to get a better look at her face, his features slowly revealing themselves as he did so. His jutting nose arrived first, cutting through the shadow like a ship's prow through black water. It was long and straight, the nostrils flared, as if he was trying to catch the scent of prey.

"What is your name, girl?"

Emily resisted the urge to step back. She forced herself to find her voice. "Emily. Emily Snow."

He stared at her for another second before responding. "Well, Miss Snow. What are you doing out so early in the morning? Hasn't your mother ever told you the streets are a dangerous place for children?"

"I'm not a child," snapped Emily. "I'm twelve."

"Is that so?" The thin man straightened. "You hear that, Mr. Blackmore? She's *twelve*."

The fat man took the whistle out of his mouth. "I heard her, sir."

The thin man turned his attention back to Emily. "Forgive me," he said. "Where are my manners?" He took a step back and bent over in a sweeping bow, the hand holding the hat brushing the wet cobblestones. "My name is Mr. Ravenhill," he said, straightening up. He frowned, brushing a smudge of dirt off his hat. "Now, why don't you tell me what you are doing here? And please don't lie. I have a nose for untruths."

As if to underline these words, he sniffed, then exhaled. Emily could smell aniseed and tobacco on his breath.

"I . . . I was on my way to Farringdon, if it please you, sir," said Emily. She'd always found it best to pretend subservience to adults.

"What for?"

"To buy a penny's worth of cress. I sell it every day, to get food for my family."

"Is that so?"

"Yessir. I took the shortcut, because Victoria Ashdown said she was going to get there first and take the best of the bunches." She trailed off and looked at the ground, waiting for the man to respond. She heard the fat one shift impatiently behind her, huffing with the slight exertion.

"What do you think, Mr. Blackmore? Is she telling the truth?"

Mr. Blackmore sucked in a huge gulp of air. "I reckon so, Mr. R. She's just a child. No sense in her to lie."

"Which just goes to show how much you know about children, Mr. Blackmore." Mr. Ravenhill tapped his hat again, then reached a decision. "But in this case, I think you are correct in your assumptions. You may go, child."

"Thank you, sir. Thank you very much." Emily stepped to the side and got ready to run. An outstretched hand stopped her. She looked up into Mr. Ravenhill's eyes.

"Where do you live?"

"Cheapside, sir. Blackfriars Road." As soon as she said the words, Emily cursed herself. Why had she said that? You don't tell anyone where you live! It was one of the first rules that Jack had taught her.

"Best not come this way again, girl. These alleys are dangerous. No telling what might happen to someone like yourself. Understand?"

She did, more than he knew. But she simply nodded. "Yes, sir."

"Be off, then."

Emily did not wait for a second invitation. She ran as fast

as her legs would carry her. At one point she heard a noise off to her right, and for a panic-stricken second she thought they had changed their minds and were coming after her. But nothing happened, and she skidded around the corner into the warm light of a gas lamp.

She stopped and crept back along the wall. She peered into the alley and saw the two men poking through the mildewed crates and heaps of rubbish, searching for something. Did that mean they knew about the creatures? Were they hunting for them?

Emily shuddered. She wasn't sure she wanted to know.

⊱ CHAPTER TWO ⊰

*In which Spring-Heeled Jack offers to help Emily
navigate the crowds at Farringdon Market. A surprise
in the shadows leads to revelations about the fey.*

SIX O'CLOCK IN THE MORNING
ON THE FIRST DAY OF EMILY'S ADVENTURES.

By the time Emily crossed Stonecutter Street and approached the iron gates of Farringdon Market, the area was already a bustling hive of activity. She knew she would be too late to get the extra watercress.

But it didn't bother her as much as it should have. She was finding it hard to concentrate on her surroundings. After what she had seen in the alleyway, everything else had taken on a taint of unreality. Emily felt as if she were trapped in a dream, that any moment now she would wake up in her bed and realize that none of this was real.

Oh, a part of her knew it was real. The part that enjoyed bedtime stories—*that* part knew. But the part of Emily that had to deal with everyday life, with finding food for herself and William, refused to accept it. It was dangerous to allow yourself such flights of fancy. Once you accepted things like that, you started to believe in princes coming to rescue you from your dreary life, in magical creatures that could fix all your problems.

Emily didn't believe in such things. She *couldn't*.

She paused for a moment and let the hustle and bustle of the market drive the events to the back of her mind. She could think about them later, when she had the time. Right now she had to focus on the real world. She took a deep breath and looked around with fresh eyes, letting the familiar, everyday surroundings drive the unreal events from her thoughts.

Emily had always loved the markets. To her they were the true heart of London, the places where the city lived and breathed.

Buyers and sellers shouted to be heard over one another, calling out to friends and acquaintances, haggling over the price of goods. Everyone—buyers, sellers, families, friends—shouted over the background din in an attempt to be heard by people no more than a foot away. To a stranger, the noises could be overwhelming, but Emily found them comforting.

The wide iron gates of the market stood open. The usual

loiterers were clustered outside, begging for a ha'penny or just waiting for something to fall from one of the many baskets and food carts coming and going through the gates.

Jack Doyle was one of them. Or Spring-Heeled Jack, as he liked to be called, named after the bogeyman who could jump through people's windows and then disappear into the night. He and a few of his friends were clustered around a potato seller, holding their hands out to the tiny firepot suspended beneath the large potato can in an attempt to ward off the morning cold.

Emily hoped he didn't see her. Jack was a year older than Emily, and while they were friends, she wasn't talking to him at the moment. She had recently found out he'd taken up with Jasper Three-Fingers, a notorious thief in the area. She'd always known Jack was a bit of a scoundrel, but now he was turning it into a real career. She'd warned him he'd end up being arrested and shipped to Australia, but he'd just laughed and said they'd have to catch him first.

She tried to use the crowd for cover as she crossed the street, but he spotted her and trotted over.

"Mornin', Snow," he said, touching his hand to the dirty hat he always wore.

"Don't call me that. You know I don't like it."

Jack bowed low. "Apologies, I'm sure. Mornin', *Miss* Snow."

"Leave me be, Jack. I'm late as it is."

Jack look pained. "Are you still not talking to me?"

"You know I'm not. I'm surprised the crushers haven't caught you and Three-Fingers by now."

"No chance. Spring-Heeled Jack is too fast for them." Jack nodded at the crowds gathered inside the market courtyard. "Want me to clear a way through? It'll be no bother."

"I'm fine, thank you."

"You sure? Looks plenty busy to me."

Emily eyed the bustling crowd doubtfully. She could hear the cries of the women selling the cresses, but she couldn't catch a glimpse of them through the mass of people. It didn't matter. There was no way she would get that extra bunch now. All she could hope for was to get her penny's worth.

"No, I'll get by."

Jack grinned. "Suit yourself." Then he darted forward and kissed her on the cheek. Emily spun around, outraged, but all she could see of Jack was his dirty wool jacket as he darted through the crowd. She wiped her cheek, glancing about quickly to make sure no one had seen.

No one was looking, so Emily took the opportunity to reach inside her coat, searching through the hidden pockets for the penny she would use to buy the watercress.

She frowned, her fingers searching more and more

frantically. Then she yanked the coat off and turned it inside out, her stomach sinking with dread.

The penny was gone.

But where—

She froze. The alley. She'd thought she'd heard a noise as she ran from Ravenhill. It must have been her penny falling from her pocket.

Emily pulled her coat back on and ran through the crowds, praying with all her being that the penny was still there. She needed that money. Without it, she and William wouldn't eat tonight.

⊢⧟ ⧟⊣

When Emily arrived back at the alley, the first hint of daylight was seeping into the sky above London, dimly outlining the edges of buildings against the gray.

Emily stopped at the mouth of the alley and peered into the shadows. There was no sign of Ravenhill and his fat friend, no sign of the creatures, so she walked slowly back along the lane, searching for the telltale glint of metal.

She couldn't see the penny anywhere. It was gone.

What was she going to do now? If she couldn't sell the watercress, she couldn't get money for food. If they didn't eat . . .

"You. Girl," said a voice.

Emily whirled around, her heart racing. The alley was deserted. She quickly turned again, half expecting to see Mr. Ravenhill stalking toward her.

Nothing.

She peered into the shadows, shadows that looked thick and threatening, capable of hiding any number of enemies.

"Over here," said the voice, clearly irritated.

Emily took a hesitant step back.

"I know you're just a stupid girl, but you're meant to walk *toward* my voice, not away from it."

Emily straightened her back. "I am *not* stupid. I've had schooling."

"Good—" The voice broke off, taken over by a fit of coughing. "Good for you. Now, why don't you prove it and actually do something *intelligent?*"

Emily narrowed her eyes and looked around. Another half hour and she'd be able to see into every corner of the alley, but right now . . .

"Where are you?"

"To your right. By the apple crates."

Emily saw the crates, three of them piled one atop the other. But there was no one there. "I can't see—"

"Just walk forward."

Emily bit down a desire to tell the voice to go and swim

with Jenny Greenteeth and slowly walked forward. The apple crates were black with damp and mildew. She leaned forward and stared behind them.

There was no one there. Where had the voice come from?

She heard a scraping noise from the bottom crate. Emily looked down and saw something emerge from between the wooden slats. It was thin and sticklike, about three times the length of her index finger.

Emily took a frightened step back. It was an arm, dangling over the side of the thin wood.

"If you leave me here, I'm dead," said a small voice from inside the crate.

Emily stopped in her tracks. *Think about this logically,* she told herself. That was what her old teacher used to say. Something was talking to her: fact. She was currently looking at a very small arm dangling from the apple crate: another fact.

Which meant that what she had witnessed that morning was real and not something she could pretend hadn't happened.

"Are you still there?" said the voice.

"I'm here," she said.

The arm lifted and waved weakly. "Then get me out of here. Before they come back."

"Before *who* comes back?"

"Take your pick. The Black Sidhe or the two men from the Order. Both of them want me dead."

The two men from the Order? Did he mean Ravenhill and Blackmore?

Emily stepped forward and lifted the two top crates from the pile. She placed them to the side, then peered into the bottom crate.

One of the small creatures she had seen earlier stared back at her. It lay propped up in the corner of the crate, one hand holding its thigh where an arrow had pierced its leg. The creature was stick thin. Its walnut-brown skin was covered in the strange blue whorls and patterns she had noted earlier.

Black eyes set in a long, foxlike face stared feverishly up at her. The creature bared its sharp yellow teeth in a grin that quickly turned into a wince of pain.

"You're a human."

"So?" said Emily. *You're talking to a faerie,* she thought.

"So this is the part where your kind usually screams and runs away," said the creature.

A faerie. A creature from the storybooks.

"I don't scream," said Emily distantly.

A creature that doesn't exist.

"How brave of you."

Emily frowned. She could tell when she was being talked down to. "You're injured," she said.

"How observant. And all this time I thought humans were stupid."

"And you obviously need my help, so if I were you, I'd think about being a bit more polite. Are you a faerie?"

"Bones, girl, do I *look* like a faerie?"

"I don't know. I've never seen one before."

The creature thought for a moment. "Fair point. No, I am not a faerie. Faeries are stupid creatures with wings. Faeries are a waste of space. I am a piskie—from Cornwall. My name is Corrigan."

Emily let this sink into her mind.

Not a faerie, she told herself. *A piskie. You're talking to a piskie.*

But she couldn't be. Piskies weren't real, either. Had she fallen and bumped her head? Maybe she was still lying in bed and none of this had really happened.

The piskie struggled to pull himself up, but his injured leg wouldn't support him. He collapsed onto his knees and looked at Emily accusingly.

"Are you just going to stand there and watch? I'm in pain here."

"Who did this to you?"

"I already told you. The Black Sidhe. They're an Unseelie tribe of Tylwyth Teg piskies from Wales. They—"

Corrigan stopped talking.

"Well?" she asked impatiently. "'*They*' what?"

"They're right behind you," he whispered, staring over her shoulder.

Emily spun around but she saw no one. She was just about to turn back and scold the creature, when she heard a noise, the scuff of something against brick. She froze and looked slowly upward.

The piskies Corrigan had been fighting lined the roof of the building that formed the alley wall. At least, Emily assumed they were piskies. They were the same size as Corrigan, but their features were hard to make out because of the denseness of the black ink covering their skin.

Corrigan said something, too low for Emily to hear. She half turned to face him, keeping her eyes trained on the rooftop. "What?" she said softly.

"I said don't move," whispered the piskie.

Too late. Something stung Emily's hand. She gave a stifled yelp and looked down. There, stuck in the soft skin between her thumb and forefinger, was one of the same arrows that was stuck in Corrigan's leg.

She pulled on it, but it wouldn't budge. She frowned and pulled harder. The skin puckered and stretched but the arrow stayed firmly lodged in her skin. Not only that, but she also imagined she felt it pulling back, as if it were somehow resisting her efforts. Emily tried to get a better grip, but the arrow jerked and sank deeper into her flesh.

Emily's breath caught in her throat. She grabbed hold of the arrow again and looked up. The piskies were all staring at her. She set her mouth, tightened her fingers, and with one sharp tug, she yanked the arrow from her flesh.

This time she couldn't stop a cry of pain from escaping. The arrow tore her skin as it came free, bringing with it a bubble of dark blood.

She looked up again. The piskies were moving, raising tiny bows and arrows.

Emily didn't wait another second. She whirled around and swept Corrigan into her hand, hiding him beneath her coat. A small satchel fell from his shoulder as she did this. She caught it and stuffed it into one of her pockets, then turned and sprinted for the entrance to the alley.

She heard the piskies whistling to one another, obviously sending some kind of signal, but she didn't look back. She burst out of the lane and took the first turn she came to, then another, and another, picking random passages through tenement buildings and courtyards, darting down secluded pathways and mews in the hope that she would be able to lose the creatures. When she thought herself far enough away, she slowed down to get her bearings and headed out into the main streets, which were slowly starting to fill up with people.

Emily looked around, then slipped into the recessed

doorway of a sweetshop and carefully uncovered the piskie. He looked terrible. His limbs hung limp over her forearm, and for a horrible second she thought she had suffocated him. But then he groaned and swung his long face around.

"What is it?"

"The arrow. It was poisoned. You need to take me—"

Emily's heart leapt in her chest. "But I was hit as well! One of the arrows got me!"

"All the more reason to take me to Merrian. I'll give you directions." Corrigan winced and gently repositioned his leg. "He's a bit on the gruff side, but give him respect and everything will be fine."

"I'll not give him respect if he doesn't earn it," said Emily firmly.

"You will."

"Why?"

"Because he's half-giant and he could crush you with one smack of his hand."

⟞ Chapter Three ⟝

*In which Emily meets Merrian the half-giant and hears
revelations about a hidden London. Mr. Ravenhill returns.*

Seven thirty in the morning
on the first day of Emily's adventures.

*M*errian *may very well have been a half-giant,* thought
Emily, looking around the cramped bookshop, but he
certainly didn't know how to keep things clean. The front
window was so dirty she could barely see through it to the
street outside. Dust covered every available surface. Piles of
clutter and towers of books strained up toward the grimy
ceiling like flowers desperate for the sun. Emily squeezed
between these haphazard piles, afraid that the slightest touch
would bring them crashing down around her.

"Ring the bell," said Corrigan. He seemed a bit stronger
now that help was close by.

Emily saw a bell on the counter. It was the one thing in the
shop that looked as if it was routinely polished. The handle

was pale wood and featured delicate scrollwork carved carefully into the grain. The bell itself was white and shimmered with blue highlights.

Emily gently placed Corrigan on the counter and picked up the bell. The slight movement produced a clear, high tone. Emily quickly put it down.

"Now what?" she whispered.

"Now we wait."

No sooner had Corrigan uttered these words than the curtain at the back of the shop was torn aside and a huge man lumbered through, ducking his head to avoid banging it against the doorframe. He was bald, with a long braided mustache that trailed down to his chest. He glared at Emily.

"Who in the name of all the gods are you?" he shouted in a deep voice.

Emily stared up at the man in awe. She suddenly understood what Corrigan had meant about crushing her with one smack of his hand. "I'm Emily," she said. "Emily Snow."

"Well, Emily Emily Snow. What are you doin' in my shop?"

"I told her to come here, Merrian," said Corrigan.

Merrian looked down at the counter. His brows knitted in surprise. "Corrigan?" He stepped forward. "You're hurt! Was it her?" He glowered at Emily. "I'll kill her—"

"Relax, Merrian. It wasn't her. She saved me. It was the Unseelie."

Merrian looked alarmed. "The Unseelie? How—?" He stopped himself, glancing warily at Emily. "Who?"

"The Black Sidhe. They followed me in from Bath."

"Did they . . . D'you have it?"

Corrigan nodded.

"And the others?"

Corrigan shook his head sadly. "They didn't make it."

"The Queen won't be happy about that."

"I doubt she will. Merrian, could you . . . ?" Corrigan gestured to the arrow sticking from his leg.

Merrian bent over and examined the piskie's wound. He sniffed. "Nasty," he said. "Unicorn spit and . . ." He sniffed again. "Unicorn spit mixed with the dead flesh of a Sluagh."

Emily, who had been listening in a state of some confusion, looked up at the huge man. "Can you heal him?"

"Aye, I think so."

Emily held out her hand. "Can you heal me, as well? One of the arrows got me."

Merrian took hold of her hand. It looked like a doll's limb resting in his huge palm. He bent over and sniffed again. "Not too bad. You got it out quick enough. I'll give you a poultice, though."

Merrian opened a drawer and took out a tiny glass vial. He handed it to Corrigan. "Drink this while I look for the ingredients. It'll take away the pain." Then he moved off to the shelves and started taking down dusty jars, muttering to himself.

"Who are the Unseelie?" Emily asked.

"The Unseelie are those who call the Dagda their King," said Corrigan. "Our enemies. We've been fighting them since the last war."

"Who's *we*?"

"The Seelie. Those who follow the Queen."

"Oh." Emily watched Merrian's back as he bustled about the shelves. "Why are you fighting?"

Merrian glanced over his shoulder. "We never used to. Well, we *did*, but not on this scale. The Dagda and the Queen used to be allies, but they had a falling out. They split, and so did the fey. Those that followed the Dagda to Wales became known as the Unseelie. Those who stayed here to follow the Queen became the Seelie." Merrian sighed. "Used to be so much simpler. Us against humans. For thousands of years, that's how it was. Oh, don't get me wrong. There have been plenty of wars between the fey, but *mostly* it was us against you."

"Rubbish," scoffed Emily. "Why don't we know about it then?"

"Some do," said Corrigan. "This is good stuff, Merrian. Does the job." He turned back to Emily. "There have always been groups of humans who know about us. They form themselves into armies, secret societies. That Mr. Ravenhill you met? He's in one. The Invisible Order, they call themselves."

"And what do they do?"

Merrian lined up five jars on the counter. He opened them and took out bits of bark and leaves. "They try to kill us," he said bluntly, then stuffed the pieces into his mouth and started chewing.

"But . . . *why?*"

Corrigan shrugged. "It's the way it's always been. They don't think we belong here."

"So, you're telling me that faeries and unicorns and piskies and all kinds of strange creatures live here in London?"

"Not just London," said Corrigan. "All over. But yes. We're just good at hiding."

"Not that good. I found you."

"That . . . should never have happened," said Corrigan. "Our glamour was weakened. We were concentrating on the fight, you see. If you'd come into that alley a few seconds later, you probably wouldn't have seen us."

"But I can see you now."

"Only because I'm letting you," said Corrigan smugly.

Merrian spat the chewed brown mess into his hand. He scooped some up with a finger and held it out to Emily. "Here. Put this on the wound. It'll draw out what poison is left."

Emily grimaced and took the warm sludge. She pasted it over her wound.

"What were you doing in the alley, anyway?" asked Corrigan.

"Looking for my penny. I dropped it when Ravenhill grabbed me. I meant to use it to buy watercress." She sighed. What was she going to do now? Maybe William would get a ha'penny from Mrs. Derry if he did a good job.

"Here," said Merrian gruffly.

Emily looked up. Nestled inside Merrian's huge palm was a shiny shilling. "A reward. For saving Corrigan here."

Emily stared at the money. With that she would be able to buy proper food, and even have some left over for boiled plum puddings. *And* baked 'taters. Her mouth watered at the thought. She looked into Merrian's eyes, unsure.

"I can see ye're a proud girl. And there's nothin' wrong with that. But this isn't charity, right? It's reward for a job well done. You saved the life of Corrigan here. This is payment."

Emily reached out and took the coin. "Thank you," she said.

"Don't mention it. Now, I think ye should go. Get back to your little world and forget everything that happened today."

"How am I supposed to do that?" Emily asked in surprise.

Merrian shrugged. "I thought that was something you humans were good at." He bent down and gently prodded

Corrigan. The piskie had fallen asleep. Or passed out. Merrian grunted with satisfaction and put a small amount of the poultice on his leg.

"Will he be all right?"

Merrian glanced up, his huge brows drawn together. "Should be. I think you got him here in time."

Emily nodded. She lingered, unwilling to let the events of the morning slip away so readily. She took one last look before she left the shop, trying to freeze in her mind the image of a half-giant bending over a sleeping piskie, then stepped out into the watery gray morning.

Emily bought two baked 'taters and held them beneath her jacket so she could feel their warmth against her stomach. She usually spent most of the day walking the streets, trying to sell the watercress, but today she was free. For the first time in a very long time, she could simply relax, maybe even nap. The mere thought of this sent a shiver of anticipation through her. That's what she would do. She would eat her potato, then climb under the blankets and sleep away the morning. Later she could go out to find some supper.

She looked up at the gray sky as she turned the corner into Blackfriars Street. The clouds were low and heavy, looking fit to burst.

Emily entered her room and put the two potatoes on the chest of drawers in the corner. She was just about to unwrap hers when she heard a noise behind her. She turned quickly, but saw it was only William, still asleep in bed.

It took a moment for this to sink in, then she hurried over to the bed, suddenly fearful for her brother. He'd only just got over the flu, and she'd heard it could sometimes come back worse than before.

Emily carefully laid her hand against William's forehead. It was cool to the touch. No fever.

William stirred. His eyes fluttered open and he stared sleepily at Emily.

"Em?" He yawned and sat up.

"What are you doing?" Emily asked. "You're supposed to be at Mrs. Derry's shop."

William glanced at the small slice of gray sky visible through the net curtain. "Too cold," he mumbled.

"Too cold?" Emily couldn't believe her ears. Here she was, up every day before it was even light, and he was complaining about it being too cold?

She opened her mouth to shout at him, but then stopped herself. She and William had been arguing more and more often lately, ever since he'd turned nine and started spending all his time with the other boys from the street. She still saw him as her little brother, in need of her protection, and sometimes he was. But more often than not he was trying to find his own place in the world, and Emily was terrified there would come a time when he wouldn't need her anymore. She'd thought about asking Jack to have a word with him but had eventually decided against it. Jack wasn't exactly the kind of person Emily wanted giving advice to William.

"You know we need the money, William. I can't *do* this . . ." Emily trailed off, the words dying on her tongue. What was the point? She'd said it all before. She turned away from William and picked up his potato, dropping it onto the bed.

Emily sank into the old rocking chair, her back to her brother. She knew it wasn't fair. He was only nine years old. He shouldn't have to worry about money, about working. But it wasn't fair to her, either.

She could hear him moving around behind her, pulling on his clothes, by the sound of it. Then she felt a cold draft as he pulled the door open.

"It wasn't like this when Ma was around," he said.

Emily turned around. William was standing at the open door. "Where are you going?" she asked wearily.

"Exactly where you told me to go. To see Mrs. Derry." William stalked out of the room, slamming the door behind him and leaving Emily alone with her thoughts.

He was right, of course. It *hadn't* been like this when Ma was around. That day she didn't come home was the day Emily had become an adult, whether she liked it or not. That was the day she had to take responsibility for herself and William, who was only seven at the time.

It hadn't always been that way. They had been well off once. Her da ran a mill outside London. Emily had gone to school, had been quite an intelligent girl, according to her teachers. She had a gift for solving puzzles, they said.

But then came the day her da went away on business and didn't come back. Ma had to sell the house, and they'd moved to Cheapside to try and make a new life for themselves. Her schooling had been one of the first things to go.

Emily didn't like thinking about it. She had to accept the fact that her parents were gone and somehow carry on.

Her thoughts turned to the events of that morning, to faeries and piskies, hidden wars and half-giants. It was all so . . . *impossible*. And she'd been told to just forget about it. How on earth was she supposed to do that? Never again would she be able to simply walk down the street and think that everything was normal. She'd always be looking out for the signs. Every movement glimpsed from the corner of her eye would hold the possibility of a hidden world, separated from hers by a couple of streets and a hint of magic. Every strange noise that woke her in the middle of the night would make her think of secret battles fought along the rooftops of London.

How could she possibly forget all that?

Emily shifted slightly. As she did so, she felt something press against her side. She reached into her coat and pulled out the small satchel that Corrigan had been carrying. She had forgotten to give it back to him.

Curiosity overcame her and she opened it up. Inside was a piece of parchment, folded over and over to fit inside the small space. Unfolded, it was about the size of her hand and felt smooth, thick, more like fabric than paper.

But it was blank. Emily stared at the paper in disappointment. She turned it over, held it up to the light, even tilted it at an angle to see if the writing had perhaps faded, but in the end she had to admit that there was nothing there.

Why would Corrigan be carrying such a thing?

The room suddenly dimmed, as if a large cloud had passed across the sun. Except there was no sun today. Heavy gray clouds hung threateningly over the city. Emily looked out the window and almost cried out in shock.

The shape of a man was silhouetted against the light. The shape was tall and thin, and as she watched, it bent slowly forward until Emily could see the outline of a top hat.

Ravenhill.

How had he found her?

Then she remembered. She had told him what street she lived on. How could she have been so stupid?

He cupped his hands against the glass and tried to peer through the window, but the net curtain blocked his view. Emily looked around, wondering what to do. What did he want? She hadn't seen him since this morning in the alley. There was nothing to connect her to the fey, no reason he should think she was involved. He had said so himself.

Whatever his reasons, Emily realized she had to get away. She didn't want him in her home, didn't want him seeing her here. It would be too much of a trespass.

Emily quickly returned the satchel and paper to her pocket. Keeping her eyes on the shadow at the window, she stepped to the door and pulled it open.

Mr. Blackmore, Ravenhill's fat friend, stumbled into the room. He looked as if he had been eavesdropping at the door. Emily tried to dart past him, but he caught hold of her arm and pulled the door closed, so they were both standing in the hall outside.

"Not so fast, miss, beggin' yer pardon." He raised his voice. "Mr. R. In here."

Emily struggled to break free, but Blackmore had a very strong grip for someone who looked so soft and round. "Let me go," she snapped. "You've no right."

"Sorry, miss. Just doin' as I'm told."

The front door to the tenement opened and Mr. Ravenhill ducked into the corridor. He took off his hat and looked around with an air of distaste.

"Filthy place," he muttered. Then he turned to Emily. "Miss Snow. *So* good to see you again. Are you well?"

Emily craned her neck to see outside, making sure there was no sign of Will. He was long gone. That was something at least.

"Now," said Ravenhill. "After we . . . *bumped* into each other this morning, I did some thinking, didn't I, Mr. Blackmore?"

"You did, Mr. R. You said to me, 'Mr. Blackmore, I've been thinking about that little girl.'"

"Quite. And do you know what I was thinking?" he asked, staring directly into Emily's eyes.

Emily shook her head.

"I was thinking"—his hand shot out suddenly and gripped hold of Emily's chin, squeezing it painfully between his long fingers—"that Emily Snow is nothing but a filthy little liar."

Emily tried to pull her head away, but Ravenhill kept a tight grip on her chin.

"Do not fight, Miss Snow. It only angers me. Now. Let us start again, shall we? What were you doing in that alley? What did you see?"

He relaxed his grip on her chin so she could speak.

"I told you the truth. I was going to the market."

"Ye-es," said Ravenhill, stretching out the word. "And that was the truth. Insofar as the truth to the question I asked. You are very intelligent for one so young. I underestimated you. So I ask again. What did you see in that alley?"

"Nothing."

Ravenhill took a deep breath. "Smell that, Mr. Blackmore? It is the stench of untruth." He turned his attention back to Emily. "You saw them, didn't you?"

"Who?" Emily was getting more and more scared. Ravenhill knew that she knew. She had to get away.

"Do you want me to name them?" asked Ravenhill softly. "I'm disappointed in you, Miss Snow. You saw . . . *them.* The Little People. The Good Neighbors, the Lordly Ones, the Darkling Fey—whatever you want to call them. You saw them, didn't you?"

He leaned forward until his large nose was almost touching hers. "I can smell them on you," he whispered.

Emily struggled again. "I don't know what you're talking about."

"Oh, but you do, Miss Snow. Have they tricked you? Or are you involved of your own free will? Do you think them *delightful*? Like the stories in the books? Because they're not, Miss Snow. They are dangerous, evil creatures who would like nothing better than to destroy humankind. That is why we exist, you see. To make sure they do not succeed in their plans."

Ravenhill let go of her chin and stood up. "Now. I think you should come with us to somewhere a bit more . . . *pleasing* to the eye."

He reached out for Emily, and for a brief moment she thought he was reaching for the satchel. Before she could stop herself, her hand clamped over the pocket where she'd hidden it. Ravenhill smiled, and it was one of the scariest smiles Emily had ever seen. It split his face open like a wound.

"Miss Snow," he said, and Emily could hear the tremor in his voice, the barely suppressed excitement. "Are you . . . *concealing* something from us?"

"No."

"You are!" He clapped his hands together like an excited child. "Is it . . . Is it something *they* gave to you?"

Emily shook her head.

"Mr. Blackmore, today is a most glorious day. Hold her."

Before Emily could do anything, Blackmore grabbed hold of Emily's arms. Ravenhill leaned forward and reached into her coat. He withdrew the satchel, opened it, and pulled out the thick parchment.

"What is it?" he asked.

"It's nothing. Just some paper. I'm going to write a letter, that's all. Give it back."

"Oh, I don't think so, Miss Snow."

"Hoy," said a voice. "What are you doing? Let her go."

Emily almost fainted with relief. Jack stood in the doorway to the tenement, glaring at Blackmore. So fierce was his stare that the fat man actually released her arms and took a guilty step back.

Ravenhill, however, was not the least bit intimidated. He flicked a bored gaze over Jack, taking in his tattered wool coat and his dirty hat.

"Be gone, boy. Miss Snow and I were just having a little chat. I'm from Scotland Yard."

"You're a policeman? A bobby?"

"Indeed I am."

"Then I'm Queen Vic's butler," said Jack, pulling out a knife. The blade was dull and rusted, but it had a point, and that was all that mattered. "You just let her go, you hear? Otherwise this could get unpleasant."

Ravenhill's eyes widened slightly. Then he started to laugh, a low, unpleasant chuckle. After a moment's hesitation, Blackmore joined in, although he kept a nervous watch on the blade in Jack's hand.

Jack's face tightened with anger. Before he could do anything that would land him in trouble, Emily made her move. She barged past Ravenhill, grabbing the satchel and parchment from his hands. She dodged a clumsy attempt by Mr.

Blackmore to catch her and pushed Jack out the door of the tenement.

"Run!" she shouted into his surprised face.

Then she took her own advice and sprinted out into the streets of London.

┅═ CHAPTER FOUR ═┅

The wrath of the Dagda. Black Annis and Jenny Greenteeth
awake from their watery slumber.

INTERLUDE.

Ｈis name was Scaithe, and he was an Unseelie piskie, a member of the Black Sidhe. He was wounded, a gash that ran from the front of his shoulder all the way around his back and down his spine. He held the hawk's feathers with one hand, the other dangling uselessly by his side.

Scaithe crouched low against the bird, dodging the wind that threatened to unseat him. The clouds whipped past like streamers of mist, leaving droplets of moisture on his black clothing. The hawk flew as fast as she could. She understood the urgency of his message.

The Dagda, his King, wasn't going to be happy. When the Dagda had first discovered the parchment was missing, he had flown into a fury so terrifying that his anger had drawn a storm to their mountain. Once it had passed, trailing a path of destruction across the lowlands of Wales, he had the Black Sidhe after the thieves. They were expected to bring back what was stolen or not return at all.

Scaithe felt a twinge of fear. Surely the Dagda would understand? He didn't have the parchment, but that was hardly his fault. He was bearing important intelligence, after all. The Cornish filth had help. Help from a human. How could they have anticipated that?

The hawk screeched a warning and banked sharply. They dropped through the air, leaving the concealment of the clouds. The border mountains appeared below them, their snow-covered peaks blinding Scaithe as the sun flashed between the clouds. Scaithe squinted and leaned forward, whispering directions to the hawk. The bird dropped until they were skimming over the white-and-gray clifftops.

Yellow-green scrub grass poked out from between the ragged stones, pushing up through clumps of snow and ice. His people were like that grass, Scaithe thought. Holding on for dear life, barely surviving in a hostile environment. How long before the faeries were all wiped out, shoved into the corners of the world to await their deaths?

He sighed. The battle had made him melancholy. That always happened, even when they won.

As they flew deeper into the mountains, into the treacherous, mist-shrouded areas impassable to humans, Scaithe felt a small surge of relief. He was safe now. Scaithe hated the city. It was dirty and suffocating. He needed the clear air of the mountains to survive.

The mist thickened into a fog, but the hawk knew where she was now. She flew confidently, as if something was calling to her, guiding her through the wall of gray.

Scaithe eventually fell into an exhausted doze. He was awoken some time later by the bird's shrill call. He yawned and leaned over to see where they were.

The mist had disappeared. They were approaching a deep basin, a huge space that looked as if it had been scooped out of the mountains by a giant hand. The basin was leagues across, encircled by towering cliff faces, and covering the bottom were sweeping grass fields and deep, ancient forests, all coated in a thick layer of fresh white snow.

In the center of the basin was a lake, and in the middle of the lake, an island.

The Dagda's Court.

The hawk folded her wings back and dropped through the air. The ground rushed toward them at a terrifying speed, the wind whipping furiously. Scaithe was soon close enough to see flashes of color beneath the snow; a hint of winter green, a flash of dark brown.

The hawk soared over the still waters, the lake so calm it

mirrored the sky perfectly. Scaithe leaned over and could see the bird's reflected underbelly, skimming calmly across the icy waters.

And then the hawk opened her wings wide and they slowed down with a lurch. She flapped a couple of times, then slowly dropped into the branches of a tall, leafless syca-more tree on the shore of the island. Scaithe leaned forward and stroked her feathers.

"Thank you, old friend."

The hawk turned her head to look at him. She held out a wing and started preening, cleaning and tucking her feathers back into place.

Scaithe got the message. He slid off her back, landing atop the thick snow. His breath clouded the air.

He heard snuffling off to his right. A large black dog padded silently into view, stark against the white snow. The dog was one of the Dagda's favorites. Scaithe's presence was required.

He climbed onto the dog's back and it sprang into action, loping up the incline toward the middle of the island. Scaithe caught glimpses of some of the others—faeries, brownies, and piskies, a few of the hollow men. They all watched silently as he passed, their dark eyes troubled at his lone return.

There was a small hill at the exact center of the island.

On its crown sprawled a giant oak tree, its branches reaching down to form a concealing shelter around the trunk. Scaithe slid off the dog's back and waited. After a moment the green leaves, untouched by winter's hand, rustled, as if a soft wind had disturbed them. The intertwined branches creaked and pulled apart, revealing a perfectly round opening.

Scaithe took a deep breath and walked forward. The branches and leaves closed instantly behind him. After a few moments, he left the shadowy tunnel and found himself standing on green grass.

He looked around. He was surrounded by his people: brownies, kobolds, gnomes, goblins, the stocky alfar with their beards trailing in the earth, and piskies. Faeries flitted through the air, quick streaks of white light.

"He's angry," one whispered.

"He's going to skin you," said another.

"Feed you to the dogs."

Scaithe batted the irritating creatures away. They flew up into the boughs of the tree so that it seemed as if every branch was decorated with tiny glowing stars.

The lights revealed what he had come here to see.

The Dagda, King of the Unseelie, was sitting upon his throne, deep inside the trunk of the massive oak.

His face was in shadow. He sat unmoving as Scaithe

walked forward and bowed his head respectfully. The fey all around him fell silent, watching with glittering eyes and bated breath.

"What news?" asked the Dagda. As if in response, the leaves rustled an echo of his words, like voices heard through a wind. *What news?*

Scaithe swallowed. "We followed the thieves, sire. All the way to Londinium itself."

"And? Did you retrieve my property?"

"Sire, we did not."

A wave of unease undulated through the watchers. Scaithe looked around nervously.

"They had help. A human girlchild. There was nothing we could do. She was too fast."

The Dagda leaned forward, revealing a smooth, cruel face. "A girl?"

"Aye. She helped the one who stole the parchment. Corrigan."

"What did she look like?" asked the Dagda.

Scaithe searched his memory. "Black hair. Young." He shrugged. "I am sorry, sire. It is hard to tell with humans."

"Did she look like this?"

An image appeared in the air before Scaithe, an image of a young, frightened girl standing before a burning building. Even through a coating of soot, Scaithe recognized the slightly rounded features, the large brown eyes, the dark hair.

"That is her."

The Dagda let out a long, slow breath. "The time has finally come," he said, a look of hunger writ plain across his features. "I think it is time to wake Black Annis and Jenny Greenteeth," he said softly. "They have been too long from this world, and it is time they finished the task they were given all those moons ago."

Jonathan Bridgewater, or "Grubber" to those who knew him, wasn't important in the grand scheme of things. He was just a boy. He wasn't going to accomplish great things or change the world. He wasn't even going to grow up to raise children of his own.

That's because he was about to die.

A low, broken stone wall bordered the section of the Thames River where Grubber waited for the tide to go out. When the water was gone, and all he could see was the thick, evil-smelling mud that made up the bottom of the river, it would be time to get to work. He saw his fellow mud-larks staring over the misty water, waiting just as he did, hoping that today they would make that big find. Maybe a chest fallen overboard from a transport ship all the way from India. Or some silk from China, wrapped in waterproof paper.

Something you could sell and make enough money from to live happy for a year.

He was so busy daydreaming he almost missed the rustle of movement among his fellows. He snapped back to attention and saw that the water had disappeared behind the thickening mist. It was time.

He made his way down the stairs and stepped gingerly into the cold mud. His bare feet sank up to his ankles. He saw the others around him, indistinct in the mist, vague shadows and shapes that faded from view as each mud-lark took to his own jealously guarded area.

Grubber pulled a foot from the sucking mud, then placed it carefully in front of him and gingerly prodded the ground. One time he'd stood on an old nail and it had gone right through the skin between his toes. It had become infected and he hadn't been able to work for two whole weeks.

He surveyed the dark, glistening mud as he made his way slowly forward. He could hear the water lapping some distance ahead, a quiet, mournful sound, muffled in the mist. Everything else was silent. Even the usual sounds of the mud-larks calling to one another were absent. He looked around uneasily. There was something not right about the day. It was like waking up from a bad dream in the middle of the night. He had that same queasy feeling deep in the pit of his stomach.

"Hello?" he called. There was no reply, but he shook his head, assuring himself there was nothing to worry about. The others were somewhere close. If he shouted loud enough, they'd come.

Grubber resumed his search, eyes constantly roving across the mud. He found two brass nails and picked them up, slipping them into his pocket.

The mud soon became softer, so that he sank halfway to his knees. Before long he was exhausted and panting for breath. It was as if the mud were actually trying to grab hold of his legs and pull him under.

The dirty water at the tide line was the same color as the mud itself. It gurgled and wrapped around his legs, pulling him off balance. He staggered, then righted himself, digging himself even deeper into the mud. He looked along the shoreline but could see nothing of interest. He squinted, but the mist—now more of a thick fog—swirled forward like a cloak and blanketed his vision.

What was that? Grubber leaned forward and peered into the distance. It looked like a pile of clothing washing in and out at the tide's edge. He lurched forward, fighting with every step to keep his balance. Maybe it was clothes washed overboard from an Indian steamer. He could sell them to Mrs. Mills and get a fair few shillings.

But his excitement was short-lived. As he drew closer he

saw that the clothes were old—in fact, they looked more like a clump of slimy black-green seaweed than the dyed cotton he had hoped for.

He splashed to a stop in front of what he now saw was an old dress. It undulated gently on the waves, spread out as if there was someone still filling its shape. There was no point in taking it. As soon as it was out of the water, the material would fall to pieces.

He was right about one thing, though: there was a lot of seaweed clinging to the dress, especially around the neck-line. In fact, the seaweed floating limply in the water looked almost like a head of greasy hair.

He smiled and shook his head. His ma always said he had too much of an imagination.

And then, as he watched, the seaweed lifted slowly out of the water.

Grubber stared in horror as the dress he had thought empty filled out, white-green arms appearing from beneath the water to push the sodden mass upright. The seaweed wasn't seaweed at all but really *was* hair, hung lank and dripping, framing the pale, skeletal face of a young woman.

Grubber's mind raced. Had she fallen overboard? Had she tripped and been washed out with the tide? But then his common sense took hold. This wasn't an ordinary woman. Her eyes were as black as pitch, her face so thin the skin barely stretched over her cheekbones. Every inch of her body that he could see was pale green except for her nails. They were long and black.

And then she smiled, a huge, unnatural grin that cut her face like a rotting wound. Her teeth were black and pointed.

"Well, well," said a voice behind Grubber. "If it ain't Jenny Greenteeth herself."

Grubber whirled around to find himself facing a figure in a sodden dark cloak, dripping with water. The apparition reached up and lowered the hood, revealing the cruel, pinched face of an old woman. She stank of stagnant water, and when she opened her mouth—as she did now to smile cruelly at Grubber—murky brown liquid dribbled over her chin.

"And what have we here, young Jenny?" she asked, staring down at Grubber.

"Don't know, Black Annis," said the woman with the seaweed hair, who was now right behind Grubber.

Grubber's eyes widened in fear at the mention of the old lady's name. He started to shiver violently.

"Our names are still known around these parts, Jenny."

"Our names will always be known, Miss Annis."

"Of course they will," purred Black Annis. She held her arms wide open in a luxurious stretch. "Looks like our services are required again, young Jenny. The Dagda has brought us back from our tombs—" Black Annis paused as if she was listening. Then she clapped her hands together softly. "It's *her*, young Jenny."

"Who, Miss Annis?"

"Her. *The girl.* We've been brought back to make amends, Jenny."

"Can I feed first?" whined Jenny Greenteeth. "I'm so hungry."

Black Annis waved her hand benevolently. "Go ahead. But keep him quiet."

"They're always quiet, Miss Annis," whispered Jenny Greenteeth. She placed her two skeletal hands on Grubber's shoulders. "Always."

And then Grubber was pulled backward into the water. His last sight was that of Black Annis, a creature from nightmares and stories, dancing a slow dance, her hands held out as if encircling the shoulder and waist of an invisible partner.

⊷Chapter Five⊷

In which Emily returns to Merrian's shop and discovers what a True Seer is. The attack.

Ten o'clock in the morning
on the first day of Emily's adventures.

Snow, wait!"

Jack caught up with Emily and grabbed her by the arm. He looked around to make sure no one was watching and pulled her into an alley.

Emily pulled herself free. "What?"

"*What?* Is that all you can say? Emily, who were those men? Are you in trouble?"

"No—yes . . ." Emily stopped herself before she let anything slip. "Look, I don't know what's going on, Jack. I can't answer your questions."

"But what did they want? What was that thing you grabbed from the tall one?"

Emily's hand flew to her pocket. The satchel was still there.

"Was he really a bobby?"

"Course he wasn't."

"Had the smell of authority, though. I'll give him that." He frowned at Emily. "You tellin' me you really don't know why they were after you?"

Emily hesitated, unsure what to do. Jack sensed her reluctance.

"Come on, Snow. I can help. Whatever it is. I've always watched over you and Will, haven't I?"

The urge to tell Jack everything that had happened that morning was strong, almost overwhelming. But he wouldn't believe her. She hardly believed it herself.

"I can't tell you, Jack. You wouldn't understand."

"Try me."

Emily shook her head. No. She wouldn't involve Jack in this. It was too dangerous, not his problem. "Thank you, Jack, for helping out back there. But this is something I have to do myself. Maybe I'll catch up with you later? At the coffee shop?"

Jack said nothing, his mouth set in a thin line. Emily could see he was unhappy about it, but he knew better than to argue with her when her mind was made up.

Emily hurried back out of the alley, trying to ignore the look of hurt on his face.

She returned to Merrian's shop. It was the only thing she could think of to do. She had to give Corrigan back his satchel, and if she returned home there was a good chance Ravenhill would be waiting. She was glad William had gone to Mrs. Derry's shop. At least that would keep him out of harm's way for the rest of the day while she figured out what to do.

Emily pushed open the door to the bookshop. Nothing had changed since she had been there earlier. Piles of books still looked as if they were about to fall over with the slightest touch. Dust still filled the air.

"Hello?" she called.

No answer. Emily walked forward and picked up the bell from the counter. It rang once, a pure, sweet call. She nervously replaced it and waited.

A second later the curtain whipped aside and Merrian stood there, his huge shoulders pushing up against the doorframe.

"What are you doing here? How did you find the shop?"

Emily was taken aback. "Um . . . Corrigan told me the way this morning."

"Yes, but you're not supposed to remember that," said Corrigan, climbing up onto the counter. Emily noticed that he was barely limping anymore. He had a fresh bandage wrapped around his leg, but the wound didn't seem to be bothering him at all. Perhaps the fey healed faster than humans? "In fact, you shouldn't be able to see us, either."

Corrigan and Merrian shared a brief look. Emily knew that kind of look. It was what adults did when they were discussing grown-up subjects and thought the children wouldn't notice.

"Why are you looking at each other like that?" she demanded.

"What do you want?" asked Merrian, avoiding the question. "I thought I told you to forget about us. You should do as you're told."

Emily started to feel angry. Here she was, trying to help them, and all they did was scold her.

"Does that mean you don't want to know that Ravenhill found out where I live? That he took a small satchel that *someone*"—she glared at Corrigan—"left in my pocket?"

Corrigan sat bolt upright. "What are you talking about?"

"Your satchel. You left it in my pocket."

"And Ravenhill got it?" demanded Merrian.

Emily nodded. Merrian stepped around the counter and knelt in front of Emily. His head still towered far above hers. "Girl, this is very important. Does Ravenhill still have the satchel?"

"What's so important about it?"

"None of your business," snapped Corrigan.

"Oh, really?" Emily shot back. "Well, if it's none of my business, maybe I should just be going."

"Wait," said Merrian. "What's in the satchel is important, Emily. It's why the Black Sidhe were chasing Corrigan."

"Why I'm the only one left alive while all my friends are dead," Corrigan added.

"Does Ravenhill still have it?" repeated Merrian.

Emily sighed. "No. I grabbed it back from him."

She fished out the satchel and handed it over to Merrian. He held it up and breathed a sigh of relief. "You have no idea," he said softly, "how much trouble we would all be in if the Order got hold of this."

"Why?" asked Emily. "What does it do?"

"That, I cannot tell you."

Emily hated people keeping secrets from her. She tried to hide her disappointment as Merrian handed the satchel across to Corrigan.

"Tell me, lass," he said, turning his attention back to Emily, "did you notice anything strange when you traveled here?"

"Strange? Like what?"

Merrian gently pushed her to the door. "What do you see?"

Emily looked outside. "People. Gray clouds. Wet streets. Horses. Carriages."

"You're not *looking*, Emily. How did you find this shop? Because you shouldn't have been able to. It has a glamour cast over it. When you came here, you were walking through the streets, the way you normally do. But when you got close, what happened?"

Emily shrugged. "I imagined the shop in my head. I knew I was on the right street, so I just tried to remember where it was." Emily was unsure what Merrian wanted her to say. "I knew it had to be here, and it was."

"Try and get back into that frame of mind," said Merrian. "Then look outside again. Carefully, this time."

Emily tried to think about how she found the shop. She had felt distracted, because most of her thoughts were on Ravenhill, but in the back of her mind, she had still been thinking about the shop. She tried to repeat the feeling now, letting her mind drift, but still focusing on Merrian's words. Then she looked at the people walking along the street, their heads down to the ground as they hurried about their business. She saw nothing unusual.

But then she realized this wasn't true. As she watched, it was as though people, previously hidden to her, somehow *faded* into view. Only, that wasn't right. They had always been there, she just hadn't been able to see them. Her eyes simply . . . *skipped* over them.

They were the fey, walking along the street as if they didn't have a care in the world. And the normal, ordinary Londoners couldn't see them. They walked right past them without giving them so much as a second look.

A man walked past with a bag of coal over his shoulder. The bag bulged and moved, as if a cat or some other animal were inside. But then a small head poked up out of the bag, and another, and another: three small olive-skinned creatures were stealing a ride. A woman approached Emily, her skin white as freshly poured milk. As she passed by, Emily saw that the back of her body was entirely hollow, like a scooped-out doll.

Emily turned to watch her go, amazed.

"I was right," said Merrian, satisfaction heavy in his voice. "You're a True Seer."

She glanced at Merrian. "A what?"

"A True Seer. Some of your people have the ability to see through our glamour, to see us when we'd rather stay hidden. When you saw the fight this morning—when the piskies' glamour was weakened—it must have woken your talent. It's happened before, many times. No doubt it will happen again."

"What happens to these Seers?"

"Sometimes the Invisible Order finds out and recruits them. Sometimes they go mad. Sometimes they write books, paint paintings." Merrian shrugged. "Sometimes, they just carry on with their lives."

"Has it always been like this?" Emily gestured outside. "I mean, have you always been here?"

Merrian nodded. "For as long as London has existed. And long before that."

Emily turned her attention back to the street. Two tall, elegantly dressed women walked past, but it was clear to Emily they weren't human. Their limbs were too thin, too stretched. Their eyes were beautiful and golden, yet at the same time cold and cruel, as if they had never given or received any kindness, and worse still, didn't care. A small trunk floated along the ground behind them. As Emily watched, they plucked a dirty bonnet from the head of a young woman and dropped it into the trunk. The woman didn't notice a thing.

"What are they doing?"

"Shopping. Well, *taking*. They're hoarders. They take everything and anything, as long as it's made by a human."

"Why?"

"No idea. Never bothered to ask them."

Emily was about to ask how many of these "True Seers" there were, but at that moment Ravenhill suddenly stepped into view, framed in the open doorway.

"Hello, Miss Snow. May I join the party?"

Merrian cursed and yanked Emily out of the way, pushing the door shut. But not before Ravenhill threw something through the narrow gap. Emily felt a wet splash across her face, and Merrian growled in pain. He turned a key in the lock and staggered back, holding his arm out before him. Emily saw that the skin on his forearm was smoking, and an ugly wound was opening up before her eyes. He staggered to the counter and grabbed some of the leftover paste from that morning, slapping it over his arm.

"What was that?" asked Emily, frightened.

"Holy water," said Corrigan. "Don't worry, it won't affect you. Merrian, what do we do?"

There was a hammering on the door behind them.

"You need to complete your mission and get the parchment to the Queen. If the Order gets it, there'll be hell to pay."

Corrigan grabbed the satchel and strapped it to his back.

"Take the girl with you. She knows too much to let the Order get her."

Corrigan hesitated. "Are you sure?"

"Aye, I'm sure. Hurry up. Go out the back way."

"What about you?" asked Emily.

Merrian smiled coldly, and Emily almost felt sorry for Ravenhill. Almost.

"I'll delay them," he said. "I've a few tricks up my sleeve. Don't worry about me."

There was another bang on the door. This time it rattled on its hinges.

"*Go*, Corrigan. I'll see you later."

Corrigan hesitated. A pane of glass shattered behind

them as a stone flew through the window, hitting one of the book towers. The falling books hit another pile, and this one fell against a cabinet, smashing the glass and sending bottles and jars crashing to the floor.

Corrigan jumped from the counter onto Emily's shoulder. "Come on," he shouted. "Through the curtain."

Emily darted behind the counter. She took one last look over her shoulder and saw Merrian arm himself with a club and turn to face the front of the shop.

Emily ran through a kitchen and yanked open the back door. It led to an overgrown garden, choked thick with grass and nettles and a tall thorn tree. A gate led into a litter-strewn alley.

Emily stepped through the gate. As soon as she set foot in the alley, there was a shout off to her right, and she turned to see Blackmore running toward her. Emily turned and ran in the opposite direction. The exit to the alley was about fifty paces ahead, a bright gap between the walls, a promise of escape and safety. But as she drew closer, the light was blocked out by the silhouette of a man.

"Don't let her through!" shouted Blackmore from behind her.

The man spread his arms and legs wide, trying to block off as much of the alley as he could. Emily couldn't stop. There was no other way out.

Instead, she picked up speed.

"What are you doing?" shouted Corrigan. "Are you blind as well as stupid?"

Emily ignored the piskie. As she drew closer, she could make out the face of the man ahead of her. He was grinning, confident he would stop her.

Emily glanced over her shoulder to see Blackmore lagging behind, huffing and puffing.

She was no more than ten paces away from the end of the alley.

Five paces.

Four.

And then Emily reached up and grabbed hold of Corrigan. He cried out in surprise, but that was nothing compared to the shout he gave when Emily bent back her arm and threw him high into the air over the man's head.

The man straightened up in shock, his head tilting back as Corrigan sailed above him. Emily dropped to the mud, skidded between his legs, and pushed herself up again, still on the move. Corrigan was now falling from the sky, tumbling end over end. Emily put on an extra burst of speed, just managing to catch the piskie before he crashed into the ground.

She gripped him to her chest, put her head down, and ran as though her life depended on it.

Which it probably did.

⊹≕Chapter Six≕⊹

In which Emily walks among the fey and discovers a hidden world.

ELEVEN THIRTY IN THE MORNING
ON THE FIRST DAY OF EMILY'S ADVENTURES.

Emily felt rather strange hurrying through the streets of London with a piskie perched on her shoulder—a piskie no one but she could see or hear.

Although, at the moment, she found herself wishing she *couldn't* hear him.

"I can't believe you did that," said Corrigan. "What if you hadn't caught me?"

"But I did."

"But what if you hadn't?"

"Then you would have a few scratches, wouldn't you?"

Corrigan didn't say anything. Emily glanced at her shoulder and saw that he was sitting with his arms folded. Sulking.

Let him, thought Emily. At least she'd get some peace and quiet.

Now that Merrian had shown her the fey, she found that with a little concentration, she could see them everywhere. Here was a small, dirty dwarf with an unhappy-looking flying sprite tied to a piece of string so it couldn't get away. There was a bald woman wearing a cloak totally covered in thick, hairy spiders the size of Emily's hand, spiders that turned their glinting eyes in her direction as she walked by. And most astounding of all, she saw a trio of what appeared to be children, but all with fox heads. They walked along the street, their tongues lolling out of grinning mouths that showed sharp, dangerous teeth. Emily paused to watch them pass. How on earth had she missed all of this before?

They walked on for about another twenty minutes, then Corrigan stiffened and straightened up on her shoulder. "Stop," he ordered. "Don't go any farther."

"Why?"

Corrigan looked around. Emily did the same. They were alone on the road. "Go back and take the first right. Hurry up."

"Why? What's down this road?"

"Take a look for yourself," said Corrigan.

Emily looked. At first she couldn't see anything, but then she noticed the glint of eyes behind a hedge. A moment later, a group of piskies leapt over a wall and stood on the pavement some twenty paces ahead of them. They looked like the piskies Corrigan had been fighting that morning, except the black tattoos on their skin were different.

"Is that the Black Sidhe?" she asked fearfully.

"No. That's a different tribe. They are Unseelie, though. Another two steps and you would have taken us into the Dagda's territory. We'd already be dead."

Emily took a nervous step backward.

"Keep going," said Corrigan. "They can't have heard about the parchment; otherwise they'd have attacked us by now."

Emily turned and hurried back the way she'd come. She cast a nervous glance over her shoulder. The piskies were gone.

"Is the whole of London separated into territories, then?"

"Not all. Some of the city is neutral, but most of it's fair game. We fight, we win, we take their territory. We fight, they win, they take ours. Turn left here," he said, pointing down a side road.

Emily turned into King Street, where she'd been many times before. She walked on for another few minutes before Corrigan directed her into a mews that led between two tall buildings and fed them out onto a quiet road.

"Stop here," said Corrigan.

Emily stopped. She looked around but could see nothing of interest, just the street stretching away to either side and a row of tenements in front.

An old, one-eyed man pushed a rickety junk cart toward them. There were three small creatures in the cart, about half the size of Corrigan, sorting through the rubbish and placing it in neat piles. The man glanced at them as he passed, giving Emily a sly wink and tipping his hat to Corrigan.

"Brownies," said Corrigan distastefully. "Scavengers." They watched the man push his cart around the corner. "One thing you should know about our Queen," Corrigan said. "She doesn't take betrayal lightly."

"What do you mean? What kind of betrayal?"

"Any kind. That man with the rubbish cart? He was a guest of the Queen. He left, but he talked about what he saw." Corrigan shook his head. "Very silly."

"What happened?"

"The Queen sent her huntsman after him. The Dark Man, they call him."

"And?"

"And the Dark Man took his eye. Plucked it right from the socket. When the Dark Man has your scent, there's no hope for you. He'll follow you to the ends of the earth if the Queen commands it."

Emily shuddered. This Dark Man sounded like a monster. She hoped she'd never have occasion to lay eyes on him.

"Come on, let's go," said Corrigan. "No point in delaying this any longer."

Emily looked around. "Go where?"

Corrigan pointed to a three-story tenement across the road. "There."

Emily frowned. "Doesn't look very magical to me."

"Is that right? Well, allow me to apologize on behalf of all of my people for not living up to your expectations. We make do with what we can. Now just go and knock, will you?"

Emily crossed the road and approached the door. It was an entirely unremarkable example of its kind, not at all the kind of thing you would associate with faeries. The wood was painted gray, but the old paint had peeled away and now littered the dirty doorstep. The only thing of interest was a small circle of thorns that had been nailed to the wood. A seed from a fruit Emily couldn't identify had been tied into the center of the circle with twine.

"What are you waiting for? Knock."

Emily hesitantly knocked on the door. There was a moment of silence, then a loud clumping sound. She could hear the grating noise of locks being pulled back, then the door swung open to reveal a creature only slightly shorter than Emily. His skin was the color of chestnuts. He had a small nose that constantly twitched and suspicious black eyes. He squinted up at Emily.

"Let us in, Alfrig," said Corrigan.

The creature's eyes widened in surprise. "Corrigan? That you?"

"Who do you think? You going to let us in or what?"

Alfrig squinted at Emily. "This one's a human."

"See, that's why you're the gnome in charge of the door, Alfrig. Observant, that's what you are. Of course she's a human. I'm taking her to see the Queen. Now, you goin' to stand here yackin' all day or what?"

Alfrig thought for a moment, then stepped aside. "You keep an eye on her, then, Corrigan. I'll not be held responsible."

"Yes, yes, fine. Onward, Miss Snow."

"I'm not a horse, you know."

"More's the pity. A horse doesn't answer back."

Emily clicked her tongue in irritation and stepped into the tenement.

"Straight ahead. Out into the gardens."

Emily walked along the short passage and undid the latch on the back door, letting it swing slowly open on creaking hinges . . .

. . . to reveal a vivid burst of color and movement.

The garden was vast and overgrown, a wild patch of ground choked with trees and bushes, flowers and weeds. Tenements bordered the garden on all four sides, protecting the plot of land from the outside world. These other buildings also housed faeries. Creatures hung from the windows and crawled across the rooftops. Everywhere she looked, she was reminded of drawings and paintings she had seen, of brownies, spriggans, elves, and kobolds, small and large, ugly and fat, pretty and lithe.

Goblins—or at least what Emily assumed were goblins—waddled around, their ugly faces sharp and pointed. Skinny creatures with golden eyes slid between tree trunks. And faeries flitted between trees, tiny flickers of color that lit the shadows between the heavy growth.

"What is this place?" she said softly.

Corrigan glanced at her with satisfaction. "I was waiting for you to show a little wonder. You're very serious for a twelve-year-old. This is one of the doorways to Underlondon. We have them all over the city."

"Under London?" asked Emily.

"*Underlondon*. It's a place, not a description." He seemed about to say something more, then shook his head. "You'll see. Come on."

He hopped off her shoulder and headed onto a path through the long grass. Emily looked back over her shoulder. Alfrig was closing the tenement door and she could just see the dreary streets of London through the opening. Two horses clattered past, pulling an omnibus behind them. The scene looked so normal. Like everything else in her life up till now.

Then the door closed, and she turned around, watching Corrigan disappear into the undergrowth. She stepped out after him.

The path led into the trees. They hadn't looked so dense from the outside, but once beneath their overhanging branches, Emily felt as if she was walking through a huge forest.

"Where are we going?" she asked as Corrigan hopped over a moss-covered rock. She had to concentrate to keep the piskie in sight, his coloring a perfect camouflage amidst all the browns and greens.

"I already told you. Underlondon. The clue's in the name."

Emily thought about this for a second. "We're going underground?"

"Correct."

"Into the sewers?"

"*Below* the sewers. But yes, we have to go through them first."

The path gradually disappeared beneath the thickening ferns as they walked deeper into the forest. Emily thought they must be near to the other side of the garden by now. In fact, they should have reached it. It was as though the forest was bigger on the inside than on the outside.

"Here we are," declared Corrigan.

Emily saw the piskie standing at the edge of a circular clearing. The grass in the clearing was short and neat, a deep, rich green. Clumps of daisies and bluebells were scattered around, their yellows and blues so vibrant they looked like paintings.

Directly in the center of the sward of grass was a small mound. Corrigan stopped before it and turned to Emily.

"Close your eyes," he said. "You can't see this."

Emily did as instructed. But as soon as she heard Corrigan muttering under his breath, she opened her eyes a crack to see what he was doing.

He was moving his fingers about in a strange, intricate dance. A moment later, a golden red line shot up from the bottom of the hill, turned to the left, then shot back down to the ground, leaving behind the shape of a door. The glow brightened so much that Emily really did have to close her eyes. When she looked again, a dark opening had been cut into the hill. Corrigan turned to Emily with a grin.

"Come on, then."

Emily hesitated only briefly, then stepped through the opening.

⊰ Chapter Seven ⊱

In which Emily travels through the realm of Underlondon.

As Emily crossed the threshold, she caught the briefest glimpse of an earthen tunnel extending away before her, then the door sealed shut and she was plunged into darkness.

She froze, unable to see even her hand in front of her face. She waited for her eyes to adjust, her breathing heavy in her ears. Where was Corrigan? Had he just left her here? Emily swallowed nervously.

A scuttling noise came from somewhere above her. She quickly backed up against the wall, imagining some huge spider creeping along the roof. Loose earth crumbled from the wall off to her left, pattering onto the floor. She imagined strange worms as long as her arm tunneling through the walls, blindly seeking her scent. How would she get out of here?

"What are you doing?"

The voice was right in front of her. She screamed and lashed out with her foot. She heard a grunt of pain, then something falling to the floor.

"*Bones*, girl! What did you do that for?" moaned Corrigan. "That *hurt*."

"Sorry," said Emily, feeling slightly guilty. Then she straightened up. "Anyway, it's your own fault. You shouldn't have left me here alone."

"*My* fault?"

"Yes."

She heard him sigh. "It doesn't matter. Come on, this way."

"I can't see," said Emily.

"What?"

"I can't see. It's too dark."

"Oh, for—"

Emily sensed movement, then light burst into the tunnel once again as Corrigan opened the doorway and disappeared outside. Emily cast a quick glance at her surroundings. No spiders. No worms. It was just a tunnel, carved roughly into the earth. Tree roots snaked through the roof and walls, their thin tendrils drifting lazily.

Emily heard Corrigan's voice outside. She couldn't hear the words, but she could tell he was fighting with someone. Then there was an outraged squeal, and Corrigan stomped back into the tunnel, carrying an old bottle in both hands. Inside the bottle was a faerie, banging angrily on the glass. Emily couldn't hear what she was saying, but by the look of pure hatred on the tiny creature's face, Emily didn't think she really wanted to.

The door closed, but this time the darkness was held at bay by the white glow coming from the angry faerie. Corrigan handed Emily the bottle and walked away.

Emily gingerly raised the bottle to her face. The faerie was sitting with her arms folded in a sulk.

"Sorry," she said. She waited, but the faerie didn't seem keen to accept her apology. Emily gave up and hurried after Corrigan, holding the bottle to light the way, trying not to jounce the poor creature around too much.

The tunnel started to slope downward. Corrigan was moving fast, but Emily's longer stride enabled her to quickly catch up with him.

"A word of warning. Don't talk to *anybody*. If someone offers you any food—don't take it."

"Why? What will happen?"

"You'll be stuck here until whoever gave you the food becomes bored with you. Either that, or you'll die of old age."

They walked down the sloping tunnel until they came up against a brick wall. Emily stood back as Corrigan laid his hands against the wall and muttered something under his breath. The bricks separated with a grinding noise and swung aside. Emily could hear the sound of rushing water coming from the other side of the hole.

Emily followed Corrigan through the hole. They were standing on a stone ledge in a huge tunnel that disappeared into the darkness to either side. A torrent of dirty water flowed through the tunnel just below the path.

"What is this place?"

"One of the old rivers," said Corrigan. "The Tyburn, I think. There are loads of them down here. They all join up with the Thames, but as your lot kept building, they had to brick them up to make room for the city. They're still here, though. You can't just kill a river. It carries the blood of the city."

Turning into a narrow corridor, Corrigan led them along the path, through dry sewer beds, and onto rickety bridges that spanned the underground rivers. As Corrigan wended his way through the sewers and tunnels, Emily was soon lost. They walked for what felt like an hour or so, and Emily was quickly tiring when Corrigan stopped at another dead end. Again, he touched the wall and muttered a word under his breath. The wall shuddered, dust sifting into the air. The bricks ground their way to the side, revealing another passage, this one lit by floating balls of orange light.

"Leave her here," said Corrigan, indicating the faerie in the jar.

"Shouldn't we let her go?"

"If you want. But you won't be able to see when we come back out."

"Oh. Of course." Emily put the faerie down on the ground. She was banging at the glass again, and Emily felt a surge of guilt at leaving her like this. But they shouldn't be long, should they? All they were doing was handing over Corrigan's satchel. She'd be back out in no time. Then after that she would go and check on William. Emily knew he was safe at the shop, but she wanted to make sure, just for her own peace of mind.

They stepped through the opening, which scraped closed behind them. Emily studied their surroundings as they walked. They seemed to have left the manmade tunnels behind and were now in what looked like warrens. The walls were rough, the marks of chisels clearly visible, and the ground was paved with broken stones.

Corrigan saw her staring. "The Alfar did this."

"Alfar?"

"Alfar—the dwarves. Before most of them disappeared. They carved all this."

"Where did they disappear to?"

"No idea. We think the Order got hold of them. A few hundred years ago."

Corrigan hurried on ahead. The tunnel again sloped

downward, and Emily thought they must be miles below London by now.

Eventually, the tunnel widened, and Emily began to see signs of life. Creatures like Corrigan scurried around, disappearing into tunnels that branched off the main thoroughfare. A faerie flew past Emily's head, its golden glow lighting the tunnel before it disappeared around a bend up ahead. A jumble of sounds rebounded off the walls and washed over Emily in a confused mishmash of echoes and voices.

Then they rounded the corner, and the wall of noise and sight slammed into Emily's senses like a slap across the face, bringing her to a sudden stop.

The scene put her immediately in mind of London Bridge, with its homes and shops lining the bridge itself. Except that instead of people bustling around selling their wares, drinking with friends, and stealing from strangers, it was the fey.

Creatures of all shapes scurried between stalls and over the roofs of shops. There were so many, and they were so varied in looks, that Emily could have spent all day there and not seen two that looked the same. Tall, short, fat, tiny, ugly, beautiful, pale, dark, blue, brown. Scarred, smooth, eyeless, noseless, mouthless.

Corrigan nudged her and she started walking again, inspecting the stalls as she passed by. They sold an astonishing variety of goods. One stall was completely covered with glass vials filled with an assortment of liquids and powders. A tall, dark woman with white eyes gazed down at Emily.

"And what is your fancy, little girl? Trying to win the heart of a young man?" She cocked her head and looked hard at Emily. "But perhaps you are a little young for that. What else? A cure for the wasting disease? No? Take a look, then. Everything you see is perfect for shinecraft."

Emily picked up one of the vials and read the label. *The First Laugh of an Unchristened Babe,* it said. She put it back and picked up another, this one containing a liquid that glowed white: *One Soul, Freely Given,* read the label.

Corrigan hastily guided her away, casting nervous glances at the woman.

"Come again, little girl," she called.

Corrigan took her deeper into the crowd. As they walked, Emily noticed faeries hovering in the air above their heads, forming neat, stationary lines.

"They get paid to light the tunnel," Corrigan said, catching the direction of Emily's gaze. "Two beetles for every hour."

"What do they do with the beetles?"

"What do you think? They eat them."

They walked on through the crowds, Corrigan pausing every now and then for a brief exchange of words. Emily drew suspicious looks, but even so, she found the fey curiously unaffected by a human girl in their midst. She asked Corrigan about it.

He shrugged. "It's not as rare as you might think. And besides, most people know me well enough to know I wouldn't bring you here unless I had a good reason."

They eventually stopped before a small, unassuming shop front. As Emily and Corrigan approached, a group of strange-looking creatures exited the shop. They had the bodies of horses but the heads of old men. They grinned and leered at Emily, showing large yellow teeth.

"Phookas," said Corrigan. "Don't speak to them. Pains in the backside, they are."

Emily did as instructed and the phookas passed them by, grunting and neighing. A moment later, the door to the shop opened again, and three tall, sad-looking men came out. Emily wondered where they were all coming from. The shop didn't look big enough to hold so many people.

Corrigan opened the door and led the way inside. Emily followed, blinking as her eyes adjusted to the darkness. What she saw left her feeling slightly puzzled. The only item in the shop was a large bed against the far wall. Snuggled beneath the covers, the blankets pulled right up to their necks, were a wizened old man and woman, both of them about the same size as Emily. They had a distinctly gnomish look about them, like Alfrig back at the tenement door.

"Close that door," snapped the woman.

"It's freezing in here," said the man.

"Freezing," agreed the woman.

Emily quickly pushed the door closed. She didn't think it did much good, as she could still see the light outside the shop through gaps in the wooden slats.

The woman leaned forward and peered at the two of them. "Corrigan. That you?"

"Yes, Mrs. Stintle."

"That you, Corrigan?" asked the old man.

"Yes, Mr. Stintle."

The man turned to the woman. "It's Corrigan, dear."

"I can see that. You think I'm blind?"

"What do you want?" she asked Corrigan. "Did you bring us that blanket you promised? We're freezing in here."

"Ah . . . no. Sorry. Been away on business. Next time, I promise."

"*Hmpph.* We know what your promises are worth, don't we, dear." She nudged the old man hard in the ribs. He winced and glared at her.

"Ow. What was that for?"

"I was saying we know what his promises are worth. Don't we?"

"Yes. But there's no need to break my ribs, woman."

"Who's the girl?" The woman nodded in Emily's direction.

"It doesn't matter," said Corrigan quickly, heading off Emily's offended reply. "We need to get below."

"Below?" said Mrs. Stintle.

"Below?" said Mr. Stintle.

"Below," agreed Corrigan.

"Well, what are you waiting for? You know what to do."

Corrigan jerked his head in the direction of the back wall. Emily followed him over.

"What *do* we do?" she asked curiously.

"We hold on," he said. "Very tight."

As soon as he had uttered these words, there was a lurch under Emily's feet, then a horrendous screaming noise and an explosion of steam from beneath the floorboards. Emily saw the old man and woman pulling on some kind of lever. Then the floor shifted beneath her and they began to drop downward.

"Probably best to sit down," said Corrigan. "You don't want to fall off."

Emily sat as the floor rose above her head. They were sinking straight down through a long tunnel that had been cut into the very earth itself. Small globes of golden light were attached to the walls, illuminating the darkness.

They sank like this for about ten minutes, then the walls of the tunnel fell away and they entered a vast open space.

Emily's mouth dropped in amazement.

"Home sweet home," whispered Corrigan.

The place was so big that at first she couldn't take it in. Her eyes were drawn to the lights, hundreds, thousands of glowing orbs hanging in the air. They lit the darkness with a golden glow, as if the sun were just sinking after a glorious summer's day. Except . . . the lights *weren't* hanging in the air. They were attached to the branches of the biggest tree Emily had ever seen. It was ten times the height of Big Ben, and the trunk was so thick it would take hundreds of people to encircle it. Thousands, maybe. The massive branches arched up into the huge cavern. Emily realized that the whole tenement building she lived in would easily fit inside one of the branches.

As they dropped lower, Emily saw that the tree was occupied. She could see hundreds of openings in the branches and trunk, small windows through which she caught glimpses of the fey going about their daily lives.

"Do you . . . do you all live in the tree branches?" she whispered.

"Not all. Only the favored." Corrigan pointed to the side. Emily leaned over and saw that the tree's roots snaked over the ground—huge, twisting walls of dark wood that formed avenues and streets, with windows and doorways cut into the roots so the fey could live inside. It was an entire city living inside a single tree.

"How long have you all lived here?" she asked in amazement.

Corrigan looked at her. "Do you still not understand? We were here *before* you. That tree was planted when we came here from Faerie. Your lot built your bricks and mortar over the top, taking land that was ours."

Emily was about to respond when the platform stopped moving about halfway down the trunk.

"Come on, then," said Corrigan, stepping onto a branch. Emily followed. The branch formed a wide walkway leading to the trunk. Corrigan touched the slightly shimmering bark, and a round door swung open with a damp, creaking sound. Warm light washed over them.

"Are you ready to meet the Queen?" asked Corrigan.

"Probably not," said Emily.

But she followed Corrigan anyway, right into the heart of the faerie tree.

⊹⊱Chapter Eight⊰⊹

*In which Emily enters the Twilight Court
and meets the Faerie Queen.*

The walls inside the tree were smooth and polished, the grain of the wood teased and coaxed into subtle patterns and pictures. Emily didn't notice them at first, so slight were the variations in the wood. It was only when they walked past a golden lamp that she caught a glimpse of spirals and strange runes.

She stopped to get a better look. Corrigan reached up and grabbed hold of her hand. "What are you doing? The Queen knows we're here. She's not someone you keep waiting."

He led them through the huge tree trunk, along corridors and up wide staircases. Every now and then they passed a window, and Emily would strain to catch a glance outside.

They passed more of the fey, most of them tall and

aristocratic—taller, even, than a normal person. Their clothing was light and colorful, flowing behind and around them as if on a breeze. Their long, thin fingers constantly smoothed the material into pleasing creases.

The fey looked down at Corrigan and Emily as they passed, their pale faces radiating distaste and curiosity in equal measures. Corrigan glared at them, and Emily heard him muttering something about "stuck-up fancy-pants."

After a while, they heard music. It was faint at first, the distant song of a violin. Then a piano joined the violin, forming a sad and mournful tune. Corrigan seemed to grow nervous, fidgeting and looking around anxiously.

He led them into another passage. This golden tunnel was empty but for two tall fey standing beside a large double door. They wore armor made of polished wood and had white hair that was braided down their backs.

"Who are they?" whispered Emily. "They look different from the others."

"The Tuatha de Danaan. The aristocracy. The Queen's soldiers." He paused and turned to Emily. "Don't say anything rude. All right?"

Emily drew herself up, offended. "I'm not rude."

Corrigan raised his hands in surrender. "Right. Fine. Of course not. Then don't say anything . . . *plain*. Just . . . hold your tongue."

As they walked down the passage, the music became louder, and Emily could hear the sound of laughter.

Corrigan stopped before the two guards. They didn't even look down. Emily stood nervously behind him.

"Hoy," he called.

No response. Emily frowned. They were doing it on purpose. She knew their type. Nothing but bullies.

"Excuse me," she said icily. "I believe we are to see your Queen."

The music stopped in the room beyond the door. The fey looked down at her. Their eyes were the blackest pitch with small white pupils. Emily had seen the same coloring on the eyes of some of the other fey, but on the Queen's guards the effect was much more disconcerting. She could see no emotion there. Just cold, hard . . . *emptiness*.

"What did I say?" Corrigan whispered furiously. "Didn't I say to keep your big mouth shut?"

"But all—"

Before she could finish, the fey guards stepped aside. Now Emily could see the doors clearly for the first time. There was a pattern carved into the surface, standing out against the wood in heavy relief. The carving was of a hill, and on top of the hill were seven trees, spaced evenly around its crown. Inside this circle of trees, faeries and goblins, gnomes and piskies danced under the sun.

A second later, the doors swung silently inward. When Emily saw what was in the room beyond, she took a nervous step back.

She found herself looking into a vast ballroom, the floor a mosaic pattern of black and white. The fey stood around the edges of the room, dressed in fine clothes that were a hundred years out of date. They stared at Emily and Corrigan, pale and cold, some with fans in front of their faces, others wearing masks carved to resemble woodland creatures: here a crow staring at her, there an owl with black eyes glinting behind the holes, and a rat with a golden glance.

Around these tall, graceful creatures were an assortment of other fey. Some she had seen already—the strange people with their backs hollowed out, creatures with the heads of foxes. But there were others, as well. Tiny creatures rode around the chamber on the backs of squirrels and rats. Some of them flew on robins and hawks around the high rafters. Creatures slightly taller than Corrigan served drinks among the gentry. The servers were old and wizened, like older versions of Alfrig and Mrs. and Mr. Stintle.

"You will enter," said a voice, and Emily found herself obeying even before she knew what she was doing. She walked past the ranks of the fey, their eyes following her every step. She looked down at her feet and noticed how tatty her shoes were compared to everything else around her. She shouldn't be walking on such fine tiles dressed like this.

"Look upon me," said the voice.

Emily looked up and saw the most beautiful woman she had ever laid eyes upon. The Fairie Queen was tall and pale, her hair the red of sunsets upon freshly fallen snow. Her eyes were golden, glowing with warmth and power. She wore a gown so light it floated about her, like spiderwebs on a breeze.

The Queen sat on a throne carved from dark wood and molded to her shape, so that she seemed to be a part of the carving. Emily heard giggling and saw that there were fey children behind the throne. They reached out to touch the Queen's gown, stroking the fabric while staring at Emily and whispering amongst themselves.

"Corrigan. What news?"

Emily blinked and saw that Corrigan was down on his knees before the Queen. Emily hastily did the same, even though she hadn't intended to. It seemed right, somehow.

"Good news, Queen Kelindria."

There was a rustle of excitement among the courtiers. The Queen said nothing.

"We infiltrated the Dagda's island. It was difficult going, my Queen. It took us many nights. But we regained the parchment."

A murmur rippled through the room. The Queen smiled at Corrigan and held out her hand. Corrigan stood and quickly took the satchel from his back, removing the blank piece of parchment. The Queen took it with trembling fingers and held it up to the light, her eyes shining with excitement.

"You have done well, Corrigan." The Queen focused her attention away from the parchment. "Am I right in assuming that this girl helped you?"

"She did, my Queen. But she also led the Invisible Order to Merrian's shop. Ravenhill, of all people."

The courtiers muttered angrily, some of them glaring at Emily. What had Corrigan said that for? That hadn't been her fault. Why was he trying to get her into trouble?

"Is Merrian well?"

"I do not know. He held off the Order while we escaped to bring you the parchment."

The Queen nodded, then turned to Emily. But before she could say anything, there was a commotion from somewhere behind her. Emily glanced over her shoulder to see what was going on.

Most of the courtiers had gathered behind Emily as she stood before the Queen. Now they quickly fell back as *darkness* flowed through their midst. It was the only way Emily could describe it. A dark form moved forward. Tendrils of shadow branched off from the heart of the blackness, touching, feeling, probing anyone and anything that was unlucky enough to be close by. Emily stumbled aside, banging up against a pillar. She felt something against her leg and saw Corrigan standing behind her, watching the shadow with fearful eyes.

He looked up at Emily. "The Dark Man," he whispered.

Emily's eyes were drawn back to the shadowy mass as it stopped before the throne. The tendrils drew back toward the figure, receding to form a cloak and hood that totally enclosed his form, lending him human shape. At the Dark Man's feet was a wretched-looking creature. He was about the size of a human male but looked vaguely elflike, with sharp features and pointed ears, and so skinny Emily thought he was in danger of snapping in two.

"Well met, Lieutenant," said the Queen. "I see you found our traitor. Where was he hiding?"

The Dark Man spoke, but it seemed to Emily that his words entered her brain without going through her ears.

He was sheltering amongst our brethren on the continent.

Queen Kelindria seemed surprised. "Really? I take it they did not know he had fallen from Our favor?"

They did not. I questioned them most carefully.

The Queen's mouth quirked in a smile. "I'm sure you did." She waved a hand. "Take him away."

The Dark Man nodded. The shadows spread out from

his body once again and enveloped both himself and his prisoner. When the elflike creature saw the tendrils creeping toward him, he cried out in fear. The shadows crawled across his face and over his mouth, muffling his scream.

A second later, the space before the Queen was empty. Emily looked around and saw shadows pool beneath a pillar, then the shadow crawled across the wall and slipped through the doorway.

The Queen turned her attention back to Emily. "Do not concern yourself with that. The elf was a traitor. He deserves everything he will get. But come. You will walk with me now, Emily Snow."

You will walk with me didn't mean, as Emily thought it did, that she and the Queen would go for a walk on their own. Rather, it meant that the Queen and Emily would walk, and the whole court would trail along behind them, a long line of fey jostling for a position close to the front. The fey children trailed immediately behind Queen Kelindria, holding her dress and staring distrustfully at Emily.

They left the huge tree and descended into the city below. The twisted roots towered high on either side of them, rough walls with windows and doorways carved into the wood. Emily stared, distracted, until the Queen spoke.

"I wish to tell you something of our history, Emily. So you may see how important it is that you saved Corrigan's life."

The Queen called something to the guards up ahead. Emily didn't understand a word she said. It sounded like small sticks clicking together while accompanied by a flute. Emily didn't even think her mouth was capable of such sounds.

Two of the smaller roots veered off to the right, creating a smaller roadway. The guards led them down this path, away from the town.

"Do you know of the Dagda?" the Queen asked.

"Merrian said you and he used to be allies. But something happened."

"Yes, you could say that," said the Queen dryly. "The Dagda's ambition has always been to conquer your people. He wants to bring the armies of Faerie through the doorway between our worlds and wipe you out. My people, the Seelie fey, have no desire for such a thing, so we fight to stop him and his followers. We have always wanted to live side by side with you. We think the world is large enough for both our races. But alas, a human called Christopher Wren did not agree. Do you know who he is?"

Emily shook her head.

"He was an architect. A scientist. And a very prominent member of the Invisible Order, as well as the Royal Society.

After the Great Fire of sixteen sixty-six, it was Wren who rebuilt most of London. He and his little secret society of murderers and sneaks were responsible for starting the last war between our races."

The Queen fell silent.

"During the war, Wren and his Invisible Order somehow got hold of the key to Faerie and locked the door. Then he hid the key. Only he knew where it was, but there were rumors that he left clues to those who would follow him in the Order, should they ever have need of the key again. The parchment Corrigan brought to me is Wren's first clue to the key's whereabouts. We have been searching for it for the past two hundred years."

"But . . . the parchment is blank."

The Queen smiled. "Yes. Another of Wren's precautions. There is an item that was stolen from us—the Stone of True Seeing, we called it—that we must retrieve from the Order. The stone sees through all falsehoods and enchantments. It can reveal things that are hidden. When the parchment is looked at through this stone, the hidden clue will be revealed." She sighed. "Unfortunately, the stone is locked away under the Royal Society in a vault made of iron, and iron is one of our weaknesses. Its touch alone can kill us."

The ground started to slope upward, and the Queen fell silent. As they climbed higher, Emily saw a small circle of trees around the crown of the hill. There were seven of them, and except for one sickly looking tree, they were all dead.

The Queen stepped into the circle and gently touched the last surviving tree. As she did so, a withered leaf detached itself from a branch and drifted to the ground to join the decaying pile around the roots.

"This is all that's left of the Twilight Court," said the Queen, her beautiful face filled with regret. "These trees are from Faerie. Once upon a time, they were healthy, green. Now, they die."

"Why are they dying?" Emily asked.

"We have been too long from our world. When the last of these trees die, our time will be at an end. That is why we seek the key. We wish to open up the doorway and travel back to our world before it is too late. For that was Wren's plan, you see. To cut us off from our source of life and watch us wither away into dust."

The Queen fell silent once again, gazing sadly around the small circle of trees. She turned to Emily. "But such is no concern of yours. You have already done more than enough to aid us, and we thank you for that. It is time for you to return to your own life. Corrigan will take you home."

CHAPTER NINE

Kidnapped! In which Emily has to make a decision.
Black Annis watches.

THREE O'CLOCK IN THE AFTERNOON
ON THE FIRST DAY OF EMILY'S ADVENTURES.

Much of the trek back up to London passed in a daze. Emily did her best to ignore Corrigan, who was perched on her shoulder imperiously issuing directions. She kept going over the information volunteered by the Queen, turning it over and over in her mind until it stopped making any sense at all.

After all that had happened to her, she was looking forward to the familiarity that awaited her at home. She had to figure out what she was going to do for William's supper tonight, not worry about a magic key that could open a doorway to Faerie. Even repeating the words in her head made her feel faintly ridiculous.

They eventually emerged from the tenement building,

Alfrig slamming the door behind them. Emily blinked up at the gray afternoon sky. It was raining cold, windblown shards that prickled like icy fingers against her skin. She shivered and pulled her coat tight.

Corrigan flicked her ear. "What's wrong with you? You haven't said a word the whole way back."

Emily frowned. She reached up and plucked the piskie from her shoulder and unceremoniously dropped him into a dirty puddle. He looked up at her in amazement.

"Did you just throw me into a *puddle*?"

"Why did you tell the Queen I led the Invisible Order to Merrian's shop?" snapped Emily.

"But . . . you *did*."

"I was bringing you the parchment! And you said it like you wanted me to get into trouble or something."

Corrigan waved his hand dismissively. "Oh, don't mind that. It's just my way."

"Just your way? What does that mean? That you lie about those who save your life?"

"Well . . . I wouldn't go *that* far." Corrigan pushed himself to his feet and tried to squeeze the water from his jerkin.

"I certainly would."

Corrigan frowned. "Fine. Think what you want to think. Who cares? Once I've taken you home, we never need to see each other again. How does that sound?"

"Fine by me. And I don't need you to walk me home. I know the way."

"The Queen told me to see you to your door," said Corrigan. "And that's what I'm going to do."

"Do what you want," said Emily, and stalked off down the street. After a few steps Corrigan called to her.

"Emily, wait!"

"Why should I?" she shouted over her shoulder.

"Because there's something I need to say. It's important."

Emily rolled her eyes in exasperation. She turned, folding her arms tightly across her chest. "What is it?"

Corrigan held out his arms. "Can you give me a lift?" he asked with a wicked grin. "I'm a bit tired."

As soon as Emily turned onto her street, she knew something was wrong. She stared at the small crowd of people gathered outside her tenement. Mrs. Hobbs was waving her arms about angrily.

"It's not even as if I'm heavy," complained Corrigan, struggling to keep up. "You could easily carry—" He bumped into her legs. "What are you doing?"

"Something's happened," whispered Emily, feeling the dread rising up inside her.

William. Something had happened to William. But how?

He was supposed to be working at Mrs. Derry's shop. That was the only reason she hadn't been worrying about him all day. He was supposed to be safe. She started to run. The crowd of women stopped talking when they saw her coming. Emily recognized most of them as neighbors from surrounding tenements.

She tried to run inside but Mrs. Hobbs grabbed her before she made it into the building.

"There's nothing to see, Emily. Will's gone."

Emily stared wildly at Mrs. Hobbs. "What was he doing here? He was supposed to be at the shop!"

"Mrs. Derry came over a bit sickly and sent Will home early. First I knew of any trouble was when I heard him screaming. A godawful racket, it was. By the time I got downstairs there was no one there."

"Did you see who did it?"

Mrs. Hobbs shook her head. "As I said, there was no one here when I came downstairs. We've called the bobbies. Best to wait—"

Emily shook off Mrs. Hobbs's hand and ran into the darkened passageway.

"Who's going to pay for the damage?" called Mrs. Hobbs. "That's what I want to know."

Their door was hanging from its hinges. The room looked as if a fierce wind had surged through, catching everything in its grasp and flinging it against the walls until almost nothing was left intact. Only the heavy bed was still in one piece. The rocking chair was destroyed, the splintered arms embedded in the walls as if thrown there with fearsome strength.

"William?" she called. But she knew there would be no answer. William was not here. He had been taken.

Ravenhill? It had to have been him. He must have waited for Emily to return but settled for her brother instead.

She felt a deep, abiding anger rise up within her. How dare he? Ravenhill had violated her home, her family. She wasn't even meant to be involved in this. It had all been an accident. And now her brother was missing, taken by some stupid secret society for who knew what reason.

Corrigan had entered the room and was standing with his back to her, staring at something on the wall. She followed his gaze and saw a black mark painted onto the torn wallpaper close to the floor. It was a circle with a strange, twisted rune inside.

"What's that?"

"It is the mark of the Unseelie," Corrigan said.

"The Unseelie?" said Emily, her thoughts struggling to keep up with the events. "Why would Ravenhill draw that on the wall?"

Corrigan turned to face her. "It wasn't Ravenhill, Emily.

This was the work of the Black Sidhe, the Dagda's servants."

"Those piskies you were fighting? But why? Why would they take—?"

"It's because you helped me. They think you've chosen your side in the war."

Emily stared helplessly at Corrigan. "War?" she said angrily. "I'm not *involved* in your war. All I did was help you, and now look where it's got me! They've taken my brother, Corrigan. What am I supposed to do about that?"

Corrigan stared at her for a moment, a strange expression on his face. "There . . . might be a way," he said eventually.

"A way? A way for what?"

"To get your brother back. Or, at least, to find out where he is being held."

Emily dropped to her knees before Corrigan.

"How? Tell me, Corrigan. Tell me how I can rescue William."

There was reluctance on Corrigan's face.

"It is dangerous, Emily Snow. Very dangerous."

"I don't care. I'll do anything!"

Corrigan stared at her, then wryly shook his head. "Do you know how old I am?"

Emily frowned, taken aback. "What? No, of course not."

"I'm two thousand four hundred and twenty-three years old."

Emily stopped, surprised. "Really?"

"Really."

"That's old."

"Emily Snow, you have no idea."

"But what has that got to do with William?"

Corrigan smiled. "Nothing much. It's just that over the years, I've heard many people say they would do anything if only they could attain this or get hold of that. Rarely do they mean it."

Emily stared fiercely at the piskie. "Well, I do," she said firmly.

"I know," said Corrigan, smiling.

"Good. Now what do I have to do?"

Corrigan straightened up. "The way to get your brother back is to retrieve the Stone of True Seeing. As the Queen said, it can see through untruths, but it can also find lost objects, as long as they are known to you."

"But didn't the Queen say the Invisible Order had it?"

"Buried somewhere beneath the Royal Society in an iron vault with walls ten feet thick, yes."

"So what am I supposed to do?"

"You'll have to break into Ravenhill's office, steal the key to the vault, then get the stone," said Corrigan simply.

Emily stared at Corrigan, aghast. "I can't do that! I'm not a thief."

"They stole it from us in the first place," Corrigan reminded her.

"I don't mean that. I mean, I wouldn't have the faintest idea how to go about it."

But Jack would, she thought. Maybe she should have taken him up on his offer of help.

"I'm sure we'll come up with something," said Corrigan. "But that doesn't matter yet. We have to make preparations first."

Emily blinked. "What kind of preparations?"

"We have to pay a visit to the Sisters," said Corrigan mysteriously.

Across the street from the tenement in which Emily lived, hidden from view in a dirty alley, Black Annis and Jenny Greenteeth watched Emily and Corrigan hurry away.

"I'm hungry, Miss Annis," whined Jenny.

"Hush, now. You've only just eaten."

"There was nothing on him. Just skin and gristle. I want a fat one."

"Then you'll have to wait till our path takes us through the West End, won't you?"

"Can't I have her? She looks tasty."

"No," said Black Annis, watching Emily disappear around

a corner. "The Dagda wants that one all to himself. And we owe him, so we do as he says." A rat poked its head out of a pile of rubbish. Jenny Greenteeth let out a squeal of delight and pounced on the startled creature.

Black Annis closed her eyes and tried to think, which was difficult to do with the crunching sounds coming from behind her.

⊁CHAPTER TEN⊰

*In which Emily meets the Sisters and the Colonel
tells her a gruesome story about India.*

THREE THIRTY IN THE AFTERNOON
ON THE FIRST DAY OF EMILY'S ADVENTURES.

Corrigan wouldn't tell Emily who the Sisters were, and she was too sick with worry to bother asking him about them more than once. All she wanted was to get the stone and take it to Queen Kelindria, so that she could find her brother.

Corrigan had her stop before a drab, two-story house nestled between a pub and a furniture shop. The house had a small, well-kept garden fenced off by a low stone wall. Corrigan slipped over the wall and Emily pushed open the gate. It squealed in protest and slammed shut behind her.

The door was painted bright green. Above the brass knocker someone had painted a closed eye. Emily studied it curiously, wondering what it represented.

She reached for the knocker. As her fingers brushed the

cold metal, the painted eye snapped open and swiveled in her direction. Emily let out a yelp and snatched back her hand.

"What's wrong with you?" demanded Corrigan. "It's just an eye. Open the door."

Emily hesitantly reached forward and turned the doorknob. The door swung silently inward, revealing a long hallway with thick red carpeting. A tall grandfather clock stood against the far wall. Emily could hear the ticking from where she stood. There was something . . . odd about it. As the clock measured off the seconds, she found herself trying to correct the sound in her head. The rhythm was off-kilter. Not much, just enough for her to realize something was wrong.

"Come on," said Corrigan, stepping inside the house.

Emily carefully wiped her feet, then followed Corrigan through a door that opened off the hallway. It led to the front parlor. The room was lit by tall lead-lined windows facing out onto the street. A man was sitting on the couch, his back to Emily. He was dressed in a fine suit and he held a polished cane across his lap. He turned in her direction as she came in.

Emily gasped. The man had only one eye. Where the other should have been there was just a gaping black hole. His good eye widened in surprise. He quickly turned away, and when he turned back Emily saw that he had covered the hole with an eye patch.

"My girl! I do beg your pardon. I had no idea . . . That is,

I thought I was alone with Miss LaFleur. Please. Accept my most humble apologies. Did I scare you?"

"No," said Emily defensively.

The man smiled slightly. "Ah. That is good. No harm done."

Emily could keep her curiosity in check no longer. "How did you lose it?" she asked.

"Ah, lass, that's a story indeed. I was in India. A great snake bit me on the head while I slept. The thing had my whole head in its mouth. I managed to beat the beast off, but some of the poison worked its way into my skull."

Emily's eyes were round with wonder. "What happened?"

The man shook his head with a mildly amused look on his face. "I cannot tell you. It is too monstrous!"

"Tell me!" Emily demanded. "You can't start a story like that and not finish it. It's against the rules."

"Is it now?"

Emily nodded. "And a fine gentleman such as yourself wouldn't want to break the rules."

"No," said the man thoughtfully. "I suppose I wouldn't. All right." He leaned forward. "The whole side of my head swelled up until it was the size of a loaf of bread. The pain was intense. I was insensible. Raving like a madman. And then one day—" He made a gesture with his hand, opening his fist and spreading his fingers.

"What? 'And then one day' what?"

"Then one day my eye popped. Like an overripe tomato."

"No," breathed Emily.

"Oh, yes. Terrible mess, but it relieved the pressure. I recovered and came back to Mother England. Unfortunately, the glass eye I had fitted in India was an inferior product. It fell out at church. Smashed onto the floor. The vicar was not happy, let me tell you." He spread his arms wide. "Which brings me here."

He leaned back against the couch, smiling at Emily.

"Here?" Emily said. "Where exactly is—?"

Before she could finish her sentence, a door at the other side of the room opened and a tall, black-skinned woman walked in. Emily couldn't help but stare. Her skin wasn't black like some of the workers Emily had seen down at the docks, but black as a piece of coal. She glanced briefly at Emily and placed a small box on a glass table.

"I'll be with you in a moment, dear," she said, opening the box. "I think this will suit you perfectly, Colonel. It took me a full week to construct. Your coloring is quite unique."

She took out something small and round and handed it to the Colonel. He examined it with his good eye, bringing the object up close and peering at it intently.

"Incredible," he whispered. "It seems almost alive." He handed the object back to the woman. "You have outdone yourself, madam. Would you be so kind . . . ?"

Miss LaFleur smiled. "Of course." She leaned forward and lifted the patch from the Colonel's eye. Then she brought the object up and did something that Emily couldn't see.

A moment later, the Colonel turned to face Emily, a large smile on his face. "Well? What do you think, girl? Not so scary now, eh?"

Indeed! Whereas before there had been a gaping ruin where his eye should be, now he had his eye back. It was as simple as that. Emily stepped forward and peered at him suspiciously. Not quite. The eye was almost identical, green flecked through with blue and brown, but when the light hit his face, the reflection from each eye was slightly different.

"It's glass," she said accusingly.

"Of course it is." The Colonel stood up and examined himself in the large mirror that hung over the mantelpiece. "Manufacturers of glass eyes are plentiful, but Miss LaFleur is the best craftswoman in the business." He turned this way and that, studying his reflection from every angle. A smile of satisfaction spread across his features. He turned back to Miss LaFleur and took her hands in his. "Madam, you have indeed outdone yourself. Allow me to treat you to dinner."

"You have already paid me, Colonel."

"I know. Consider it a token of my gratitude. How about Verrey's?"

Verrey's? Emily looked at Miss LaFleur in amazement.

Emily had heard that the food at Verrey's was the best in London. What was she waiting for? Emily would say yes straightaway. Her mouth watered at the mere thought. Finally Miss LaFleur pursed her lips and nodded.

"Very well, Colonel. I accept your invitation."

"Excellent." He released her hands, then picked up his cane from the sofa. He bowed to Emily. "My dear."

The Colonel left the sitting room. Emily heard the front door close and saw him walking along the pavement, happily swinging his cane in circles.

"Now," said Miss LaFleur from behind her. "What do you want, Corrigan? And make it quick. I need to test this one."

"Go ahead," said Corrigan. "That's part of the reason we're here anyway. The Queen needs a favor."

Miss LaFleur raised an eyebrow. But before she said anything, a second door leading into the room opened and a girl a few years older than Emily walked in. She had the same color skin as Miss LaFleur, the same shape to her face. Emily wondered if she might be Miss LaFleur's sister.

The girl stared at her. Emily found the intensity of the scrutiny unsettling, but she refused to look away. Miss LaFleur's lips quirked in a tiny smile and she held a hand out to the side. The girl walked forward, still staring at Emily, and they linked fingers.

As soon as they did this, their bodies seemed to change.

They drew close together, and Emily got the strange feeling that there was only one person standing before her instead of two. Their breathing became as one, and Emily realized they even blinked at the same time.

They turned smoothly and left the sitting room through the open door. Corrigan scrambled up Emily's back and perched on her shoulder.

"Go on, then. And stop staring. It's rude."

"Is she fey?"

"Course she is. But chosen because she looks close to your lot."

"And are they really sisters?"

"No. They're actually the same person, split in two."

"What do you mean?"

"There was some spell that went wrong. Miss LaFleur is actually three thousand years old. But she's aging backward. Her other self is a few hundred years old but is aging upward."

"Oh." Emily thought about that for a second. "What will happen when their ages meet?"

"That," said Corrigan wryly, "is the question."

✢⟫Chapter Eleven⟪✢

*In which the All-Seeing Eyes watch Emily. A magical artifact
stolen from Merlin. Inside the Royal Society.*

Four o'clock in the afternoon
on the first day of Emily's adventures.

Emily followed the Sisters through the door and found herself standing at the top of a set of unlit stairs.

"Down you go," said Corrigan.

"Actually," said Emily, reaching over and grabbing hold of Corrigan, "I think you can walk on your own two feet now. I'm tired of carrying you everywhere."

She placed him on the floor and he glared up at her indignantly.

"But I'm not heavy!"

"That's not the point. I'm not your servant."

Corrigan muttered something under his breath, then turned and stomped down the stairs. Emily lost sight of him in the darkness, but then a door opened and he was outlined in the dim glow from within the room below. He stepped through and let the door swing shut behind him.

Emily sighed and trudged down the steps. She pushed the door open and entered a dim room, finding herself standing behind an old wooden shop counter. The only source of light was an oil lamp that cast a wavering orange glow up the wall and across the ceiling. Everything else was shrouded in darkness.

"Hello?"

A moment later she heard the rough scrape of a Lucifer match and a smoky light flared in the blackness, revealing the shadowy planes of Miss LaFleur's face. She lit another lantern, then turned up the flame until the room slowly emerged from the darkness.

"Don't stare," said a voice from behind Emily. "They don't like it."

Emily turned quickly to find the girl standing by her side, the one Corrigan said was the young version of Miss LaFleur.

"Don't stare at what?" she whispered.

In answer, the girl raised her eyes and looked over Emily's shoulder. Emily slowly turned around.

The walls of the room were filled with shelves. And on these shelves were jars and containers of every conceivable size and color. Large glass jars almost as big as Emily was.

Tiny ones no larger than her hand. Strangely shaped ones that curved and turned in upon themselves.

They all contained glass eyes.

Emily stared around in awe. There were thousands of them, each one different from the last. Green eyes. Blue eyes. Brown and even yellow. Cat's eyes, dog's eyes, bird's eyes, and mice's eyes. (The last she knew only because of the crude drawings stuck to the containers.)

Emily shivered, suddenly sorry she had chased Corrigan off her shoulder.

"Corrigan?"

"What?"

Emily glanced in the direction of his voice and saw Corrigan sitting on a long table next to the lantern. She slowly walked out from behind the counter.

The eyes followed her movement.

Emily froze, wondering if she had imagined it. Then she took one step forward.

Every single eye in the room swiveled to follow her path. Emily swallowed nervously.

"I told you not to stare," said the girl, skipping past Emily to once again link hands with Miss LaFleur. Miss LaFleur smiled fondly at her younger version and stroked her cheek.

"Don't tease the poor child," the older woman said.

Emily shuffled closer to Corrigan. "What are we doing here?" she whispered.

"Miss LaFleur here is going to help us get into the Royal Society. Well, I say *us*, but I mean *you*."

"How will she do that?"

Corrigan turned to the tall lady. "You still have someone on the inside?"

"Corrigan, I've had someone inside the Royal Society ever since the Invisible Order took up residence there. But you'll have to wait a moment. I need to test out the Colonel."

Emily watched as Miss LaFleur cleared a space on the cluttered worktable, sweeping strange instruments and half-finished glass eyes into boxes and jars. Then she pulled aside a dirty sheet covering a round piece of thick green glass, cloudy and covered with chips and imperfections. It stood almost as tall as Emily.

"It's the eye of a dragon," said Miss LaFleur as Emily leaned in to inspect it closer. "Used to belong to Merlin. Before I stole it from him, that is."

Miss LaFleur ran her hands over the glassy surface. A dim white light pulsed from within, spreading sluggishly out from the center until it formed a ring close to the edge of the glass. Another light pulsed, this one red. It grew in strength until it was a solid circle sitting within the first ring.

It took Emily a few seconds to realize what she was

looking at. An eye. The red circle was the pupil. But before she could say anything, Miss LaFleur ran her hands over the crystal once again, and the light faded, only to be replaced a second later by a moving image.

Emily frowned. She saw a pair of feet walking along a cobbled pavement. Then the image shifted again and she saw shops off to the side. A hansom cab trundled by on the right. An elegantly dressed lady was seated by the window. The image turned to fix on the lady for a moment.

"There you go. It works," said Corrigan. "Hurry up. I need to see the inside of the Society."

"Not as clear as I'd like," muttered Miss LaFleur. "But what can you do? It will suffice."

Emily suddenly realized what was going on. "His eye. You bewitched the colonel's glass eye so you can see what he sees."

"Took you long enough," said Corrigan.

"But that's not right. How many eyes—?"

Miss LaFleur smiled grimly. "How many glass eyes do I have spying for me? Thousands, I think. I've never counted."

"Do they know that they are spying for you?"

"Of course not! According to my patients, I am simply one of the best makers of glass eyes in the city. People come to me when an accident or disease takes an eye from them. I supply them with a product of exceptional quality, and in return, I occasionally use those eyes to spy for Queen Kelindria."

"But—"

"What's the problem?" asked Corrigan. "It doesn't hurt anyone. Just don't do anything embarrassing in front of someone with a glass eye." He smiled wickedly. "Besides, you should be thankful. Miss LaFleur's collection is going to help you find your way around the Royal Society."

"I thought you said we were going to look inside the Invisible Order."

"We are. But the offices of the Order are within the offices of the Royal Society."

Emily looked blank. The Queen had said something similar when she was telling her about Christopher Wren, but Emily didn't have any idea what the Royal Society *was*. Corrigan clicked his tongue in irritation. "It's very simple, girl. The Royal Society was created in sixteen sixty as a cover to hide the goings-on of the Invisible Order. The Order had been going for centuries before that, but they needed someplace to gather. So Christopher Wren and a few of his mates created the Royal Society as a cover. Course, since then, the Society's become a proper institution for scientists and mathematicians and the like. But the reason it was created was to hide the activities of the Invisible Order. And it's filled with iron. The cursed stuff is everywhere. That's why none of us have ever been able to get inside. All clear now?" He turned to Miss LaFleur. "Is this going to take long?"

"Hold on."

The young girl crossed the room and stopped before a bookshelf crammed full of ledgers.

"It should be number twenty-four," said Miss LaFleur. "No—twenty-five."

The girl took out a ledger and brought it to the table. Miss LaFleur blew the dust away. The spine creaked with disuse when she opened it. She ran her long finger down the pages, muttering to herself. At last, she looked up. "Here we go. We have three in Somerset House. The caretaker is on duty now."

"Wait," said Emily. "Do you mean there are three people with glass eyes working there? Isn't that a bit of a coincidence?"

Corrigan looked uncomfortable. "It was deemed necessary to always have a way of seeing what was going on with the Invisible Order."

It took a while for Emily to understand. "You mean you *caused* them to lose one of their eyes?"

"Not really. They had . . . accidents. Remember the Dark Man? He . . . arranged things."

"But that's horrid!"

"It was necessary," said Miss LaFleur. She checked something on the ledger, then spoke softly. The image on the crystal faded, then slowly coalesced into a red-carpeted corridor lined with wood paneling. A hand was industriously polishing the wood.

"Right." Miss LaFleur unfolded a large sheet of paper that she took from the ledger. "This is what we know so far of the layout of the Royal Society. It goes underground as well, but we haven't managed to get anyone down there." She frowned at the crystal. "Our spy is . . . here." She tapped the paper. Emily leaned forward and saw that it was a map drawn in ink. But the map was incomplete. Vast sections were simply blank spaces. "Perhaps you can help us fill in some of these gaps. But for the meantime, we watch."

Emily spent the next hour watching through the eyes of the caretaker as he went about his duties at the Royal Society. It was boring and tedious, and she soon developed a headache, but she had to admit, she did have a clearer picture of where she would have to go to steal the stone. Corrigan even pointed out the door she had to go through to get to the Invisible Order's offices. The caretaker didn't go into the office, but Emily had its position locked in her head.

She began to think her task might not be so hard after all.

But then she remembered. She still needed help to get *into* the Royal Society.

And the only person she knew who could offer her that help was Jack.

That meant she would have to tell him what was going on. She wouldn't lie to him. Not if he was going to help her do something potentially dangerous.

"Come on," she said to Corrigan. "I want you to meet someone."

⊁ CHAPTER TWELVE ⊱

*In which Emily asks Jack for help and they take
a brief boat trip on the Thames.*

I still don't see why I have to give your boyfriend the second
sight," complained Corrigan as they hurried through the
early-evening streets, the drizzle soaking them to their skin.
"Just spin him a story."

"He's not my boyfriend," snapped Emily. "And that might be
how *you* do things, Corrigan, but not me. I won't lie to him. We
need Jack if we want to get into Somerset House, so we tell him
the truth. And if there's even the remotest chance of him believ-
ing me, he needs to be able to see the fey. It's as simple as that."

"But I could get into trouble," whined the piskie. "The
Queen doesn't like us showing ourselves to your lot."

"No, not unless it suits your own needs," said Emily, walking on.

There was only one place Jack would spend a miserable afternoon like today: Mr. Miller's coffeehouse. Jack liked to sip the bitter drink and pretend he was all grown up, even though he had once told Emily he didn't like the taste. He said he did it because he had to act older than his gang, even though they all were the same age. He said if he didn't act like a grown-up, they wouldn't follow his instructions, and they'd all be in Newgate prison by now.

Emily found Jack seated by the front window of the coffeehouse, surrounded by his gang of thieves. He took a sip from a small cup, and Emily saw the tiny flicker of distaste dance across his features. Emily hurried across the street, pausing while a horse pulling a rickety-looking carriage clattered past. She stopped just beyond the window. Jack, seated closest to the glass, saw her immediately. His eyes widened and he started to say something, but Emily put her finger to her lips, beckoning him outside.

He said something to his gang and rose from the chair. Then he stretched and yawned, winking at Emily as he did so.

Emily shook her head in exasperation. Why couldn't he do anything without showing off?

Emily moved away from the window and took shelter beneath the awning of a shop. Jack soon joined her, briskly rubbing his hands together.

"Emily!" he said. "I've been worried sick. Is everything all right?"

"No," said Emily. "It's not." She hesitated, unsure how to proceed. "Jack," she said. "I'm going to show you something, but you have to promise not to do anything . . . abrupt. Don't pull out that knife I saw this morning. Don't shout or run away or anything like that. It's important."

Jack stared at her doubtfully, then nodded. "All right," he said.

Emily took a deep breath. "Corrigan?"

Jack frowned. "Who's Corrigan?" he asked.

"I am," said Corrigan from his position by Emily's knee.

Jack looked down.

"Boo," said the piskie.

Jack gasped and stumbled backward into the rain, his eyes fixed on Corrigan. He lifted a shaking finger.

"Snow," he said distantly. "What is that?"

"A piskie," said Emily.

"Is it real?"

"What do you think?" snapped Corrigan. He looked up at Emily. "You sure he can help? Seems a bit stupid if you ask me."

"Behave," said Emily, nudging Corrigan with her knee.

Jack glanced up at the rain, then stepped beneath the shelter of the awning once again. He crouched down and prodded Corrigan. The piskie tried to bat his finger away.

"Hey! Get off. What—?"

"Ugly little beggar, isn't he?" said Jack.

"I *beg* your pardon!" exclaimed Corrigan. "I happen to be a very good-looking piskie. Not like you lot with your—"

But Jack wasn't listening. He stood up, leaving Corrigan to splutter into silence, and faced Emily. "Tell me," he said. "Tell me everything."

So Emily did. Starting with the battle she stumbled across that morning and ending with their recent trip to the Sisters. As he listened, Jack leaned up against the wall of the shop, staring into the rain. When Emily finished, he straightened up and cast a dark look at Corrigan.

"And now these Unseelie have got Will?"

Emily nodded. "That's why I need your help. If we can get this seeing stone from inside the Invisible Order, Corrigan says the Queen could use it to find him." Emily watched Jack as he gazed thoughtfully at the ground. "Will you help?" she asked hesitantly.

Jack's head snapped up. "Course I will, Snow. I was just thinking the best way to go about it. You know you can count on me." He flashed a grin at her. "Spring-Heeled Jack will save the day."

"Oh, well, that settles it," said Corrigan sarcastically. "All our problems are over."

When Emily had watched through the enchanted eye, the rooms of the Royal Society hadn't seemed overly large. She'd thought it might be a single-story building. Or something that looked like her old school, with a slate roof that glistened wetly in the rain and tiny windows that let in the smallest amount of light.

She certainly hadn't expected this. The building was enormous. It stood three stories high and was shaped like a massive *U*. Emily stared at it between gaps in the never-ending traffic of clattering carriages and trotting horses.

It would take days to search all the rooms inside. There would be hundreds of them.

Jack must have sensed her thoughts. "It's not all the Royal Society," he said. "The building is called Somerset House. The Society keeps offices here, but so do other groups." He pointed off to the right. "I think the rooms you are looking for are over there."

"How will we get in?" asked Emily. "There are so many people about."

"I've been thinking about that," said Jack. "The other side of Somerset House borders the Thames. There are arches and doors built into that side of the building so people can get in by boat if they want. All we have to do is get to one of those doors and I'll get us inside. No one will see us under there."

"How do you know so much about it?" asked Corrigan. Emily thought he sounded impressed, though he was doing his best to hide it.

"I was hired as a scout a while back to check out the Adelphi Theatre." He pointed along the street. "It's that big building down the way. The Thames was the same route I suggested to them."

"Stealing's wrong, you know," said Emily primly.

Jack let out a crow of laughter. Passersby glanced at him and frowned. A well-dressed lady veered around them so as not to come too close.

"What's so funny?"

"You. 'Stealing's wrong, you know.' What do you think we're about to do? Have a picnic in Hyde Park?"

"This is different. We're only taking what doesn't belong to them."

Jack shook his head ruefully. "Don't think the bobbies will agree with you there."

"When are you going to do it?" asked Corrigan.

"Later on tonight." Jack looked at Emily. "Meet you at the Adelphi at ten? Will you be all right till then?"

"Why wouldn't I be?" asked Emily, offended. "I only asked for help, Jack. That doesn't mean I can't do anything by myself."

Jack held his hands up. "Fine. Where will you be? In case I need to find you," he added, seeing Emily's brows come together angrily.

Emily thought about it. "Maybe I'll go home," she said. "I can get a few hours' sleep."

"But will it be safe?" asked Jack. "What about the Unseelie?"

"They won't be back," said Corrigan. "They already took a great risk when they kidnapped William. They won't expose themselves again."

"Anyway," said Emily. "I'll just hide under what's left of the bed."

Jack thought about it and nodded. "Probably a good idea, actually. No telling how long we'll be awake tonight. Till ten, then."

Jack turned and disappeared into the crowd. Emily glanced at Corrigan. "And you?"

Corrigan shivered. "Well, obviously I can't come in with you. I can feel the iron from here." He was thoughtful for a moment. "Do you know Seven Dials?"

"Course I do."

"Good. Head up Great St. Andrew's Street till you come to a side alley. It's called Oberon's Court. Follow the alley until you reach a fey tavern called the Unicorn's Head. I'll be there waiting."

"There's no alley called Oberon's Court in Great St. Andrew's Street," said Emily.

"Trust me," said Corrigan. "It's there."

⊶ ⊷

The rain had stopped by the time Emily arrived at the Adelphi Theatre later that night. She could even see one or two stars glittering through the departing clouds.

She stood across the street and watched the toffs dressed in their fancy suits and furs filing inside to watch the play. She'd love to see a show like that. The closest she'd ever come was visiting the penny music halls, but the noise and drunken laughter and all the smoke had been too much for her, and she'd had to leave. Anyway, she hadn't understood half the songs they were singing. Everyone else seemed to find them hilarious, but Emily had just thought them silly.

Now, a *proper* play. One performed by actors, with proper music—*that* she would love to see.

Emily huddled down in her thick coat and tried to keep herself warm. She'd gone home—just as she said she would. But she wished she hadn't. She'd huddled beneath the bed and managed to grab a couple of hours' sleep, but her dreams were filled with images of William being held against his will by a creature that was a combination of Ravenhill and the Dark Man. It had Ravenhill's face but had black eyes

130

and skeletal wings, and it reached out with clawed hands to enfold William in its grasp.

Emily had woken up with tears in her eyes and had quickly left her old home. She didn't want to return there ever again.

She had paused to buy some food with the shilling Merrian gave her that morning, and it had gone a long way to restoring her flagging energy. Despite her fitful sleep, Emily felt refreshed, ready to face whatever lay ahead of them.

There was still no sign of Jack, though. What if he had changed his mind? What if he thought it too dangerous?

"Miss me?"

Emily jumped. Jack had appeared at her side, an impudent grin on his face. He grabbed hold of her hand and set off down the street. "Come on. Everything's all set."

He led her past the theater doors and down a narrow alley that led around the back of the building to a long metal railing. On the other side of the railing flowed the thick and murky waters of the Thames. On the opposite shore, barges and wherries were tied up for the night, and farther along the bank she could see the small towboats that were used to offload the contents of the merchant ships. Even from here she could hear the dirty water slapping sluggishly against the slime-coated hulls.

Jack moved along the railing to a set of stairs. At the

bottom of the steps was a small rowboat. The smell of sewage filled Emily's nostrils. She gagged and straightened up. "Do we have to go that way?" she asked.

"We do if you don't want to be seen. Come on. Just cover your mouth."

Emily reluctantly followed Jack down the slippery stairs, one hand pressing her sleeve across her mouth and nose. Jack stepped into the boat, and the little vessel pitched alarmingly in the water. There was already a large puddle of black liquid sloshing about inside.

"Is it safe?" she asked.

Jack looked up from where he was sliding the oars into the water. "Of course it's safe. We're not going to be in here long. Come on."

Emily took one last look around, then carefully stepped onboard, trying to avoid getting her shoes wet. Not that it would make *that* much difference. They were already damp from the rain this afternoon. But at least they didn't stink.

Jack untied the frayed rope that had been holding the small boat in place and dipped the oars into the water. He pulled, and the boat slowly started to crawl along the river. Emily tried to remember how far down the street Somerset House was. She thought about asking Jack, but he was concentrating on rowing, so she decided against it. She didn't think it was too far.

A dead dog floated past them, carried away with the current. Emily heard someone shouting *"Thief!"* in the distance, then the piercing whistle of the crushers as they gave chase. The sound of drunken laughter spilled over from a barge in the distance. A door slammed open and she could just make out a square of warm light, then the silhouette of someone leaning over the barge railings. There was the sound of something wet hitting the water.

They passed the first of a series of large arches cut into the wall. Emily peered inside and could just make out the dark glint of water in a tunnel, but she couldn't see where it went.

They passed three more arches, but at the fourth one, Jack quickly started rowing with only one oar, spinning the boat around like a leaf in a stream. Then he pulled on both oars until they slipped inside a dark passage.

The sounds of the river lapping against the hull echoed eerily inside the tunnel. A moment later, they bumped up against a small wooden pier. Jack quickly threw the rope over a mooring post and clambered from the boat.

"You coming?" he whispered.

But Emily was already climbing out onto the pier. It led to a small set of stairs that ended at a thick, imposing-looking door. Jack leaned down to inspect the lock.

He straightened with a smile and pulled a thin package about the length of his forearm from his jacket. "I'll have you inside in thirty seconds," he said, unfolding the leather covering and selecting three thin metal tools. Then he turned his attention to the door.

He didn't get them inside in thirty seconds.

It took him only twenty.

⊰≡ CHAPTER THIRTEEN ≡⊱
In which Emily and Jack sneak inside the Invisible Order.

ELEVEN O'CLOCK IN THE EVENING
ON THE FIRST DAY OF EMILY'S ADVENTURES.

The door opened into a dimly lit, tiled corridor. Emily didn't recognize the corridor itself, but the pattern of the tile was familiar. She had seen it earlier as she followed the caretaker through the halls and passages of the Royal Society. The man had an unfortunate tendency to stare at his feet while walking.

She felt oddly relaxed. Up till this point, she still hadn't been sure what would be waiting for her once she got inside. Oh, she'd watched through the eye that afternoon, but it had all seemed so . . . unreal. At least here was confirmation that what she had seen *was* real.

Jack was busy fixing the lock so that the key wouldn't be able to turn the mechanism any more.

"Just in case," he said in response to Emily's questioning look. "Now we can get in and out whenever we want to. Well . . . at least until someone calls in a locksmith."

"That didn't seem very hard," said Emily.

"Well, it wouldn't," said Jack proudly. "Not to an *outsider*. If you was in the know, you'd understand how hard all this was."

He marked off his accomplishments on his fingers as they walked down the corridor.

"I mean, first there was the scoutin'. That took all afternoon—"

"You said you already knew how to get in because of another job."

"Well, I didn't say *which* afternoon, did I? Then I had to get the boat and row it across the river without being seen. Not to mention the wear and tear on my tools. Very intricate mechanisms, you see. Got to be careful how much you use them—"

"Yes, yes," snapped Emily as she looked about for a familiar landmark. "Jolly well done. Couldn't have done it without you and all that." She placed her ear against a door. There was no sound coming from within, so she gently pushed it open. A dusty storeroom lay beyond, filled from floor to ceiling with old crates. Emily frowned and closed the door again.

The corridor ended at another door. The carpet here was green with a diamond pattern. She couldn't remember seeing that through the dragon's eye. She pulled the map from her pocket and stared at the neat drawings, searching for something familiar.

"What are you looking for?" asked Jack, peering over her shoulder.

"This doesn't look familiar. I don't remember seeing any of this."

"Oh." Jack was silent for a moment. "Maybe that's because you're not inside the Royal Society yet."

Emily looked up from the map. "What?"

Jack shrugged. "This was the easiest place to get inside. The place you're looking for is in another wing."

Emily resisted the urge to yank on Jack's ear like she sometimes did with William. "Just lead the way," she ordered.

Jack saluted. "Yes, ma'am."

Jack was good at what he did. Emily had to give him that. If he hadn't been guiding her, she would have been lost in a second. And that wasn't even taking into consideration the three locked doors he got them through.

But eventually Emily started to recognize her surroundings. They entered a corridor lit with a ruddy golden glow by a series of ornate gas lamps attached to the walls. The light fell across thickly carpeted floors and walls cluttered with paintings, the subjects of which ranged from landscapes to mischievous-looking faeries to the Great Fire of London. It was this painting that told Emily she was in the Royal Society; she remembered the caretaker cleaning the frame earlier that day.

Emily pushed her hair behind her ears and peered both ways along the corridor. For all intents and purposes, this wing was deserted. But she knew that didn't really mean anything. Corrigan had told her the members of the Royal Society kept strange hours, so any number of them could be hidden away in their offices, doing whatever it was they did here.

"Which way?" whispered Jack.

Emily tried to remember the path the caretaker had walked. "Down here," she whispered, turning right and hurrying along the corridor. She shivered, feeling totally exposed. If someone were to step through one of the numerous doors that lined the corridor, they would be spotted straightaway. What would her excuse be? There was nothing she could say that would sound believable.

Then make sure you don't get caught, she told herself sternly, putting on an extra burst of speed.

She followed the caretaker's footsteps until she came to

a small, dark corridor that branched off to the left. This was where Miss LaFleur had said the Invisible Order had its offices. Emily's map didn't show any detail here. She was on her own.

Marble pedestals sat in recesses along the walls, and at the end of the corridor was an imposing door painted pitch-black.

She turned to Jack and saw a look of doubt pass briefly across his face.

"Is there a problem?" she asked.

"No. Why should there be a problem?"

"Jack."

Jack tore his gaze away from the immense door. "What?"

"Can you open it?"

"I'm almost certainly positive I can."

Emily's eyes narrowed. Jack hastily raised his hands in surrender. "Sorry. Yes, I can open it. It'll just take a bit of time." He took out his tools and got to work.

"I hope you *can* unlock it," said Emily. "I would hate for word to get around the streets that you aren't a very good thief."

Jack looked over his shoulder. "You're not helping, you know." He turned back to the lock, then paused. "And you have a very cruel sense of humor."

Emily watched for a while as he wiggled the three long

pieces of metal inside the keyhole. She eventually got bored and headed back down the corridor to look out for anyone approaching.

The corridor was still deserted. With any luck they would be in and out before anyone saw them. She only hoped that she would be able to find the stone. Emily smiled grimly. She was getting ahead of herself. She only hoped she would be able to find the *vault*, never mind the stone. Just then, a noise froze her in her tracks.

She peered around the corner and saw the door at the far end of the passage open. A young man wearing round spectacles and carrying a huge pile of books staggered through and closed the door behind him. He paused to readjust everything in his arms, then headed in Emily's direction.

She ran to Jack. "Someone's coming!" she whispered. "Are you nearly done?"

"You can't rush these things, Emily."

"Well, you'd better learn how!"

"You're not helping," said Jack through gritted teeth.

Emily balled her fists in frustration. She ran back along the corridor and listened. She could hear the young man muttering to himself. She risked another look, then jerked her head back. He was almost on top of her.

Emily ran to Jack and grabbed him by the collar, yanking him so hard he toppled off his feet. He rolled over onto his knees and spun to face her, but Emily raised a finger to her lips and hastily retreated into the shadows formed by one of the marble pedestals. Jack quickly shuffled forward and crouched down next to Emily a split second before the man turned into the corridor.

They were no more than an arm's length from the door. The young man walked toward them, still muttering to himself. Emily strained to hear.

". . . see why I should have to work. It's not fair. Not fair at all." The young man paused before the door, and a book slipped from his pile and fell to the floor with a heavy thud. Emily felt her heart freeze. Jutting out from beneath the book were Jack's lock picks, rolled in their cloth cover.

The man bent down to pick up his book. Emily held her breath. His fingers curled beneath the open cover, almost touching the picks. But he just missed them. He lifted the book and placed it back on the top of his pile, then raised his knee to balance them as he managed to get his hand inside his trouser pocket and withdrew a heavy iron key.

He unlocked the door, then placed the key back in his pocket. With one hand, he opened the door and stumbled in, almost losing his balance as he tried to keep hold of his books.

The door swung closed behind him, and Emily and Jack rose to their feet.

"That was close," said Jack softly.

"Yes, it was," hissed Emily. "Why did you leave your picks on the floor? He could have spotted them!"

"But he didn't, did he?"

Emily opened her mouth, ready to reply, but the sound of a distant door brought her back to the task at hand.

She tested the door and found it still unlocked. A large library lay beyond. Soft light illuminated wooden shelves that climbed all the way to the ceiling. Books were crammed into every available space. Four large desks occupied most of the floor space, their surfaces piled with papers and ledgers.

There was no sign of the young man. He must have left through the door on the opposite wall.

Emily stepped into the library. Jack scooped up his picks and followed, looking around in awe.

"I've never seen so many books in one place," he said. "Wouldn't it be something to be able to read?"

"I can read," said Emily absently.

Jack looked at her, his eyes wide with wonder. "Truly?"

"Yes. I used to go to school, you know. Before Da disappeared."

"Will you read to me sometime?"

Emily was a little nonplussed by the change in Jack's attitude, from cocky thief to pleading boy. "I'll read to you," she said. "*If* we manage to get out of here without being caught."

Jack smiled at her. "You worry too much. I've got you this far, haven't I?"

"Yes, but I honestly have no idea how."

Jack took another look around the library. "I always knew there was something different about you, Emily Snow. Now I know what it is."

"What?"

"Education. You've got class, you have. You've got smarts."

Emily snorted and turned away, trying to hide a flush of pleasure. She started toward the door. "Pity the same can't be said about you," she said, glancing briefly over her shoulder.

Jack just shook his head in amusement and followed.

⇥ CHAPTER FOURTEEN ⇤

In which Emily and Jack are trapped inside Ravenhill's office.

<small>MIDNIGHT ON THE SECOND DAY OF EMILY'S ADVENTURES.</small>

T he library opened into another carpeted corridor.
Immediately to their left was a huge, iron-bound door that
looked like it belonged in a dungeon. A keyhole as long as
her finger was set into the pitted wood.

"Don't ask me to pick that," whispered Jack. "I don't have
the tools big enough."

The rest of the corridor was lined with more normal-
looking doors. One of them was open and Emily peered nervously inside, but she found nothing more than a cramped,
untidy office.

Emily was rather disappointed. She had expected something a bit more dramatic from the offices of a centuries-old
secret society charged to seek out and destroy the creatures
of Faerie.

"Which one?" asked Jack in a low voice. There was no sign of the young man, but he had to be around somewhere.

"Um . . ." Emily thought. "I'm not sure, actually. Probably that one."

Jack pointed to the end of the corridor, where a single mahogany door faced them, the most daunting of all the doors in the corridor—besides the iron-bound one. "There?"

"Why not?"

They crept along the corridor. When they got about halfway, Emily heard a voice muttering inside one of the offices. That must be where the young man was.

They reached the last door and Jack bent down and peered into the lock. "No problem," he whispered. "I'll have it open in a second."

"You mean like the last one?"

Jack gave her a wounded look. "I would have cracked it eventually. These things just take time."

"Just get on with it."

Jack heaved a theatrical sigh. "You're a very hard girl to impress, do you know that?"

Emily opened her mouth to retort, but Jack just raised his hands in surrender and got to work. True to his word, he had the door open in a few seconds.

"Easy," he said, getting to his feet again. "It's not even a new lock. It's over ten years old, that."

He opened the door, revealing a large office that was almost the same size as the library. An ancient-looking desk dominated the center of the room, its dark wood carved and etched with elaborate designs. Jack whistled when he saw it.

"That would fetch a shilling or two to a collector. I wonder how heavy it is."

"We're here for a reason, Jack," said Emily nervously. She was staring at the desk. There was a stovepipe hat sitting in the center of the wood. Ravenhill's hat.

"Just thinking out loud, that's all. So where is this stone of yours?"

Emily tore her gaze away from Ravenhill's hat. "Actually, I don't think the stone's in here."

Jack frowned at her. "Then what are we doing, if you don't mind me asking?"

"Looking for a key to the vault where it *is* kept."

"Ah." Jack looked around. "Any ideas?"

Emily also glanced around. Paintings and bookshelves lined the walls. To the side of the desk, there was a filing cabinet and a massive globe of the world. A map of London hung on the wall opposite the desk, with little pins sticking into it in various locations. The key could be anywhere.

"You start with the desk," Jack said, lifting the painting closest to him and checking behind it. He moved to the next while Emily walked around the vast desk and tried the top drawer.

It slid easily open, but all it contained were papers, some new, some old and yellowing. She closed it again. The next drawer was locked. The one underneath opened partway, then stuck. Emily peered inside but couldn't see anything of interest.

"Emily!"

She looked up and saw that one of the paintings Jack was checking had swung away on a hinge to reveal a small safe.

"Can you open it?" she asked.

"Maybe."

Jack leaned forward to inspect the safe. Then he unrolled his packet of tools and took out a crowbar, which he inserted between the wall and the safe. He pushed on the bar, stopping when the safe scraped out slightly from its hiding place.

"I need some cushions," he said. "Something soft."

Emily ran over to a couch next to the filing cabinet and dragged all the cushions over to Jack. He arranged them beneath the safe.

"This might make a bit of noise," he said. "But I need to get the safe out so I can spring the rivets. Promise not to shout at me?"

"Depends on how much noise it makes," said Emily nervously, glancing at the door.

Jack applied pressure to the crowbar, and the safe slowly slid out of the hole in the wall. It teetered on the edge, then dropped heavily onto the cushions with a resounding *thunk!* Emily hurried to the door and cracked it open. No sign of anyone coming to investigate the noise.

She closed the door. Jack now had a chisel out and was holding it against one of four rivets on the top of the safe.

"See, most people try to get in through the door, but that's a common mistake. On these older safes the seals are the weak points. Just be thankful this wasn't a Milner safe. One of those would take hours to crack." Jack hefted a small hammer and glanced at Emily, eyebrows raised questioningly. She nodded quickly, and Jack struck the rivet one sharp blow. The head of the rivet flew off and smacked the wall.

They both winced at the noise of the hammer. Surely someone had heard that?

"Hurry up. Get it over with."

Jack nodded and quickly hit each of the three remaining rivets. After the last one was broken, they strained their ears, barely breathing as they listened for any sounds that would indicate discovery.

There was nothing for a while, and Emily started to believe they had actually gotten away with it.

Then she heard a door slam in the corridor beyond.

Emily hurried over to the door. She didn't open it this time, but bent down to peer through the keyhole.

She almost cried out in shock when she saw Ravenhill's distinctive silhouette in the corridor beyond. He was standing at the open door of the young man's office, and she thought she could hear their low voices.

"Jack!" she whispered over her shoulder.

Jack was trying to pry the top of the safe off, but was having some difficulty. Emily dared not speak any louder. She ran across the thick carpeting and grabbed him by the shoulder.

"Jack, it's him. Ravenhill. He's coming."

"Hold on, Emily. I've almost got it."

"There's no time!"

"Just a bit longer," said Jack, tapping the chisel gently. He looked over at her. "If anything goes wrong, head back to the coffeehouse. All right?"

Emily nodded. She hurried back to the door and put her eye to the keyhole . . .

. . . to find Ravenhill standing directly in front of the door, his leg only inches away.

Emily jerked back her head in shock. She watched as the door handle moved downward. The click of the latch releasing sounded as loud as a gunshot. She turned to warn Jack, but he was carefully lowering the top panel of the safe onto a cushion. He turned to her with a grin of triumph, a grin that quickly vanished when he saw the door slowly opening.

This was it. Ravenhill could simply kill them both now; no one would be any wiser. Would he go that far?

Emily thought he would. She could see Ravenhill's shoe as it swung slowly forward to enter the office.

"Mr. Ravenhill."

The door stopped moving. Emily watched the booted foot retreat and come down on the landing outside. Then it swiveled around.

"Mr. Ravenhill!"

Emily peered through the gap in the door and saw the young man hurrying down the hall, gesturing for Ravenhill's attention.

"What is it, Sebastian?" asked Ravenhill.

Emily could not suppress a shudder of fear at the sound of that voice.

"Hsst!"

Emily turned to see Jack signaling frantically for her to hide. She scrambled to her feet as Jack darted behind the couch. Emily looked quickly around the office. There was a set of curtains behind the desk. She ran forward and slid behind the thick velvet material.

And not a moment too soon. She had just stilled the

curtains (keeping a tiny gap so she could see) when Raven-hill entered the room.

As soon as he did so, Ravenhill stopped moving. He frowned, tilting his head upward and testing the air with his nose.

Then he turned slowly and stared directly at the mess on the floor.

He lunged across the floor and examined the safe, but luckily Jack had managed to replace the top panel so that the safe still appeared to be sealed. Ravenhill fished around in his pocket and pulled out a key. He inserted it into the safe door and was about to unlock it when Jack suddenly popped up from behind the couch and sauntered across the carpet.

Emily's eyes widened in amazement. Ravenhill's head turned slowly to follow Jack's movements. Emily could almost feel the shock radiating from him. Jack stopped in front of the door and turned to face Ravenhill. A cocky grin appeared on his face.

Ravenhill and Jack stayed frozen like this for a few seconds, neither of them moving. Then, as if on some kind of hidden signal, they both moved at the same time. Jack turned and yanked open the door, sprinting out into the corridor. Ravenhill yanked out the key and surged to his feet, no more than a few steps behind.

Emily was alone.

She let out her breath in an explosive gasp, then slipped out of her hiding place. Jack had sacrificed himself as a diversion, and she had to move quickly to make sure it wasn't in vain. She just hoped he was fast enough to escape Ravenhill's clutches.

She hurried to the safe, unable to keep a smile from her face. He'd done it. Despite all his cocky, annoying ways, Jack had actually done it.

Emily pried the top panel loose with the crowbar Jack had left lying on the floor. There were a few yellowing documents piled inside, but she ignored them and pulled out a ring of keys hidden at the bottom. There were three keys on the ring, two large and one small. According to Corrigan, one of these would open up the door to the vault, and inside the vault she would find the stone. Emily assumed one of the others was for the door at the end of the corridor outside.

She grasped the keys tightly and hurriedly left Ravenhill's office, praying she would never have to step inside again.

⊱ Chapter Fifteen ⊰

In which Emily finds more than she bargained for inside the vault.

One o'clock in the morning
on the second day of Emily's adventures.

There was no sign of the other man, the one Ravenhill had called Sebastian. He must have heard the commotion and joined in the chase.

Emily ran to the huge, iron-bound door at the other end of the corridor and inserted the most likely-looking key. It clunked its way into the keyhole, and she had to strain with both hands before it would unlock the door.

It swung grudgingly open to reveal a set of darkened stairs. Emily frowned. She needed some light.

The lamps on the walls looked fixed in place. She quickly entered Sebastian's office and paused in surprise. It was more like a sitting room than an office. A cheery fire roared in the grate. Comfortable-looking chairs were placed in a small circle close to the hearth. Bookshelves lined the wall, and just beneath a window was a small, neat desk. It was on the desk that she found what she was looking for: a small, portable oil lamp. She lit the wick from a box of matches on the fireplace and quickly returned to the stairs.

The stone was old and weathered, the centers of the steps smoothed and bowed from years of passage. She closed the door behind her. The only light came from the lamp, a small circle of flickering orange that extended barely an arm's length in front of her.

She hesitated, imagining all kinds of horrors lurking in the darkness, just waiting for her to walk into their midst.

"Come on, Emily," she muttered to herself. "Do it for William."

She took a deep breath and set her foot on the second step. Nothing jumped out at her, or reached out to grasp her ankle. Nothing slithered along the walls, or brushed against her hair.

Emboldened, Emily walked slowly downward.

The stairs soon ended in a flagstone passage. Emily held up the lamp and saw the light reflected dully off something up ahead, a huge metal door about three times taller than she was. She ran her hands over the cold metal. Corrigan was right. If iron was poison to the fey, there was no way they would be able to get close to this.

There was a large keyhole protected by a rusty cover. Emily pushed the cover aside, wincing at the loud scrape of metal on metal, and pushed the second of the large keys inside the lock. It stuck at first, but she leaned into it and pushed, and it jerked into the hole with a solid *clunk*. After she had turned it halfway, the mechanism engaged and the key turned the rest of the way of its own accord. She heard the locks releasing inside the massive door, and a second later it trundled slowly open.

Emily jumped out of the way and barely avoided being hit by the door. A dark entrance was revealed, uninviting and thick with cloying shadows, as if an air of oppression was about to waft out of the room to embrace her in clammy arms. She shivered and raised the lantern higher, but the light did nothing to penetrate the darkness.

Emily hesitated, then remembered that Ravenhill was somewhere upstairs, and Jack wouldn't be able to keep him occupied for long. She took a deep breath, held the light out before her like a shield, and stepped over the threshold.

The room was colder than the corridor outside. Emily's breath misted the air in front of her face. She held the lantern high, the light crawling halfheartedly over crammed shelves filled with all manner of items: wooden boxes, earthenware jars, ancient-looking books so large Emily would not have been able to lift them. She turned in a slow circle, examining everything around her. One shelf was filled with the skulls of strange animals, some larger than a human skull, others tiny, no bigger than her own thumb. One of the skulls looked like a horse's, but it had a large horn issuing from the center of its forehead.

Another shelf held only glass jars, all of varying sizes. Emily leaned forward nervously, thinking that perhaps they held eyes, like the jars at Miss LaFleur's shop. She couldn't quite make out what was inside them. She brought the torch closer—

Emily jumped back with a small cry of alarm. The jars were filled with some kind of thick fluid and suspended in the fluid were creatures of the fey. Dead, all of them, their faces bleached white and bloated. Just floating there in the fluid, forever.

Emily felt sick to her stomach. She had to get out of here, to see the streets of London again. She needed to feel the air on her face, hear the shouts of costers selling oranges and apples, hot nuts and coffee. The shouts of real people. The friendly face of Mrs. Eldridge peddling her watercress.

She looked around again, focusing on what she had come here for. The stone was valuable, said Corrigan, so that meant it probably wouldn't just have been tossed on the shelves with the other items. And besides, there was one more key left on the ring. It had to open something.

Emily quickly searched through the room, recoiling in disgust when she came across a corkboard with the desiccated corpses of faeries pinned to it, their wings pulled wide like butterflies.

She tried the key in four small chests but none of them would open. She was running out of time. Surely Ravenhill would be coming back soon, and he would discover that the keys to the vault were missing.

Finally, at the far end of the room, Emily found one more chest. This one was constructed entirely from iron. She inserted the key and sighed with relief when it turned smoothly in the lock.

Emily lifted the lid. The stone was inside, nestled on a piece of red satin. It was exactly as Corrigan had described, a black-gray stone with a hole in the center. Emily took it out and examined it. It didn't seem all that special. She had expected something more . . . *magical.* This just looked like a stone she would find on the shores of the Thames.

But that didn't matter. She had it. Now the Queen could help her find William. Then she could use the stone to read the spell and get back to Faerie. Everyone would win.

About to leave the vault, Emily hesitated. Would it be possible for *her* to use the stone to find William? That would save a lot of time. If she could do that, she could just hand the stone over to Corrigan while she and Jack went to rescue

Will. Emily turned the stone over in her hands. How would it work? It was magic, obviously, but did it need a magical command? She held it up to her mouth and whispered into the hole.

"Find William," she whispered.

Nothing happened. Emily lifted the stone to her eye and looked through it, thinking of William as she did so. Again, nothing. Emily sighed. Maybe the Queen was the only one who could use it.

Emily hid the stone inside her coat, then quickly left the vault, locking the door behind her. She hurried back up the steps and paused at the door leading out into the passage. She listened for a moment but didn't hear anything out of the ordinary.

She waited a few seconds more, then stepped into the hall and closed the door behind her. She contemplated taking the keys back but decided against it. Ravenhill would see the damaged safe regardless. If she kept the keys, there was no way the Order could gain access to the vault to see what she had stolen.

Feeling rather proud of her reasoning, Emily pulled open the door to the library.

And found herself face-to-face with the young man Ravenhill had called Sebastian.

His eyes widened in shock. "Who—?" he began, but he

didn't get any further, because Emily burst suddenly into tears.

"Please, mister," she sobbed. "Don't kill me. Jack made me come with him. I was supposed to be a lookout, only I'm no good at it, because it's wrong. Please don't lock me up. My mum is sick, and . . . and . . ." Emily faltered, rapidly running out of things to cry about. She risked a glance at the man and almost smiled to see the distressed look on his face. ". . . and I have to look after her. Jack forced me to do it, see. I didn't have a choice."

"Er . . . there, there," said Sebastian awkwardly. He glanced nervously over his shoulder. "Um . . . yes. I think . . ." He looked at Emily again and tried to look stern. "Have you learned your lesson, young lady?"

Emily wiped her eyes and sniffed. "Oh, yes, sir. Ever so. I won't never 'sociate with the likes of him again. He's a bad apple, he is."

"Yes. Um . . . a very *fast* bad apple, as it turns out. I hope he didn't get away with anything valuable. So you promise not to try something like this again?"

"Promise, sir."

"All right. Then I think you should just go. And quickly, before Mr. Ravenhill comes back."

Emily thought about trying to find her way back through the corridors and down to the boat. She didn't think she would be able to row it on her own. Actually, would it even be there? Jack had probably used it to escape. She looked at Sebastian, her lower lip trembling.

"Can you show me how to get out? I can't remember the way."

"I really don't think—"

Emily scrunched up her eyes, and Sebastian waved his hands in the air.

"All right," he said. "Hurry now."

He turned and guided her through the library, then along corridors and hallways and down grand-looking stairs. After about five minutes, he was hastily unlocking the front doors of Somerset House. Emily looked around the large entrance hall. There were statues all around, and massive paintings on the walls.

"Hurry, now," said Sebastian, pulling the door open onto a flight of steps. "And remember, you'd better not come back."

"You needn't worry there, mister," said Emily, almost running through the door. "Thanks." She rejoiced at the feel of cold air against her face as she hurried across the open square that fed onto the Strand. The stone was reassuringly heavy in her pocket.

From Sebastian's words, it seemed that Jack had gotten away. Emily remembered Jack had said to meet back at the coffeeshop if anything went wrong, so she made her way there through the dark, late-night streets. The coffeehouse was almost empty, with only a few stragglers left.

Jack wasn't one of them.

Had he been caught, then? Maybe Ravenhill had caught up with him after Sebastian had given up the chase.

"Looking for someone?" said a voice behind her.

Emily whirled around to find Jack lounging against a lamppost, grinning at her.

"Will you stop *doing* that!" she shouted, relief washing through her body.

"Did you get it?" he asked.

Emily nodded, her features breaking into a smile.

Jack's grin widened. "Now, aren't you glad you came to me for help?"

"Moderately glad," said Emily. "How did you get away?"

Jack spread his arms wide, like an actor on the stage. "I'm Spring-Heeled Jack, Snow. No one catches Spring-Heeled Jack."

≈CHAPTER SIXTEEN≈

*In which Emily discovers a part of Seven Dials she never knew
existed and meets a peculiar gnome called Mr. Pemberton.*

The neighborhood of London called Seven Dials was
named after an old column that used to stand in its central
plaza. Emily's schoolmaster had told her that the column had
seven dials on it with which to tell the time, and each one of
these dials faced one of seven streets that radiated away from
the courtyard like the spokes on a wheel. The column was
long gone, but the name remained. (Even though Jack had
once told her there were only six dials atop the column. How
he knew that, Emily had no idea.)

Emily had lived around Seven Dials for the past few years,
and she knew the area as well as any part of London. She
had always thought of it as a small Irish town magically
separated from the rest of the city. It was filled with the Irish,

and almost no other nationality lived here unless given per-mission. She'd heard talk about how dangerous it was, how violent the people were. But she had never experienced that.

"So you're saying there's more of them? All over London?" Jack cast a nervous glance around the street. "Are there any here now?"

"No," said Emily. "Anyway, you'd be able to see if there were. Corrigan gave you the sight, remember? When he let you see him, he gave you the ability to see all of the fey."

"I wonder what kind of treasures they have," said Jack musingly.

"Don't even think about it, Jack. They'll probably cut your hands off if they catch you."

"*If* they catch me. Which they won't. Because I'm—"

"—Spring-Heeled Jack, I know."

Corrigan had said to take Great St. Andrew's Street. Emily still didn't know why. She'd been in the street a hun-dred times over the years and she knew there was no pub there, for the fey or otherwise.

The reason Emily knew Great St. Andrew's so well was because of what was sold there: birds, dozens of different kinds. When she came during the day, she would close her eyes and let the cacophony of sounds wash over her. The chittering call of the goldcrests, the cheep of the finches, the scolding cry of the blackbirds, and the mimicry of the starlings. The birds all hung close together in their cramped cages. Yellow canaries and green lovebirds, robin redbreasts, and even strange parrots from as far away as Africa. Their color and sound always distracted her from the drabness and soot stains of the city.

But the birds were all quiet now, sleeping inside the shops.

"Do you know where you're going?" asked Jack.

"Course I do," said Emily.

Actually, she didn't, not really. Corrigan had said there was an alley halfway up the street, but Emily hadn't remembered ever seeing one. She led Jack past closed-up shops and shadowy doorways until, sure enough, as she approached the halfway point, she saw a narrow lane separating two decrepit shops. She was positive it hadn't been here before.

She looked up at the street sign: OBERON'S COURT. No, she'd definitely never seen this before.

"This it?" asked Jack.

"I think so," said Emily, peering inside. All she could see were dark shadows. The alley didn't seem too deep, but as her eyes adjusted to the dimness, she realized this was because the path turned sharply to the left about ten paces in. Emily sighed, feeling inside her coat to make sure the Queen's seeing stone was still there.

She and Jack exchanged a look, then both stepped forward.

The shadows closed quickly around them, cutting off the

light as if a bank of clouds had covered the moon. Emily and Jack hurried forward, following the alley as it turned to the left. Another ten steps and the path veered back to the right. They stayed on the path as it ran deeper and deeper into what Emily assumed were the mews and courts that ran behind the main roads of Seven Dials.

It was only when she stepped out of a final stretch of cobbled alleyway that she realized how wrong she was.

The street that opened up beyond the twisting alley was filled with fey. They darted in and out of shops, still open despite the late hour. They sat on the windowsills of wooden houses two, three, sometimes four stories high, talking to friends on the street below or to faeries hovering in the air. A large, shambling creature stalked across the street, pausing to stare at Emily and Jack before heaving a large, heartfelt sigh and moving on again. The sounds of street life were familiar to her—angry shouting, raucous laughter, the calling out of names, the wooden trundling of carts being pushed across the uneven cobbles, the clink of bottles from a hidden taproom. If Emily closed her eyes, she could think it just another night on Oxford Street.

Jack stood with his mouth hanging open, staring at every-thing with wide eyes.

"Close your mouth," said Emily. "You'll let the flies in." She remembered her da had said that to her once, after he'd read her a story about a witch trying to eat two children. He'd loved stories, did her da.

Corrigan had said to find a pub called the Unicorn's Head. Emily looked up and down the street but couldn't see any such sign. She walked up the street, Jack following closely behind her. Nobody paid them much attention. That suited Emily fine. The sooner she could find Corrigan, the sooner they could track down her brother.

But Emily couldn't find the tavern anywhere. The street curved gently to the right, then ended abruptly at a brick wall. She checked all the signs again. The pub had to be here somewhere.

"You will all die horrible deaths!" shouted a voice.

Emily and Jack both jumped. They turned in a circle, looking for the source of the voice. Crowds milled along the street, seemingly unconcerned with the threat. In fact, not one creature seemed to think anything was amiss.

"Ungrateful wretches! I was your King! You owe me *respect*. I have powerful friends, you know."

Emily looked in the direction of the voice and saw an enormously fat fey. He was the height of an adult man, but so large he couldn't even stand. He sat in a wooden wagon, his huge stomach hanging over the front and almost trailing against the ground.

"Will you look at the size of him," said Jack in awe.

The crowd closed in around the fey again, but Emily and Jack pushed through to get a closer look. He pointed at a faerie that flew slowly past. "You! Sianna. I know you. I saved you from that wretch, Shakespeare. You owe me your loyalty."

The faerie known as Sianna stuck her tongue out at him and flew away. The creature sputtered his rage.

"H-How dare you! I am Oberon! I was your King! You cannot treat me like this!"

But he was speaking to thin air, as everyone else had moved away from him. He tried to turn around, but his girth prevented him from moving anything more than his head. He clicked his fingers impatiently. "Come on! *Come on!*"

A moment later the wagon he sat in began to trundle around until it faced directly into the street. Emily hadn't noticed before, but there were about ten wooden handles sticking out from the base of the wagon, and small children with the heads of ravens were pushing on these handles.

"Hurry up!" roared Oberon. "I haven't got all day."

"A sad sight," said a polite voice at her side.

Emily looked down and saw the top of a black bowler hat somewhere around her waist. "Excuse me?"

The bowler tilted back, revealing a chubby face the color of oak wood. It was a gnome, like Mr. and Mrs. Stintle, only younger. Emily blinked in bemusement. It appeared he had a false mustache glued to his upper lip.

"Oh, no, madam. And sir," he said, nodding respectfully at Jack. "Please, excuse *me*." With these words the small creature stepped back, whipped off his hat, and executed a graceful bow. He was dressed as a gentleman, with a finely stitched waistcoat beneath his brown tweed jacket, a crisp white shirt, and a gold chain that disappeared into his breast pocket. His shoes were so clean, Emily reckoned she would be able to see her reflection if she bent over.

He also had a small walking stick, which he held hooked over his forearm.

"I see you are admiring my attire," said the creature.

"Uh, yes. Very nice. Very . . . very *gentlemanly*."

The gnome's face broke into a huge smile. "Oh, do you really think so? Truly?"

Emily found herself rather taken aback by his enthusiasm. "Um. Yes?"

"Oh, thank you so much. You don't know how much that means to me. My name is Mr. Pemberton, by the way."

"Pemberton?"

"Yes. Such a regal-sounding name, don't you think?" The gnome took out a pocket watch from the breast pocket of his jacket. He flicked open the cover and Emily saw that there were no hands on the clock face. "My, my, doesn't time fly." He snapped the lid shut and put the watch away again. Then he looked suspiciously at Emily. "You *are* a True Seer, aren't you?"

"A . . . ?"

"A True Seer. I mean, you can really see me. You're not mad and just *think* you're talking to someone?"

"No, I can see you very well."

"Excellent. Good show." He looked at Jack. "And you?"

Jack hesitated, looking at Emily for help.

"He was given the sight," said Emily. "By a piskie."

"Ah, I see. You are very lucky," he said to Jack.

"Am I?"

"Oh, indeed. It is very rare that one of your lot is given the gift. You must be very special."

Jack proudly drew himself up. "As a matter of fact—"

"You don't happen to know where the Unicorn's Head is, do you?" Emily asked, interrupting Jack before he could get started.

Mr. Pemberton flashed her a smile. "My dear! But, of course. Happy to be of service. It's right there." He lifted his walking stick and pointed past her leg.

Emily turned around and found herself facing a building that looked much the same as any other on the street. There was nothing to indicate it was a public house at all.

"Are you sure? Only—"

She was cut off when the door burst open and Corrigan came sprinting out. A tankard flew through the air behind him. He ducked, narrowly avoiding the metal cup.

"Hah! As usual, Millicent, your aim is as good as your food. Which is to say not good at all!"

He turned and saw Emily. He stumbled to a stop, casting a venomous look at Mr. Pemberton, then hurried over. "Did you get it?" he asked excitedly.

"I did," said Emily.

Corrigan grinned. He stepped away and danced a little jig. "I knew you'd come through, Emily Snow. I always knew it." He stopped and glared at Mr. Pemberton. "What are you staring at? Get lost."

Pemberton blew out his cheeks in outrage. "You, sir, are a buffoon." He bowed to Emily and Jack, once again taking off his bowler hat. "Madam. Sir. It was a pleasure."

"Nice to meet you, too. Uh . . ." Emily hesitated.

"Is anything the matter?" Mr. Pemberton asked.

"Well, it's just that . . . your mustache . . ."

"A magnificent specimen, I think you'll agree. What of it?"

"It's hanging off your lip. I think the glue must have gotten old."

Pemberton turned red and clapped a hand over his mouth. He backed away, bowing as he did so. "Fank-u," he said, his voice muffled behind his fingers. "'m frever in ur debt."

Then he turned around and hurried off as fast as his legs would take him.

❦ CHAPTER SEVENTEEN ❦
In which Emily gives the stone to the Faerie Queen
and asks for her help in searching for William.

THREE THIRTY IN THE MORNING
ON THE SECOND DAY OF EMILY'S ADVENTURES.

S o how did you get it?" asked Corrigan eagerly as they hurried through the late-night streets. "Did you have to kill anyone?"

Emily glared at Corrigan. "Don't be stupid. Why would we kill anyone?"

Corrigan shrugged. "You never know. You humans are a bloodthirsty lot. I see you've still got your little pet following you around."

"My what?" She followed his gaze. He was looking at Jack. "Oh."

Jack's face twisted with outrage. He aimed a kick at Corrigan, but the piskie danced out of the way. "This way," he said, turning a corner.

"I thought we were going to see Queen Kelindria," said Emily. "That's not the way we went before."

"We're not going to Underlondon," called Corrigan, scampering ahead.

Emily hurried after the piskie. "What do you mean? Where are we going?"

"The Queen said that if you got the stone, I was to take you to the house she uses when she's up here. Quicker that way."

They walked on through quiet streets lined by darkened houses. Emily fretted all the way. She had the means to find William in her pocket, and it seemed to her that Corrigan was taking too long to take them to their destination.

Finally, after about half an hour, Corrigan stopped before a high wall.

"We're here."

Emily looked up. The wall towered above her, and tree branches hung over the top as if reaching for the ground. The gates were made from polished wood, coaxed and shaped to look like twining branches, so it was as if the trees themselves were barring entrance into the grounds.

Emily peered through the gates. Everything was overgrown, a tangle of grass and flowers gone wild. A stone path, with thick grass between the gaps, twined around the shrubs and trees and led to a large house that was just visible through the vegetation.

Corrigan pushed open the gates. Jack made as if to step through, but Corrigan held up a hand to stop him.

"Where do you think you're going?"

"With you," said Jack, puzzled.

"Not a chance. If the Queen found out I gave you the sight, she'll have my hide. You'll have to stay out here."

Jack opened his mouth to protest, but Emily laid a hand on his arm. "It'll be all right. We shouldn't be long. Isn't that right?" she asked Corrigan.

"Eh, no. Not too long."

"You see? We'll meet you back out here."

"I'm not happy with this, Snow." Jack lowered his voice. "I don't trust him."

Emily shrugged. "I don't have a choice. Not if I want to get William back. Please, Jack. For me?"

Jack hesitated, then finally nodded. "Fine. I'll see you back here." He glared a warning at Corrigan, but the piskie ignored him and stepped through the gate.

Emily followed him through, but they had gone only a few steps into the heavy undergrowth when Corrigan took her hand and pulled her to a stop.

"Wait," he said.

Emily stood still, wondering what it was they were waiting for.

A second later she saw it: a patch of darkness, moving

slowly through the air. It drew closer to them and Emily saw that it was actually a thick, oily cloud that coiled and writhed like an angry snake. She stiffened in fear.

"What is it?" she whispered.

"The Sluagh. Dead souls. They keep the unwanted out."

The cloud stopped moving. Corrigan reached out and put his arm into the heaving mass. A second later it moved off again, disappearing into the trees.

Corrigan shivered. "I hate doing that. Right. Come on."

As they drew closer to the house, Emily saw that its top story was covered in clinging ivy. Even the windows were partially hidden.

Corrigan stepped up to the wooden door and knocked. A second later, it swung silently open to reveal a hallway littered with brown leaves and twigs. Emily couldn't even see the floor. Corrigan glanced over his shoulder.

"You ready?"

Emily gripped the stone through her coat and nodded at Corrigan. "Ready."

Corrigan stepped inside and Emily followed, the dry leaves crunching underfoot. The door closed behind her with a quiet click. She turned to look, but there was no one there.

She wondered why she was feeling so uneasy. There was something about the house: it felt . . . *haunted*. Which was silly, as she had no idea what a haunted house really felt like.

But the air held a feeling of sadness. As if whoever lived here before had a terribly unhappy life.

A flickering light came from a room at the far end of the corridor. Corrigan was heading toward it, his form outlined in the faint golden glow. He disappeared through the doorway and Emily hurried to catch up, not wanting to be left alone.

Emily stepped into the room. A fire was roaring in the grate. Three armchairs covered with dusty sheets were pushed up against the wall. Emily saw Corrigan's footprints on the floor, clearly defined in the dust. No one had been in this room for a long time.

"I thought you said the Queen uses this house."

"She does. Part of it, at least."

Corrigan approached a door to the left of the fireplace, pausing briefly to pick up an unlit torch from beside the hearth and hold it in the flames. Emily joined him, and the door swung open as they approached. She peered through and saw a very long, very dark corridor, too long to be contained inside the house. More magic.

"Where does it go?"

"To the Queen's court," said Corrigan. "Well . . . to one of them, anyway."

He stepped through the doorway. Emily bit her lip, then quickly followed. The walls of the passage were made from smooth wood, polished to a high sheen that reflected the light of Corrigan's torch and surrounded them in a rich, golden-red glow.

A door appeared up ahead out of the shadows. As they drew closer, Emily saw that it was charred and blackened by what must have been a fierce fire.

Corrigan stopped and glanced over his shoulder. "Are you ready?"

Emily tore her gaze away from the door. "Why do you keep asking me that? Why wouldn't I be ready? Let's just hurry up so I can find William. The less time he is in the hands of the Unseelie the better."

Corrigan cleared his throat. "Of course." He hesitated. "Emily . . . ," he said, but then he trailed off into silence.

Emily got the impression he wanted to say something but couldn't find the words. Instead, he turned back and laid his hand against the door.

As soon as his skin made contact, the door shuddered. Dust fell around them, flakes of charred wood dropping at their feet.

Then the door slowly opened, a line of bright light bursting through, shining directly into Emily's face. She winced and looked away, closing her eyes. When she opened them again, the door stood wide open. Emily found herself looking into a room similar to the one where she had first met the Queen. But this room was smaller, more intimate. To her relief, she saw that it was empty of the courtiers that had made Emily feel so self-conscious.

There was a raised dais at the opposite end of the room. On it was a throne identical to the one Emily had seen in the huge tree in Underlondon, and on this throne sat the Faerie Queen. When she saw Emily, her eyes widened and she looked quickly at Corrigan, her pale, beautiful face radiating hope.

"Did you get it? Did you get the stone?"

Emily hesitated, glancing uncertainly at the piskie. How did the Queen know Emily had gone after the stone? After all, she had only decided to try and get it after she had left the Queen and found out William was missing. Had Corrigan somehow managed to get word to her?

Corrigan wouldn't look at Emily. Instead, he turned all his attention to the Queen. "She retrieved it," he said softly.

The Queen broke into a huge smile and held out both her arms, almost as if she was going to run forward and hug Emily. But she didn't. She waited for a split second, then gestured impatiently from her throne, her golden eyes shining with excitement. "Come, child! Show it to me."

Corrigan prodded her in the leg. Emily walked slowly forward and stopped just below the dais. Then she reached inside her coat pocket and pulled out the stone.

The Queen drew in a sharp breath and reached down with trembling fingers. Then she took the stone in her hands, her expression rapt.

"Finally," she whispered.

Emily cleared her throat. She had fulfilled her part of the bargain. Now it was the Queen's turn. "Excuse me," she said.

The Queen, still staring at the stone, did not even look up.

"Excuse me," Emily said again, in a louder voice.

This time the Queen did look up, an irritated frown marring her perfect features. It took her a moment to focus on Emily, and even then it was as if she didn't recognize her.

Emily took a deep breath. "My brother . . . that is, William. He was taken by the Unseelie. I need to get him back. Corrigan said you would be able to find him with the stone, in return for me getting it back for you."

The Queen smiled again, but this time there was no joy in it. It was a cold smile and sent shivers down Emily's spine.

"Is that what Corrigan said, was it?" The Queen glanced at Corrigan, who was standing next to Emily. "Well then, who am I to break his word? Let us see what can be done."

She raised a hand in the air. There was a movement behind the throne, and a figure detached itself from the shadows.

It was the Dark Man, the Queen's huntsman, the stealer of eyes.

Emily swallowed nervously. She hadn't even noticed him there. He moved slowly forward, shrouded in his heavy black cloak and hood. She remembered the first time she had seen the Dark Man, when he had brought the elf before the Queen, the fear on the creature's face. What was he doing here?

The Queen raised the stone to her eye so that she was looking through it. "Now. Let us see where those *terrible* Unseelie fey have taken your brother," she said.

Emily waited expectantly, fear and anticipation battling inside of her. She had no idea what she would do when she found out where William was being held. Would Corrigan help her? After all, he owed her a favor. Maybe—

But a second later all such thoughts vanished from her mind. From her position, Emily could see through the hole of the stone, could see the Queen's eye as she peered through the opening.

And she saw that eye turn from a rich gold to an oily, viscous black. The Queen turned slowly in her throne, and as she turned Emily saw that the Queen's face, when looked at *through* the stone, was different. Her skin was saggy and wrinkled. What hair Emily could see through the hole was white and brittle. One of her fingers curled through the opening, and it was like a twig on a tree, thin and spindly.

The Queen lowered the stone, and once again sat before

Emily, beautiful, pale, red-haired. "Ah," she said with an amused smile. "I think I have found your brother, young Emily."

She made an impatient gesture. The Dark Man moved around the pedestal and knelt in front of the Queen. Then he stood up and stepped to the side, leaving something lying at the Queen's feet.

Emily looked down. It took her a moment to realize what it was she was looking at.

"William," she whispered, relief and fear surging through her with such force that it almost brought her to her knees.

For it was none other than her brother, seemingly unharmed, his eyes closed as if fast asleep.

But how . . . ?

Why did the Dark Man have her brother?

An answer suggested itself, but it was too horrific a thought for her to acknowledge. No. It couldn't be. She wouldn't believe it. That would mean Corrigan . . .

Emily quickly turned to the piskie, but he steadfastly refused to meet her eyes.

That alone was answer enough.

She whirled back to face the Queen. "*You* took him! It never was the Unseelie."

The Queen inclined her head. "It is as you say."

"But . . . *why*? What has he ever done to you?"

"Him? Nothing. But you . . . that is another story altogether. You have long been a thorn in our side, Emily Snow. I have waited two hundred years for this day, do you know that? Two hundred years of waiting, wondering how you would become involved in our fight. And now here you are."

Emily gaped at the Queen as if she were mad. "What are you talking about? I *helped* you. Why would you do this to me? Corrigan?" She turned to the piskie. This time he met her eyes. "In the alley. I saved you."

"Yes," said the Queen. "As I said, we always knew you would eventually stumble upon our kind. Now we know how."

Emily whirled back to the Queen. "You're not making any sense!" she said. "*How* could you know about me? What do you mean you've waited for this day to come? I—"

"You will be silent," said the Queen. She held out a hand, and the Dark Man gave her something. It glinted blackly in the light, and Emily realized it was a knife. Before she could react, the Queen leaned forward and held the blade to William's throat.

"One step and he dies," she said.

Emily froze in horror as a tiny bead of blood rolled down William's neck and settled in the hollow of his collarbone while he slept. No, it couldn't be sleep. He was unconscious, under some kind of spell.

"Good. Now listen carefully," said the Queen. "Most of what I told you was true. It *was* Christopher Wren who locked the doorway through to Faerie. If he could, he would have destroyed the key, but that was beyond his power. So he came up with another plan. He hid it, making sure none of his colleagues knew its location. He suspected treachery, you see, and with good cause. We had an agent inside the Order. So he made sure that only one person could find the key. The one person he truly trusted."

It took Emily a moment to realize what the Queen was saying.

"Me?" she said in amazement. "Don't be absurd—"

"I am far from absurd, Emily Snow. I am referring to you, yes. We have awaited your arrival for more than two hundred years. We were never sure *when* you would turn up, only that someday you would. And that your arrival would signal the beginning of the end."

Emily blinked, looking around in a daze. None of this made any sense.

"We don't know why he chose you. Or how you came to be involved. All we *do* know is that he somehow used magic to attune the seeing stone to you. You are the only person who can use it. You are the only person who can read the directions to the key's hiding place. That is what is on that parchment you so kindly returned to Corrigan. The directions to the hidden key." The Queen leaned back in her throne. "Wren thought himself so clever, hiding the stone in the one place we could never go. But we have had many years to plan for this day."

"But . . . even if any of this is true, why didn't you just ask me? Why go to all this trouble? If all you want is to get home—"

Queen Kelindria laughed.

"Home? My dear, I do not want to go *home*. That story I told you about us dying was a lie, part of the ruse. I want to open the doorway and bring my armies through. I want London destroyed. I will wipe out your people. It will be as though you never existed! You do not belong here, Emily Snow. This world was ours long before you crawled out of the swamps. We will take back what belongs to us." She paused and smiled coldly at Emily. "And you will help."

"I won't. I—"

The Queen pressed the blade deeper into William's flesh. He groaned softly.

"Wait!"

The Queen pulled the point away.

Emily looked around, tears blurring her vision. Corrigan was nowhere to be seen. She stood alone before the Queen.

She didn't know what to do. If she helped, she could be responsible for millions of deaths, but if she didn't help, the Queen would kill William right before her eyes.

"Come now," said the Queen. "I grow impatient."

Emily stared at her brother. It was no choice, really. She couldn't watch her brother slaughtered. She just couldn't.

So she looked up and wiped the tears from her eyes.

"Fine," she said. "I'll help."

The Queen smiled. "Good girl." She held out her hand, and the Dark Man placed something into her palm. Emily saw that it was the blank piece of parchment that she and Corrigan had taken to Underlondon. The Queen offered both the parchment and the stone to Emily. "Read it," she ordered.

Emily took the stone and parchment from the Queen's fingers and hesitantly raised it to her eye. What if it didn't work? What would happen to William? To her?

But she needn't have worried. As the hole in the stone drew level with her eye, the parchment changed. Black lines appeared, smudged and blurry as if someone had spilled water on fresh ink. But then they sharpened and formed into recognizable words, laid out in short lines like the poems she used to read at school.

"Do not think to deceive me," snapped the Queen. "Just read what you see or your brother dies."

Emily swallowed nervously. "It says . . .

"'A bird raises a saint in the wake of the fire.

A father's favorite rhyme will confirm the truth.

Speak the rhyme and the whispering shall reveal all.'"

Emily slowly lowered the stone. The Queen was frowning.

"What else?" she asked.

"Nothing else. That is all there is."

The Queen slammed her hands down hard on the throne. "Do not lie to me!" she screamed. She snatched the stone from Emily's hand. "That doesn't make any sense!" She held the stone up to her eye, looking at the parchment. Then she screamed in frustration and threw the stone to the floor.

She grabbed Emily by the chin, her fingers digging painfully into Emily's cheeks.

"I advise you to think very carefully. Either you tell me everything that is on that parchment, or I kill your brother."

Emily pulled back, feeling the Queen's nails scraping on her skin. "I'm not lying to you! That's all it says."

"Then you have until this time tomorrow to figure out what it means." She gestured to the Dark Man. "Take them to their cells."

✻ CHAPTER EIGHTEEN ✻
In which Emily loses hope.

In the darkness of her cell, Emily finally allowed the tears to fall. She'd held them in as long as she could, but it was just all too much. Everything that had happened over the past day—all the surprises, the fear, the worry, came out in a flood of bitter tears that she couldn't stop.

She'd always known life was hard. It was simply one of those things you had to accept. But up until now, even after all that she and William had been through, she'd never thought of it as cruel. Yes, there were times when they were both hungry and cold. But they got through it. Because that was what you did.

But now, for the first time ever, Emily actually felt defeated. She could see no way out of this. Either she figured out the stupid riddle and many people died, or she didn't figure it out and William died.

What kind of choice was that?

Emily sniffed. It was all that stupid Corrigan's fault. If she had never found him in that alley, none of this would ever have happened.

And what was all that rubbish the Queen said about waiting two hundred years for Emily? It didn't make any sense. None of it did.

Emily sniffed again, willing the tears to stop. What if someone walked in and saw her like this? She hastily wiped her eyes on her coat. She wouldn't give them the satisfaction.

Emily sighed and looked around her prison. There wasn't much to see. Just four walls and a floor. They hadn't even given her a bed.

A small amount of light filtered in through a narrow slit in the door, and she examined the walls more closely, wondering if she could somehow tunnel her way out.

But even that slight hope was soon dashed. The earth was so tightly packed that she doubted she could make a dent even if she had a spade. She tried to knock on the hard earth, hoping that William could hear her in the next cell, but all she heard was a dull thump. The walls were too thick even for that.

Emily retreated to the middle of the room, glaring at the

gap in the door. The fear and self-pity she felt were chang-
ing, disappearing. She could feel them draining away, pushed
out by something else, something she knew she would be
able to use to combat whatever lay ahead.

Anger. Total and utter anger.

How dare they kidnap her brother? How dare they trick
her into doing their dirty work? Just who did they think they
were, using her like that? She would not stand for it.

Somehow or other, she would get free. Then she would
take William to a safe place and . . .

And what? What would she do? She supposed hiding was
one option. If they couldn't find her, they couldn't decipher
the clue. Then they wouldn't ever find the key. Maybe she
should leave London, head to Scotland or Ireland. She once
heard her ma say they had family over in Ireland.

She wasn't sure. As long as it foiled the Queen's plans, she
wasn't fussy.

Emily sat down against the wall, trying to think of a way
out. She yawned, exhausted. She hadn't yet had a proper
sleep. She'd only managed to get a few hours' rest before she
and Jack broke into Somerset House. She'd managed to keep
going, but only because events had propelled her forward.
But now . . .

Her eyes drifted closed. She tried to force them open
again, but they closed one last time, and Emily fell fast asleep.

A noise woke her. She opened her eyes and found herself staring at the ground. She must have lain down sometime. She yawned and sat up. How long had she been asleep? She felt refreshed and invigorated. Not that it would do her any good, stuck in here.

A second later she realized the noise she had heard was a key turning in the lock. She scrambled to her feet just as the door swung open, flooding the small cell with lantern light. There was a figure silhouetted in the doorway. She couldn't make out the features, but the height and stance identified him immediately.

"Corrigan," she said in disgust. "Go away. And tell your Queen to get someone else to bring any messages. I won't deal with you."

Corrigan stepped inside the cell. As he came closer, Emily could see him more clearly. His face was pinched with worry. He looked nervously over his shoulder. "Queen Kelindria doesn't know I'm here," he said.

Emily scowled. "What are you talking about?"

Corrigan tried to smile, but it faltered and died on his lips. "I'm here to rescue you," he said.

"You're *what?*"

Corrigan took another step into the cell. "I didn't want

this," he whispered urgently. "The Queen said I had to tell you the Unseelie took your brother. And that the stone would help find him. That was all. I didn't know she was going to threaten him. Or lock you up."

"Oh, really? And what about her plan to bring her armies through?"

"I didn't know about that, either. Look . . . most of the fey just want to get home. We don't want to stay here. It's cold and wet. Your lot are welcome to it. All this talk of invasion . . . it's not what we want, all right? If we had the key to the door, we would leave, and we would lock it behind us. We don't want to conquer your people. That's too much like hard work."

Realization dawned on Emily. "This is another trick."

"What?"

"You're trying to trick me again. The Queen sent you, didn't she? She thinks I'll believe you. That you can 'rescue' me, and I'll find the key, and . . . and then you can just take it away from me. Just like you did with the stone."

"No, it's not like that. I know I don't have any right to ask you to trust me—"

"Correct."

"—but it's the truth. I swear." He stepped forward until he was only an arm's length from Emily. "Let me help you. I can get you out of here, take you somewhere safe."

"And William?"

"Yes. Your brother, as well. I would have come hours ago, but the Queen was keeping an eye on me."

"Hours ago? How long have I been asleep?"

Corrigan shrugged. "It's dark out now. The day's come and gone. You were brought to your cell just before dawn."

"*Dark?* You mean I've been asleep all day?" That meant the Queen would be coming for them soon. They had to get out.

But still Emily hesitated, staring at the piskie. She didn't trust him. She couldn't, not after what he had done. But he offered a sliver of hope, and that sliver was more than she'd had a minute ago. If she could at least get William to safety, then that was one less thing to worry about. Then, well, then she would see.

"Fine," she said abruptly. "Get us out of here."

Corrigan grinned, and just like that he was back to his familiar, cocky self. "Wait here," he said, and hurried to the door. He peered outside, then turned and winked at her. "You owe me for this, you know." Then he was gone before Emily could think of something suitable with which to respond.

He returned a moment later with a frightened-looking William. As soon as he saw Emily, he ran straight into her arms.

"Emily!" he gasped. "Em, don't let the faeries take me away again. Please."

Emily stroked his hair, feeling tears of relief come to her

eyes. This time, she didn't do anything to stop them. "I won't, Will. I promise. We're going to escape. Right now. And then I know a place where you'll be safe. A place the faeries can't go." She smiled, trying to put on a brave face. "Are you ready?"

"*Yes.* Let's go."

A sudden thought struck Emily. If she had been here all day, what had happened to Jack? He had been expecting them to return last night.

"Do you know where Jack is?" she asked Corrigan.

The piskie frowned. "I'm not his keeper," he said.

"Corrigan," Emily said, warning clear in her voice. "What happened to Jack?"

Corrigan hesitated, then threw up his hands in annoyance. "He was caught trying to break in."

"And you weren't going to tell me?" Emily was outraged.

"He's not important!"

"Yes, he is! Where is he now?"

"In one of the cells."

Emily could hardly believe her ears. Corrigan was actually going to leave Jack behind.

"Go and release him!" she shouted.

"Do I have to?" whined Corrigan. "I don't like him—"

"Now!"

"Fine!" snapped the piskie, and stamped back into the corridor.

⇥ CHAPTER NINETEEN ⇤

In which Corrigan helps Emily, William, and Jack escape.
The Sluagh attacks.

FOUR O'CLOCK IN THE AFTERNOON
ON THE SECOND DAY OF EMILY'S ADVENTURES.

Emily waited with William while Corrigan went to free
Jack. The corridor smelled of damp mold. The only light
came from the torch outside their cells. Emily could just see
Corrigan's shadowy form as he opened up a cell door farther
down the passage. A moment later, Jack emerged from the
cell. He saw Emily and William and ran to join them.

"Jack!" exclaimed William, darting forward to hug him.
Jack ruffled his hair.

"Hullo, squire." Jack turned his attention to Emily. "Are
you all right?"

"I'll be a lot better once we get out of this place," said
Emily.

"Follow me, then," whispered Corrigan. "And for the sake

of my skin, please keep the volume down. If we're caught, I'm dead."

As they walked through the dark passage, Emily ran one hand along the wall and held William's trembling hand with the other. Both were cold to the touch. Occasionally, pieces of the wall crumbled away beneath her fingers. The sound of the earth pattering to the floor was the only noise above William's fearful breathing.

After a few minutes, Corrigan spoke. "Stairs ahead," he whispered. "Watch yourself."

Emily found a step and hesitantly put her weight on it, pulling William along with her. The Dark Man had brought her to the cell from the opposite direction, so she had no idea where Corrigan was taking them.

She counted the stairs as they climbed. After thirty-two steps, Corrigan opened a door into a corridor. A bright light shone from the far end of the passage.

They hurried along the corridor and through a door that took them into the main body of the house they had used to enter the Queen's Court. Corrigan paused and listened, then hurried down another passage.

All the corridors they passed through were filled with dead leaves. The walls and roof were festooned with spiderwebs.

Corrigan stopped before another door and put his ear

to the wood. He listened carefully for a few seconds, then stepped back and pulled it open.

He ushered them through, and Emily found herself back in the foyer that led to the front door. Emily saw the look of worry on his face as he reached out to touch the doorknob.

"What's wrong?" asked Jack.

Corrigan hesitated. "It's the Sluagh," he said.

"What of them?" said Emily. "They let us enter the garden."

"Yes, but that was because they sensed our motives. They get inside your head. They'll know we're not meant to be here now."

"Then we run," said Emily. "No tricks or anything like that. We just run as fast as we can."

"Easy for you to say," said Corrigan.

"I'll carry you." She turned to William. His face was pale, his eyes wide with fear. "William? We're nearly there, all right? I'm going to get you to a safe place, a place where they won't be able to find you. But I need you to do one last thing for me. I need you to run with Jack as fast as you can. Don't stop for anything. Don't stop until you're in the street outside. Can you do that?"

William nodded. "What about you?" he whispered.

"I'll be right behind you. Don't worry." She turned her attention to Jack. "Get him out of the garden as quick as you can. Don't stop for anything. And don't come back in once you're outside. Promise?"

"Emily—"

"Jack, we don't have the time! Just promise."

"You sure about this?"

"Yes."

"Then I promise." Jack took William's hand. "You ready, squire?"

William nodded. Emily turned to Corrigan and held out her hand. The piskie scampered up her arm and sat on her shoulder.

"You'd better hold on tight," she said. "If you fall, I'm not coming back for you."

"There's gratitude for you," muttered Corrigan, but Emily could feel his small hands tightening around her coat. "Now listen to me. You have to think that you belong here. You have to believe that this is the only place in the world where you should be. Maybe it will confuse them long enough to get out."

Emily nodded. She placed her hand on the doorknob. "Ready?"

"No, but get a move on, anyway," said Corrigan.

"William?"

"Ready, Emily."

"Jack?"

Jack nodded.

Emily pushed open the door.

It was dark outside, and the air had the damp feeling of rain about it. Emily looked around but couldn't see anything suspicious. The stone trail beckoned invitingly, a clear path through the overgrown garden.

Emily took a deep breath and tried to clear her mind of fear. It wasn't easy. She told herself how inviting the garden looked, how nice it would be to walk among the flowers, how she had every right to be here and nothing could change that.

"Run," she whispered.

William and Jack darted into the garden, Emily following close behind. William ran clumsily onto the path and headed for the gate, looking neither right nor left. Jack stayed right behind him, his hands held out in case Will stumbled.

They were halfway through the garden now, still running hard. Emily allowed herself a brief flash of hope. Maybe the Sluagh weren't as bad as Corrigan thought. Maybe they wouldn't even see them.

Then she heard it, a low hissing sound that seemed to enter her mind directly without traveling through her ears. It vibrated in her head, causing her ears to pop. Corrigan groaned in fear. Emily looked up and saw the cloud, just as she had seen it before, an oily, writhing, serpentine mass that looked like ink in water. Except now, Emily could see faces inside the cloud. They pushed against the smoky substance, stretching it out as if they were trying to escape.

The cloud was heading straight for William and Jack. They were close to the gate, just another few steps . . .

It was no use. Emily could see they weren't going to make it. She kept running, wanting to get as close to the gate as she possibly could. But then, just before the cloud reached William, she stopped moving and dropped her guard. She thought about the Queen, how she had escaped her. About how angry she would be.

"What are you doing?" hissed Corrigan from her shoulder. "Keep going!"

The cloud halted. It roiled faster, as if a wind was blowing it from inside. Emily saw William and Jack reach the gate, saw Jack yank it open and push William through. They were free. She felt a wave of relief that quickly turned to horror when she saw the faces appear at the back of the cloud, looking directly at her with black eyes, mouths wide as if they were screaming. But all Emily heard was the hissing. It filled her head, growing louder and louder until it drowned out everything around her. She was distantly aware of Corrigan shouting at her, telling her to run, but all she could do was stare at the faces and let the hissing wrap itself around her mind. There was no escape. She knew that. She would be sucked into the cloud and forced to become one with it, trapped for centuries with the other dead souls.

Emily was vaguely aware that these were not her thoughts, that the Sluagh were in her mind and feeding her despair. But at the same time there was nothing she could do. She wasn't strong enough to fight. How many people had been drawn into the cloud? Ten? Twenty? A hundred? How was she supposed to fight something like that?

But then she saw another face push out of the mass, squeezing between two snarling masks of hatred. This face was different. It wasn't screaming. It wasn't angry. It just looked . . . sad. Other faces appeared, snapping at it with wraithlike jaws. Emily thought she could make out the features of an old, terrifying woman, and another wearing an old-fashioned helm. Like some kind of knight. But the face ignored them. It stared at Emily, and Emily stared back.

"Go now," said a voice in her head, and Emily knew it was the face talking to her. "I have waited many decades to repay my debt to you, Emily Snow. It is done."

The hissing in her head faded until it was nothing but a background buzz. Emily stumbled forward, almost falling to her knees as she became aware of her surroundings again. Corrigan was shouting at her. William was standing at the gate, tears streaming down his face. Jack was in the garden again, heading along the path toward her. The face was slowly fading, sinking back within the cloud.

"What are you waiting for?" shouted Corrigan. "Run, you stupid girl, run!"

Emily ran, skirting the black cloud. She could just make out howls of anger at her escape. Faces pushed forward, mouths snapped as they tried to stop her, but the cloud itself didn't move. Whoever had spoken to her was keeping it back.

Jack waited till she drew even with him, then pushed her ahead. William was holding the gate open. Emily sprinted through, followed closely by Jack. She quickly turned back and slammed it shut. She saw the face again, and this time saw it was the face of a girl. It gave her a ghostly smile. Then it drifted back into the cloud.

╼═CHAPTER TWENTY═╾

In which Emily and Corrigan part ways and Emily
receives help from an unexpected source.

An evening fog was forming, creeping through the streets and casting everything in a shadowy yellow half-light that made Emily wonder if they really had escaped the Faerie Queen.

Emily kept hold of William's hand. They hadn't stopped walking since they'd left the garden, and she didn't plan on stopping until she saw something, anything, that showed her she was back in her own familiar world.

Except that her world would never be familiar again. Her world would never make *sense* again. What had the voice meant by saying the debt was repaid? What debt? And how had it known her name? It was yet another in a long list of things that she didn't understand, things that implied she had more to do with events than she actually did. Everything the Queen had said about Emily causing harm to the fey, about being a pest to them—how? She hadn't even known about them until yesterday morning.

Her thoughts were interrupted by Corrigan, giving her hair a sharp tweak.

"We're far enough away," he said. "They won't find us for the moment."

For the moment.

Emily ignored Corrigan, pulling William through a mews that led to a dark, misty street. Jack followed, lost in his own thoughts. She heard sounds of life somewhere to her right, a fiddle playing a drunken tune, the crash of something breaking, then the roar of laughter. Familiar sounds. *Human* sounds.

She let go of William's hand and shrugged her shoulders.

"Off," she said to Corrigan.

"Off? We still have to—"

"I said *off*. Now."

After a moment, Corrigan climbed down her back, muttering beneath his breath. He looked so small standing there in the hazy half-light, Emily thought. She steeled herself.

"Now go."

Corrigan didn't say anything for a moment. "Go where?"

"I don't care. Just leave me alone. I never want to see you again."

Jack looked between Emily and Corrigan, confused. "Snow? What's going on?"

"He betrayed us, Jack. They all did. The whole thing was a trick."

"What?"

"It was the Queen who kidnapped William. Or at least, she ordered it. They pretended it was the Unseelie so I would get the stone, hoping they'd use it to find Will. But they just wanted the stone for themselves."

Jack turned to Corrigan. "And he knew all the time?"

"Yes."

"But I rescued you!" said Corrigan. "I thought you'd forgiven me."

"*Forgiven* you?" Emily took a deep, steadying breath. She wouldn't let Corrigan see her tears. "You lied to me. You tricked me. You kidnapped my brother. We could have been killed! Everything about you from the time I saved your life has been a lie." She paused, a thought suddenly occurring to her. "Or was that part of the lie, as well? Was the fight in the alley a show, put on for my benefit?"

"No! That was real. Emily, what did you expect me to do? She is the Queen. You saw her. You saw the Dark Man. You don't betray the Queen. Not if you value your life."

"No," said Emily softly. "You just betray everyone else."

"I had no choice!"

"You always have a choice. I'm twelve, and even I know that. How old did you say you were again?"

Corrigan ignored the question. "She'll send the Dark Man after you, Emily. You need my help."

"Your help? Look where your help has gotten me so far. Just get out of my sight."

Corrigan didn't move. Jack pulled out his rusty knife and took a threatening step forward. "You heard her. Get lost!"

Corrigan gave him a contemptuous look but didn't budge. Emily grabbed William's hand and turned away, stalking silently along the street. Jack spat on the pavement next to Corrigan, then hurried after them. Emily looked back once and wished she hadn't. He looked so lost, standing there in the fog, fear clearly visible in his eyes. Emily hesitated. Maybe he was telling the truth. And if he was, what would the Queen do to him for helping her escape?

"Emily?"

She looked down at William.

"Can we go? I really don't like it here."

Emily steeled herself and kept walking. She had made the right decision. She couldn't trust Corrigan. She had no way of knowing whose side he was really on.

After a few more steps, she turned one final time. The fog had swallowed Corrigan up, as if he had never been there.

It took them an hour to reach Somerset House, but it seemed far longer. Every time she turned a corner, Emily expected the Dark Man to be waiting for her. But all she saw was the normal, everyday life that was London: A lone coffee seller shivering by his pot. A fight spilling out of a pub, which they had to cross the street to avoid. Young children tumbling and somersaulting in the street to impress some theatergoers. It was the kind of thing she was used to seeing, and it should have been a comfort.

But it wasn't. Everything had changed. It was as if she were watching her old world from a distance, or through a window she couldn't open. It was there, same as always, but removed from her in a way that made her incredibly lonely.

Except, she wasn't *quite* alone.

"What's your plan?" asked Jack as they emerged from a side street and stopped opposite Somerset House.

What *was* her plan? She had been thinking about it ever since they escaped. All she knew was that before she did anything else, she had to get William to safety. That was her main concern. If the Queen thought Emily had lied about the riddle, she wouldn't rest until Emily was her prisoner again. If William was safely hidden away, then at least the Queen couldn't use him against her. But once William was safe? What then? What would happen tomorrow? Or the next day?

Should she arrange passage out of London for the two of them? She didn't really want to do that. London was her home. Why should she be forced to run because of the Queen? No, leaving London was a last resort. There had to be another way to deal with the Queen.

She leaned close to Jack. "The main thing is to get William to safety," she whispered, careful that her brother didn't hear. He hated being treated like a child, and he would definitely have something to say about going into hiding. She still wasn't sure how she would break it to him.

"What makes you think he'll be safe here?" said Jack softly.

"Corrigan said they haven't been able to get inside the Invisible Order for two hundred years. Too much iron. It's the best place for him."

"What about Ravenhill?"

"I reckon he'll be out looking for the stone," said Emily. "If not, we'll just find an old office or something to hide him in."

Jack thought about this, then nodded. "Sounds good to me."

"Is the boat still there?"

Jack added, "At the bottom of the stairs. Tied it up when I made my escape."

They crossed the street, retracing the steps they had taken

the previous night. The fog was so thick now that they almost missed the alley opening. She led William blindly down the lane and finally bumped up against the metal railings. She groped along until they reached the steps leading down to the Thames.

She could hear the water lapping sluggishly against the wall. Once again, the smell was almost overpowering: a mixture of sewage, rotting food, and the putrid stench of something that had died.

They descended the steps. The water lapped gently against the stone, leaving behind a dirty scum that clung tenaciously to the stairs. It was almost as if the river was trying to claw free of its ancient banks, trying to escape the rubbish that now fouled its waters. Emily didn't blame it.

Jack helped William into the boat. Emily was about to follow when she slipped on the step. One foot plunged into the water, and Jack lunged forward to grab her arm. She smiled nervously at him and climbed carefully aboard, taking her seat on the bench next to William.

Jack followed and took up the oars.

Three miles away, the Thames swirled and eddied around the barnacle-covered hull of a steamer. Ripples spread out from the large, silent ship, forming tiny whirlpools that skated slowly across the water. The whirlpools grew in size, then joined together to form two deep depressions in the river.

Two heads rose slowly out of the black holes.

Black Annis raised her head to the fog and sniffed deeply.

"She's in our water, Jenny. I can taste her. Disgusting little child."

Jenny Greenteeth smiled. "We'll get her this time, Miss Annis. You see if we don't."

"And our debt to the Dagda will finally be paid."

Jack guided the boat up to the pier, and they all climbed out and hurried to the door of Somerset House.

Emily hesitantly touched the handle, carefully pushing it down. She heard a click, and then the door swung slowly inward. She had been worried about Jack "fixing" the lock to keep it open, but it seemed he had done his job properly.

They retraced their steps through the building. The doors whose locks Jack had picked were still open. Up ahead, she saw the door leading into the Invisible Order's head-quarters. This was where their luck had nearly run out the previous night. She quickened her steps, dragging William behind her.

It seemed their luck was to stay the same. The door was locked.

Emily stared at the handle, then tried it again in case she was mistaken. She supposed it made sense. This was the door that led into the offices of the Invisible Order. They wouldn't just leave it unlocked. There was too much they needed to keep hidden.

"Emily? What's wrong?" asked William.

Emily locked eyes with Jack. He shook his head. "Don't have my tools," he said. "The fey made me drop them when they caught me trying to get into the garden."

Emily knelt in front of William, trying to look calm. "Nothing's wrong. We just have to find another way in, that's all."

There was a clicking sound from behind her. Emily spun around, her throat tight with fear, and found herself looking into the surprised face of Sebastian, the young man she had tricked into showing her the way out.

He opened the door wider, and dim light spilled out into the corridor.

"I think you three had better come with me," he said. "It seems we have a lot to talk about."

⊷ CHAPTER TWENTY-ONE ⊷

*In which Emily is finally told
the true history of the Invisible Order.*

SEVEN O'CLOCK IN THE EVENING
ON THE SECOND DAY OF EMILY'S ADVENTURES.

The young man ushered them quickly through the library and into his office. It looked no different than when Emily had come in searching for a lantern, more like a cozy sitting room than an office. The fire still crackled away in the hearth, its warmth emanating through the room. Emily longed to stand before the flames and let the heat seep into her freezing limbs.

She heard a click and turned to see Sebastian locking the door.

"Don't worry," he said when he saw Emily and Jack exchange looks of alarm. "Just making sure no one interrupts us."

Interrupts what? thought Emily nervously. She looked

around, marking the room for any escape routes. There was the window, of course, and another door nestled between the ceiling-high bookcases, but that was it. She glanced surreptitiously at the door. At least he had left the key in the lock.

The young man gestured toward the chairs that formed a circle around the fire. "Please. Sit. You all look freezing."

Emily, William, and Jack sat in the chairs closest to the fire. There was a small table in front of them, and on it was a silver plate loaded with cakes and biscuits. Emily's stomach grumbled. It had been a whole day since she had eaten.

"Help yourself," the young man said, nodding at the cakes. "It's a vice of mine, I'm afraid. But I suppose it is better than tobacco or gin. My name's Sebastian, by the way."

William and Jack both reached out eagerly to snatch up a cake.

"William!" snapped Emily.

William stopped, his face radiating disappointment. Jack froze as well, looking like a chastised schoolboy. Sebastian smiled thinly and took one for himself.

"I assure you, they're not poisoned, if that is what you are worried about." He took a huge bite, swallowed, then sighed with pleasure. "Delightful."

That was good enough for Jack. He grabbed a cake and popped the whole thing into his mouth. William watched him, impressed.

"Please, Em?" he begged.

Emily hesitated, then reluctantly nodded. William grinned and took two off the plate, stuffing them in his mouth at the same time, grinning at Jack around a mouthful of cake.

"Now," said Sebastian, "I suppose it is too much to hope that you have the stone with you?"

"What stone?" asked Emily, rearranging her features into a mask of innocence.

Sebastian chuckled. "Come now, child. Let us not insult each other's intelligence. Your little performance was quite convincing, you know. You should join the theater." He glanced at Jack. "And you have quite a burst of speed about you."

Jack nodded, accepting the praise. Emily said nothing. She leaned forward and took one of the cakes, nibbling at the edges.

"So, do you have the stone?"

Emily shook her head, and Sebastian sighed. "Ravenhill is not going to be happy." A quick smile appeared on his face. "So I suppose that's one good thing to come of all this."

Emily's surprise must have shown on her face.

"What? Have you *met* Ravenhill? A more unpleasant individual I don't think I have ever encountered. I've tried to get him thrown out of the Order—" Sebastian stopped, a guilty look on his face. "Sorry. I'm not very good with secrets.

Tend to spill the beans at the slightest provocation. That's why I'm here all the time. They don't like me mixing with the public." He steepled his fingers beneath his chin. "Why don't we make a deal? You tell me what has happened. *Everything*, mind. And I will answer any questions you have."

Emily swallowed her cake. "Any questions at all?"

Sebastian nodded. "On my honor."

"How do I know you won't lie?"

"How do I know *you* won't lie? We'll just have to trust each other."

Emily thought about it. On the one hand, Corrigan had told her how evil the Order was, and she had believed him. With someone like Ravenhill chasing you around, it was hard *not* to believe. But on the other hand, Corrigan had lied nonstop since she had found him in the alley. How much of what he told her about the Order was *actually* true?

Sebastian seemed able to read her thoughts. "I could have turned you in already," he said. "Please," he said earnestly. "You can trust me. I'm a good person."

His plea brought unexpected tears to Emily's eyes. She didn't know why, but his solemn words seemed to touch her somewhere deep inside. To trust someone with the power to help, to believe they had your best wishes at heart and no ulterior motives—it would be wonderful to feel that again. She hadn't experienced such a thing since before her parents disappeared. Oh, there was Jack and Will, but it was different with people her own age.

Emily searched Sebastian's eyes. She saw no malice there, only concern and sympathy.

"I want to help," he said quietly.

Emily glanced at Jack. "We could do with a hand," he said.

"I trust him," said William.

Emily smiled. "You'd trust anyone who gave you cake."

Still, Jack was right. They could certainly do with some help.

So Emily told him everything that had happened since she had first walked through the alley. How Ravenhill had been there, how she had helped Corrigan, the story of her brother supposedly being taken by the Unseelie, and her breaking into the Order's offices to get the stone back. She moved on to the Queen's betrayal, and how she had said the parchment would reveal the location of the key, and how angry the Queen was when it instead had turned out to be a riddle. Sebastian jotted down the words of the riddle in a notebook, then leaned back in the chair, a troubled look on his face. Emily ended with her escape and appearance at the library door.

The only thing she left out was how the Queen had acted as if she knew Emily, and all that talk about having waited for her for years. She hadn't even told Jack about that. She didn't understand it herself, and instinct told her to keep it quiet.

At last, she finished talking. "I don't like this," said Sebastian. "Not one bit." He straightened up. "Perhaps it is fortunate that you became embroiled in all this. At least now we know the Queen plans to make her move soon."

"What do you mean?" asked Emily.

"The Order and the fey have been at—well, not *peace*, that's too strong a word—but we've tolerated one another's presence for a good two hundred years now. Ever since the war. We thought things were getting better."

"But they're not?"

"It doesn't appear so. It looks as if the fey were simply biding their time, searching for this clue." He was thoughtful for a moment. "What do you know of us? The Invisible Order, I mean?"

Emily shrugged. "The Queen said you've been around for centuries. That you want to destroy the fey. She said a man called Christopher Wren locked the door to Faerie, trapping them all here."

Sebastian stood up and went over to the bookcases. He pulled out a huge book that was about half the size of William and brought it back over to the fire.

"Could you move the cakes, please?"

Emily moved the tray to the floor. Sebastian placed the huge book on the table, where it dropped with a heavy thud. The leather cover had a strange emblem on it. Emily studied it curiously. It was a circle, but the circle was formed by two thin dragons, each of them curving around one half of the circumference. At the top, their jaws were locked together in battle, and at the bottom, their tails were twined around each other.

Inside this circle was an eye with an almond-shaped pupil.

"It's a dragon's eye," said Sebastian, seeing the direction of her gaze. "This book is the *Historia Occultus*—the Hidden Histories. It contains all the known history of the Invisible Order. Diaries of our leaders, details of the fey, historical accounts—everything." He opened it up carefully and leafed through the brittle yellow paper. There was a lot of neat cursive writing on the pages, interspersed with different types of illustrations. Emily saw a painting that looked like a stained-glass window, armored men fighting an army of the fey.

"The Society has existed in one form or another throughout all of recorded human history," said Sebastian. "No one is sure how it began. Some say it was started by one man. One simple, uneducated farmer whose unbaptized child was stolen by the fey. So he formed a small group of likeminded individuals—probably those who had had their own babies stolen—and they vowed to destroy those responsible.

"Other legends say the Order was started by Merlin the Magician, although back then he was called Myrddin. The story goes that the fey took his only daughter, Inogen, and from that moment on, he vowed to save others the heartache he had endured.

"Yet other legends say Merlin was trained by the Order to be their ultimate weapon. The legend went that he was half-fey himself, so he had the power of magic and a loyalty to humans.

"Whatever the truth, with the formation of the Order, so started the first war between the humans and the fey." Sebastian looked sad. "A tragic story. The legends do not do it justice."

He absently turned another page. This one was filled with writing, lists of names in columns.

"But why are the fey here?" asked Emily. "The Queen says they have their own world to live in."

"Ah, yes, but that world is . . . ethereal. It is not the same as our world. There, ideas take shape in reality, but it is an insubstantial place, like a dream. No, the fey much prefer our world, with blood and mud and humans whom they can rule. Their goal is total subjugation of our species. It always has been. That's why they stole babies, you see. They were trying to raise humans who would be sympathetic to their cause. They were actually quite successful.

"Anyway, the Order made it its duty to stop the fey. We were always there, passing the knowledge down through the centuries. And waiting, always waiting for the war we knew would come."

"And did it?"

"Oh, yes. In sixteen sixty-six. We don't know the details—a lot of our records were destroyed in the Great Fire—but we do know that when the Order locked the gateway to Faerie, the fey went to ground. We thought—we *hoped*—that they had given up. But it seems they were simply waiting, licking their wounds."

"How did Wren lock the gate?"

Sebastian shrugged. "That information has disappeared, I'm afraid. All we know is that he somehow locked it and hid the key." He sighed wearily. "And now if what you say is true, the fey have found a clue to that hiding place. They won't give up, Emily. If there is the slightest possibility that the Queen can open the door to Faerie and bring her armies through, she will pursue that chance."

"Can you do anything?"

Sebastian sighed. "We must find the key before they do. It is as simple as that. We will have to call all our operatives in to discuss this clue of yours."

Emily straightened in her chair. "Does that mean Raven-hill will come here?"

"I'm afraid so. Most of us see him as something of a fanatic, but he has his supporters. You see, when Ravenhill joined, the Order was not much more than a gentleman's club. We all thought the worst was over, that things has quieted down. But Ravenhill didn't believe it. He started the patrols again, insisted on keeping the Order staffed. A very unpleasant man, devoted to science. But it seems that he was right."

Emily sat back, lost in her own thoughts. Before she had entered Somerset House, Emily had wondered what to do. She'd thought about running, taking William away from the city. But after hearing Sebastian, she knew the Queen would never let her go. If she thought Emily held knowledge about the key, she would send the Dark Man after her. Emily knew there would be no escape.

Which only left her with two options: She could find the key and force the Queen to go back to Faerie. The trouble was, she had no idea how to accomplish that. Or secondly, she could find the key and destroy it. With the key gone, there would be no reason for the Queen to chase Emily. Oh, there was always the possibility she would want revenge, but that was something Emily would deal with later on.

Either way, she had to make sure she found the key first.

Sebastian was staring into the fire, lost in thought. Emily cleared her throat.

"Is it really safe here?" she asked. "The Queen said it was the one place in London where the fey couldn't come."

Sebastian blinked. "Hmm? Oh. Yes, it's safe. After the fire, Christopher Wren rebuilt the Society to be a haven for those in the fight against the fey. He rebuilt much of London, actually. St. Paul's Cathedral is one of his. The man was a genius. He held the Order together, you know. After he died was when everything sort of . . . fell apart."

Sebastian stood up. "You'll have to excuse me," he said. "I must get word to the others. I have a feeling the fey will be abroad tonight, and we need to figure out this clue of yours before they do."

He hurried out through the door. Emily waited a moment to make sure he wasn't coming back, then turned to Jack and William. William was drowsing in a chair by the fire, crumbs all over his clothes. She gestured for Jack to move out of earshot.

"You've got that look about you," said Jack. "You're planning something."

"I don't think the Queen is going to leave us alone," said Emily.

"No. Not if everything Sebastian said is true."

"That means I need to find the key before she does. I need to destroy it, or use it to force her back to Faerie."

"We. *We* need to find this key. You're not alone here, Snow."

"It's going to be dangerous."

Jack shrugged. "Doesn't bother me, I'm—"

"Spring-Heeled Jack, I know, I know."

"What about Will?"

Emily shook her head. "I can't take him with us. It's too risky."

"He's not going to like that."

"I'll deal with him. Wait outside for me. And don't steal anything!"

Jack grinned and slipped through the door. Emily crossed the room, pausing by Sebastian's desk and picking up a small letter opener. She could use it as a weapon if she needed to. She tucked it away in her coat pocket, then knelt down before her brother. "William?"

William reluctantly opened his eyes. "Mmm . . . ?"

"William, I have to go—"

William's eyes snapped open in alarm.

"Don't panic. I'll be back. I'm just going to get our stuff from our rooms," she lied. "You'll be safe here. The fey can't enter the building. Too much iron."

William struggled to sit upright. "I'll come with you."

"No. You stay here. I'll be fine."

Emily saw the look of doubt on her brother's face. She knew what he was thinking. He wanted to make sure she was safe. It almost made her smile, but she knew that would only annoy him. "Jack's with me, remember? He'll make sure nothing happens."

William stifled a yawn. "I should help."

Emily firmly shook her head. "You can barely keep your eyes open. I need you alert if you want to help. Have a nap. I'll wake you when we get back. Please," she said when she saw he was about to argue. "We won't be long. Do this for me, William."

William stared at her, then sighed. "Promise you'll come back?"

"Of course I'll come back. I rescued you from the Faerie Queen, didn't I? How many little brothers can say that?"

William smiled. Emily leaned forward and ruffled his hair. "See you soon."

❦ CHAPTER TWENTY-TWO ❦

In which danger lurks in the fog
and help arrives from an unexpected source.

EIGHT THIRTY IN THE EVENING
ON THE SECOND DAY OF EMILY'S ADVENTURES.

Emily and Jack left Somerset House by the front door this time. Emily did take one detour, however. Just before they stepped outside, she slipped into one of the rooms that opened off from the large entrance hall. The room was stuffy, filled with chairs and small tables covered in newspapers. Probably some kind of smoking room, thought Emily.

She undid the latch on one of the windows and pushed it up so that it was slightly ajar. Now when she came back to fetch William, she wouldn't have to mess about around the back of the building. She could simply slip in through the front window.

Proud of this show of foresight, Emily rejoined Jack in the entrance hall, and they stepped out into the cold night.

The fog was even thicker now. It enfolded Emily in a claustrophobic embrace, tendrils of dampness brushing against her face like the chill fingers of the dead. Her world was reduced to an eerie, muffled circle of pale yellow-gray. Her brief, tiny burst of confidence slipped away, leeched out of her by the horrid weather.

She turned to look for Jack, but there was no sign of him. "Jack?" she whispered.

"I'm here." His muffled voice came from a step or so behind her. She waited until she could see his shadowy form, then reached out and grabbed hold of his sleeve.

They crossed the large square in front of Somerset House. The fog was so thick Emily was unable to see the gas lamps until she was right on top of them, and even then they were just hazy, yellow shapes materializing out of the air, like floating balls of dim light.

It had been strange listening to Sebastian tell the true history of the Invisible Order. Ever since meeting Corrigan, Emily had thought of the Order as some evil, ghastly group of men trying to hunt down and kill the poor, innocent fey. Now she found out that it was actually the fey who were bad, and the Order was actually trying to save people.

Well, that wasn't exactly true. She was sure there were some fey who were perfectly nice, just as there were some members of the Order who were perfectly horrible. If she'd learned one thing from all of this, it was to make up her own mind when judging people and not simply listen to what others had to say.

Someone shouted in the distance, the sound muffled by the fog. The sharp *clip-clop* of a horse's hooves echoed around her, accompanied by the creaking trundle of wooden wheels. The sounds grew louder, then faded away again as the horse and cart passed invisibly in front of her.

Emily wasn't sure where they should go. If she was to find the key, she had to figure out what the riddle meant. And she needed to be somewhere safe to do that. The offices of the Order might have been ideal, if it weren't for the fact that Ravenhill would be there. She'd never be able to concentrate with him close by.

Where would she be safe? She couldn't go home. Mrs. Hobbs would have cleaned up the room by now, which meant it would be filled with people snoring and making noises.

She gazed around, at a loss. The fog before her swirled oddly, forming spirals and tendrils that turned in upon themselves, almost as though a gust of wind had cut through the thick vapor. But she hadn't felt any wind.

That was when she realized she was no longer holding on to Jack's sleeve. She must have let go while she was thinking about what to do.

"Jack?" she whispered. No answer.

And then she smelled it. The murky, brackish smell of stagnant water.

"Well, well," said an invisible voice. "Look who we have 'ere, Jenny Greenteeth. I do believe it's our troublesome friend, Miss Snow. Out on her lonesome."

"Not a clever move, Black Annis," said another voice.

"No, Jenny. Not a clever move at all. In fact, I'd say it was a very silly move."

The ghastly face of the old, wrinkled woman lunged at Emily out of the fog. Black water dribbled from her mouth. "Wouldn't you agree, Miss Snow?"

Emily screamed, then turned and ran. She heard the loud cackle of the one called Black Annis behind her.

"Ooh, she's runnin' away, Jenny. I do like it when they run. Gives the old bones a bit of exercise."

"Jack!" she screamed. "Jack, where are you?"

Black Annis suddenly appeared right in front of Emily. "Boo," she said.

Emily veered to the side and ran again. She couldn't see where she was going, but she kept moving anyway. Where was Jack? Did they already have him? She needed to get back across the square to Somerset House. If she could just get inside, she would be safe.

Something clammy touched Emily's arm. She looked

down and saw a strand of seaweed hanging over her wrist. Laughter echoed from close by.

They're toying with me, she realized. There was no way she would make it to safety. They would have her before she could even get close to Somerset House.

Emily stopped and tried to get her bearings. She was somewhere in the large square outside the building, but the swirling fog cut off all sense of direction. She took a deep breath, then shouted at the top of her voice.

"Jack!" She let out a frightened yelp when a voice seemed to answer, right by her ear.

"We've got your little Jack, poppet. There's no one to help you now." Emily whirled around, searching frantically through the fog. The voice hissed in her other ear. "Jenny Greenteeth's going to eat your face."

Emily darted around. Again, she saw nothing. She sobbed with frustration, then turned and ran blindly from the voices.

By sheer luck she ran in the right direction. The steps leading up to the door of Somerset House materialized out of the fog, and she ran straight toward them.

Black Annis and Jenny Greenteeth slid into view at the bottom of the stairs. Emily skidded to a stop. Jenny held Jack by the back of the neck. He struggled in her grasp, but Jenny only tightened her fingers, her dirty claws digging into his skin. He stopped moving.

"Well, this has been a lark, and no mistake. Ain't that right, Jenny?"

Jenny just stared at Emily, hunger plain in her dark eyes.

Emily reached into her pocket and took out the letter opener she had picked up from Sebastian's desk. She held it out before her, hoping her hand wouldn't tremble.

"Oh, will you look at that, Jenny. She has a knife." Black Annis moved forward. Emily backed up a step, then braced herself. "And what are you going to do with that, little girl? Weren't you ever told that knives are dangerous?"

Black Annis reached out. Emily watched, mesmerized, as the clawlike hand unfurled toward her. The hand drew closer, closer . . .

. . . then stopped. The fingers curled in upon themselves. Emily blinked and looked up. Black Annis was staring at the blade. She let out a hiss of frustration.

"Why don't you just put down the knife, poppet? We don't want to hurt you. Our King just wants a quiet word, that's all. He's nice, the Dagda. Very fair. He told us to bring you to him."

During this speech, Black Annis didn't once take her eyes from the blade. Then Emily realized why. The blade was made of iron.

Barely allowing the thought to register in her head, she darted forward and sliced the blade along Black Annis's hand. There was a hiss, like water on a hot stone. Black Annis jerked back with a strangled, mewling cry that was more animal than human. Greasy smoke drifted up from her arm as thick black blood oozed from the cut.

"Aah, see what she's done, Jenny? Undone! Undone by a child."

Jenny Greenteeth stepped toward Emily, her hand still gripping Jack's neck, and this time Emily did stumble backward. "I'm going to eat her, Black Annis. Nobody cuts you and gets away with it. Nobody."

But before anyone could make another move, there was a shout from above and an indistinct shape dropped from somewhere and landed between Emily and Jenny Greenteeth.

It was Corrigan.

And he was brandishing a tiny bronze sword about the length of Emily's finger.

There was a frozen moment of silence. Corrigan brandished his sword in a flamboyant circle.

"Hah!" he said.

Then Jenny started to laugh. Even Black Annis, clutching her hand in pain, let out a snicker. Corrigan pulled himself to his full height, indignant.

Emily knew this was about to end badly. She locked eyes with Jack, raising her eyebrows. He nodded almost imperceptibly, then, while Jenny was distracted by Corrigan, drove his elbow hard into her ribs. Jenny's grip loosened, and Jack jerked forward. Emily bent over and snatched Corrigan into her arms, then turned and ran. She had briefly contemplated trying to get past Black Annis and Jenny Greenteeth to regain the safety of Somerset House, but that meant she would be trapped in there when Ravenhill arrived, and she didn't want that.

She heard Jack's footsteps behind her. Emily kept running as fast as she could, fearing that if she slowed, she would feel Jenny's claws on her neck.

"Right! Turn right!" shouted Corrigan.

"Why?"

"Because if you don't, you're going to run straight into a wall."

Emily veered to the right, half-glimpsing the walls of Somerset House. "Can you see?" she shouted, her breath coming in ragged bursts.

"Of course I can see!"

"I mean through the fog. Can you see through the fog?"

"Oh. Yes."

"Guide me, then. Get us as far away from here as possible."

Silence greeted her words.

"Corrigan?"

"Say 'please.'"

⇤CHAPTER TWENTY-THREE⇥

*In which Corrigan comes up with a plan
that involves a visit to the Landed Gentry.*

The fog remained thick as Emily and Jack ran from Black Annis and Jenny Greenteeth. At one point, they even jumped onto the back of a carriage and let it carry them through the streets until the driver sensed the extra weight and slowed down to see what the problem was.

"Did you two have any kind of a plan, or were you just planning on swanning around the city all night?" asked Corrigan.

"I do have a plan, actually," snapped Emily. "I just need a place to hole up for a while, so I can figure out that stupid riddle. Somewhere I don't have to keep looking over my shoulder every few seconds."

Corrigan lapsed into a thoughtful silence. "A safe place, you say?"

"Yes. Somewhere I won't be bothered."

"Hmm."

"What? Do you know somewhere?"

"Unfortunately, yes."

"Why 'unfortunately'?"

"You'll see," said Corrigan grimly. "Here. Take this road on the right."

Emily and Jack turned onto the road. They walked on in silence for a while. Then Corrigan cleared his throat.

"Don't you two have anything to say?"

"Not really," said Emily. "Why?"

"Not even a 'thank you'? I saved your lives back there. Who knows what would have happened if I hadn't stepped in."

"What?" said Emily and Jack simultaneously.

"You just jumped in and . . . and waved that stupid sword about," said Emily.

"That creature was about to step on you," said Jack.

"Rubbish," scoffed Corrigan. "She was terrified. I could see it in her eyes."

"You're mad," said Emily, softening her voice. "But you could have been killed."

"Yes, well . . . ," said Corrigan awkwardly. "Just returning the favor, wasn't I? And that means we're even now. You saved me, I saved you. I don't owe you anymore. Agreed?"

"You think that's all it takes to get us to trust you?" said Jack hotly.

"Boy, I couldn't give a Sluagh's rotten carcass whether you trusted me or not," said Corrigan. "You could drop dead right now and I wouldn't even notice."

"That's enough," snapped Emily.

Jack and Corrigan lapsed into a sullen silence, and they walked on. The darkness and fog had transformed the city into a ghost town. It was as if she, Jack, and Corrigan were the only living souls walking the streets. And when they did encounter any people, they loomed out of the fog as indistinct shadows, spirits drifting through the night, making no sound at all.

"Where are we?" asked Emily nervously.

"We're close. That's St. James's Theatre up ahead."

Emily wondered how he could tell. The hazy building he indicated looked just like every other structure they had walked past, giving indistinct impressions of bricks and windows.

"Turn left here," said Corrigan.

Emily stopped before the mouth of a narrow alley. She peered nervously into the darkness.

"Hurry up. We're nearly there."

Emily steeled herself, then plunged into the narrow passage, Jack following close behind. She could feel the damp

233

walls on either side, brushing up close against her arms. Corrigan guided them across a road and down another alley that led into a small, hidden court. Someone had drawn chalk hopscotch squares on the uneven flagstones.

"You have to jump the sequence," said Corrigan.

"Excuse me?"

Corrigan gestured at the hopscotch drawing. "You have to do it. To open the door."

Emily looked at the chalk drawings. Compared to everything else that had happened to her, playing hopscotch in the middle of the night was mild by comparison.

Emily found a stone and tossed it onto the drawing. Then she hopped through the sequence, jumping over the square the stone had landed on. She got to the other side, then turned and hopped back, grabbing the stone as she passed.

"Now what?" she asked.

"Now we go down."

Emily turned around to find that the square where the stone had fallen had vanished, and in its place was a dark hole in the ground. She leaned over the hole and found a narrow flight of stairs leading down into the gloom.

Jack joined her. "Where does it go?" he asked.

"Down."

"Very funny."

"It goes somewhere I don't want to go, but at the moment we don't really have much choice. We have Black Annis and Jenny Greenteeth chasing us on one side, the Dark Man on the other, and the Invisible Order probably searching for us, as well. I think I'd rather take my chances down there."

Corrigan hopped off Emily's shoulder and disappeared down the stairs, followed by Jack. Emily ducked her head to avoid the edge of the flagstone and started her descent. There was a rough wall to her right, but nothing to her left. She got the impression of a vast, empty space, with nothing stopping her from plummeting to her death should she put a foot wrong. She kept her hand against the wall, just to be safe.

"How come nobody ever finds these places?" she called out. She could just see Corrigan up ahead, a vague shadow hopping down the shallow steps with Jack following carefully in his wake. "Surely someone knocking down a wall in their cellar could fall into one of these hidey-holes?"

"It's not as simple as that," said Corrigan, glancing over his shoulder. "Which isn't to say that some of your kind don't fall through. They do." Corrigan hopped down a few more stairs. "But these hidey-holes aren't exactly *under* London. Well, they are, but they're touched by the magic of Faerie, so to speak. Little puddles that got caught here when the door closed. There are fewer now. One day soon, the last one will probably wither up and vanish. But we use them while they last."

The stairs ended at the entrance to a high tunnel. Emily stared up at the ornate arches that supported the distant roof. Water dripped steadily from the ceiling, forming a small stream that ran beneath her feet.

They followed the tunnel for what seemed like an hour. A change in the light up ahead told Emily that they were finally reaching the end. And they were—a rather abrupt end.

The tunnel opened up into a chamber that was so vast, Emily couldn't see the other side. And for some reason, the tunnel ended high up on the wall of the chamber so that there was a drop of about a hundred feet below them. Huge pillars supported the distant roof, fading into the distance. A ramp attached directly to the wall descended to the ground.

As they stepped onto the ramp, Emily carefully leaned over the edge to see what was below them.

What she saw took her breath away.

It was a village, but a village unlike any she had ever seen. Houses had been built into every available space—up against the pillars, up against the walls, sometimes on the roofs of other houses. And where space had run out, the builders had simply moved upward. Structures clung precariously to the walls, held up by stilts and pillars. Flickering lamps lit streets that wound through and around the houses like pieces of tangled string.

As they drew closer to the ground, Emily saw something else that filled her with wonder. The houses and streets weren't made from the traditional bricks and mortar. They were made from junk. Anything that could be taken from the streets above had been brought here to build the dwellings. She saw one small house built entirely of broken glass. Every time the faerie inside it moved, flashes of broken color sparked through the air. Another house was made completely of metal street signs. A crude tenement building had been built by piling twenty or so hansom cabs one atop the other.

"What is this place?" whispered Emily.

"You'll see," said Corrigan.

At the bottom of the ramp was a small booth, and inside the booth was one of the chestnut-colored gnomes. The creature stared at them for a full five seconds before seeming to realize they were there. Then he jumped, banging his head on the roof.

"I say," he said indignantly. "I say, what are you doing, creeping up on someone like that, what what what?"

"Uh . . ." Emily stared uncertainly at the creature. He was dressed in a similar fashion to the gnome with the fake mustache—Mr. Pemberton. He wore a thick jacket, a silk cravat, and an immaculate hat. He even had a pipe hanging from his mouth. She looked to Corrigan for help, but the piskie was staring at the creature with a look of disgust.

"Just let us in, will you?" snapped Corrigan. "We've got important business."

The gnome fished around in his waistcoat for a second, then pulled out a gold watch and opened the lid.

"Apologies, good sir. But you call at a most ungodly hour. I'm afraid everyone is now abed."

Corrigan jumped up to the lip of the booth's window and grabbed hold of the gnome's cravat.

"Fetch me Pemberton right now. Otherwise I'll pull those clothes off and throw them in the mud. Then I'll take that watch and break it into pieces with that ridiculous pipe."

The gnome swallowed fearfully. "One moment, if you please," he said.

Corrigan released him. "Good man. You're a real gentleman, you are."

"You think so? Why, thank you, kind sir. I do try. I—"

"Don't push your luck."

"Of course."

The gnome bowed nervously and backed out of his booth. Then he turned and ran as fast as his short legs could carry him, zigzagging back and forth across the street. Corrigan sighed and shook his head.

"What was all that about?" asked Emily.

"I warned you, didn't I? They call themselves the Landed Gentry. They live down here and try to copy you lot. And when I say copy, I mean copy *everything*. The way you dress, the way you speak, your society. They even have a Queen who calls herself Victoria. They want to be like you; they want to *be* you."

"Can we trust them?" Emily asked dubiously.

"Oh, yes. That's about the only thing I can say for them. They love it here. They have about as much reason as you do to keep London as it is. They've already said they'll have nothing to do with the Queen *or* the Dagda. They're neutral, like Merrian. That's why they live down here. Trying to form their own little society."

"Is that the same Pemberton—?"

"Aye, the same one. Seeing him earlier is what gave me the idea. Can't stand the irritating creature, but beggars can't be choosers, eh?"

"Wait, did you just say Merrian was neutral?" asked Emily. "I thought he worked for the Queen."

"Hmm? Oh, no. He sides with whoever he thinks is right."

"Did he know that the Queen planned on bringing her armies through to London?"

"Bones, no! He would never have helped the Queen if

he knew that. I'll have to get word to him that things have changed. He won't be happy when he finds out what she planned, let me tell you. He's another one that likes London as it is." Corrigan looked past the small hut and groaned. "Here we go," he said.

Emily peered around the hut and saw two gnomes hurrying toward them. One was the gatekeeper, and the other was indeed Mr. Pemberton, in a scarlet dressing gown pulled tight around his belly. He still wore his mustache, and this time it seemed to be staying in one place.

When he saw Emily and Jack, he broke into a huge smile. He bowed to Emily, then took hold of Jack's hand and pumped it up and down.

"My lady! Good sir! Delighted to see you both. So glad you could join us." He cast a dark glance at Corrigan. "Shame you had to bring your servant, but we can't have everything, can we?" He turned his back on Corrigan and gently guided Emily and Jack past the gatehouse and onto the street. Emily looked down and saw it was paved with bottle tops, thousands upon thousands of them.

"Now. Tell me. What can I do for you?"

Emily looked over her shoulder at Corrigan. He shrugged his shoulders in resignation, then nodded. Emily was rather surprised to realize that this was enough for her. It meant she trusted Corrigan. She knew she shouldn't, not after what he had done, but the piskie seemed genuinely intent on helping her now. And no matter what Jack said, he *had* risked his life back at Somerset House. If Corrigan said the gnome was trustworthy, then she believed him.

So Emily told Mr. Pemberton the story. Everything.

⊰⊱Chapter Twenty-four⊰⊱

*In which Emily, Jack, Corrigan, and Mr. Pemberton
struggle to decipher the riddle.*

Ten thirty in the evening
on the second day of Emily's adventures.

Emily felt as if she had gone back to school.

The room Mr. Pemberton had led them to was an exact copy of a schoolroom, although she supposed *copy* wasn't the proper word. The building was a school that had been built to, as Mr. Pemberton put it, "educate the fey into the ways of proper Victorian Society," and Mr. Pemberton was the head teacher.

Emily and Jack each sat down at one of the desks. Luckily for them, the gnomes had pilfered their supplies from London above. They were able to fit quite comfortably, though Emily imagined everything was a bit on the large side for any gnome children.

Emily looked around wistfully at the familiar surroundings. She had enjoyed school. Actually, that wasn't entirely accurate. She enjoyed *learning*, even if she wasn't always fond of the school itself, and the teachers in particular.

"Right," said Mr. Pemberton. "Excuse me? Pay attention at the back, please."

Emily turned around to find Corrigan staring out the window. He threw Mr. Pemberton a disgusted look.

"The object of this gathering is to decipher Emily's puzzle."

He turned to the huge blackboard, brandishing a stick of chalk. "Emily, if you please?"

Emily unconsciously straightened her back and recited the riddle.

"A bird raises a saint in the wake of the fire.
A father's favorite rhyme will confirm the truth.
Speak the rhyme and the whispering shall reveal all."

As she talked, Mr. Pemberton wrote the words on the board in neat, cursive script. He stepped back and surveyed his handiwork.

"Hmm," he said after a while. "Tricky."

"Really?" said Corrigan. "And here was me thinking this would be easy."

"Silence in the classroom!" shouted Mr. Pemberton.

Emily, Jack, and Corrigan all stared at him in surprise. Mr. Pemberton flushed red and shrugged in embarrassment.

"Apologies," he said. "Old habits die hard." He turned back to the board. "Let's take it one step at a time, shall we? The first line is too vague. It could mean anything. We'll leave that for the moment. 'A father's favorite rhyme.' Does your father have a favorite rhyme?"

"My father disappeared when I was seven. I don't know what his favorite rhyme was."

"Oh. I'm very sorry, Emily. I didn't mean—"

"The clue's in the first line," argued Corrigan. "'In the wake of the fire.' Notice how it says 'the' fire, and not 'a' fire. What else can it be talking about?"

Mr. Pemberton's eyes widened. "The Great Fire. Sixteen sixty-six."

"Exactly."

"Fine," said Emily. "Sixteen sixty-six. The Great Fire of London. But how can a bird raise a saint? Does it mean raise a saint from the dead?"

Mr. Pemberton frowned. "I've never heard of any such thing."

"Neither have I," said Corrigan.

They lapsed into silence. Emily began to grow frustrated. She was good at riddles. She should be able to get this. The riddle was a clue about the location of a key to open the door to Faerie. The door was locked by Christopher Wren. That was fact.

So Christopher Wren himself had written the clue. The Queen had said as much to Emily. And somehow . . . *somehow*, he wrote the clue for Emily, knowing that she would be searching for the key. *How* he knew that was another matter altogether. But . . .

Emily stopped mid-thought and stared at the board. A bird raises a saint. A bird . . . Christopher Wren. A wren was a bird . . .

"Christopher Wren," she said suddenly.

The others looked at her.

"Christopher Wren," she repeated. She pointed at the board. "A bird raises a saint. A wren is a bird. If Christopher *Wren* wrote the clue, doesn't it follow that he was referring to himself?"

Corrigan and Mr. Pemberton looked back at the board.

"Could it be?" mused Mr. Pemberton.

"Could it be?" repeated Jack, impressed. "I can't read or write and even *I* can tell she's got it."

Corrigan looked at Emily. "Well done, girl."

Emily blushed at the praise. "It was nothing. I just—"

"Yes, yes. Don't get full of yourself, now."

Emily snapped her mouth shut and glared at Corrigan. He grinned and winked at her.

"Now," said Mr. Pemberton, "how did Mr. Wren raise a saint?"

Emily thought about it some more. Didn't Sebastian say that Wren was responsible for rebuilding much of London after the Great Fire? He'd said that he designed and built St. Paul's Cathedral—

Emily went absolutely still. It was so simple when you knew the answer. She started to smile.

"What are you smiling at?" Corrigan asked suspiciously.

Mr. Pemberton turned from the board and studied her face. "I do believe Miss Snow has the answer."

"It's St. Paul's Cathedral," said Emily simply. "Christopher Wren raised St. Paul's after the fire. He built it."

Corrigan stared at the board. "But he built nearly every other church in London as well," said Corrigan. "St. Mary's, St. Peter's, St. Michael's . . ."

Mr. Pemberton cleared his throat. "Maybe so, but none of those matter when we take into account the final line. 'Speak the rhyme and the whispering shall reveal all.' That can only refer to the Whispering Gallery at St. Paul's. None of his other churches had such a thing." He turned to the others. "Agreed?"

"What's the Whispering Gallery?" asked Jack.

"It is a balcony that runs around the inside of the cathedral. Apparently, if you stand on one side and whisper something, anyone standing on the opposite side will be able to hear what you said. Something to do with the acoustics."

"Yes. Well done," said Corrigan. "It's just a pity we don't know what she's supposed to whisper, isn't it?"

Mr. Pemberton's air of excitement faded, and he fell into one of the chairs. "Good point," he said.

They both turned expectantly to Emily.

"What?" she said defensively. "I've already said I don't know."

"You *do* realize how important this is?" said Corrigan.

"Yes!" said Emily. "Yes, I know how important this is. Do you think I'm an idiot? All I did was save your life"—she pointed at Corrigan—"and ever since then, I've been chased, lied to, attacked, had my home destroyed, my brother kidnapped, been forced to become a thief. I'm tired of it! I. Don't. *Know!*"

An embarrassed silence followed. Then Corrigan cleared his throat.

"So what you're saying is, you don't know?"

"Leave her alone," snapped Jack. "She's doing her best."

Emily felt the hot tears begin to flow. She stood up and ran toward the door.

"Emily?" called Jack.

"Leave me be!" Emily called. "Just, everyone . . . leave me alone." She pulled the door open and stormed out of the classroom, then ran down the hall and out into the street, where she sank down onto the pavement. She was so tired.

All she wanted was everything to be back to normal, for everything to return to the way it was.

She'd felt exactly the same way in the days after their ma disappeared.

She was ten when it happened. At first all she'd felt was sorrow and fear. She and William hadn't known what to do, how they would survive. William barely even understood what was going on.

But after those first few days, the sorrow and the fear were pushed out of the way by more pressing matters. Who would look after them? Who would feed them, clothe them? There was no way Emily would let them take her and William to the workhouse, so it had fallen to her to try and bring some money in.

That was when the anger set in. Anger that first her da, then her ma, could just leave them like that. She knew, deep down, that something must have happened to them. But that didn't stop the anger and the resentment. She was just a child. She was supposed to have stories read to her by her da. Instead, she was barely scraping out a living selling watercress.

It wasn't the work she minded—she would have had to do that anyway. It was the responsibility. She loved William dearly, but it was hard to have to look after him all the time.

Then over the next few weeks, the self-pity set in. Why did it have to happen to her? Why not someone horrible, like Victoria Ashdown? What had she done to deserve all this?

She'd snapped out of that when she came home one day to find William weeping uncontrollably in the corner, calling out for their ma. Emily had held and rocked him until he stopped crying. That was the day she grew up, the day she knew she simply had to do what had to be done.

What she was feeling now—the anger, the self-pity— she had gone through it all before, and she knew it was pointless.

Emily straightened up and wiped her eyes. The road she had been staring at was made from old shields—round, oval, square, rectangular—all of them laid down and held in place with some kind of clear glue. About twenty paces farther up the street, the shields changed to metal dinner trays, brass and silver, many of them lacquered or painted and all of them covered with the same substance.

She became gradually aware of an itch at the back of her mind trying to get her attention. Something had triggered it. Something she had just been thinking about. Was it something about William? No, she didn't think so. Her ma? Her da?

Something stirred. Something to do with her da, then? What had she been thinking about? Her da disappearing?

No. What else then? Having stories read to her by her da?

That was it. Something about stories.

The stories her da used to read to her came from one battered book, a book that Ma said had belonged to *his* father before him. She felt a twinge of sorrow. The book was probably destroyed now, lost in the mess that used to be their home.

But something about the book was important. She tried to remember what it had looked like. The cover was made from battered and scuffed red leather. A verse from an old nursery rhyme had been scrawled onto the first page.

Emily's eyes opened wide. She vaguely remembered her father telling her that those few lines of rhyme were his favorite.

She closed her eyes to think. What was the rhyme? She tried to imagine the page in her mind, to see the untidy scrawl on the yellowing paper. She remembered thinking it was a curiously sad rhyme. How did it go?

She had it!

Emily ran back inside the classroom. Corrigan was standing on a desk trying to wrest a piece of chalk out of Mr. Pemberton's hand. Jack was watching them with an amused look in his eyes.

"I said no," snapped Mr. Pemberton. "The chalk isn't for drawing lewd pictures with."

"I've got it! I remember the rhyme!" Emily shouted.

All three of them turned to face her in surprise.

"If clouds or mists do dark the sky,
Great store of birds and beasts shall die.
And if the winds do file aloft,
Then war shall vex the kingdom oft."

Corrigan released Mr. Pemberton's hand. "You're sure?"

Emily nodded. "It was in a book my da used to read to us."

"I think you've cracked it," said Mr. Pemberton thought-fully, turning to the board. "This line here. 'A father's favorite rhyme will confirm the truth.'" He stared at them expectantly. "That confirms that it's St. Paul's Cathedral, surely?"

"Why?" snapped Corrigan. "Explain yourself, gnome."

"Well, the verse Emily just recited. It's only one verse of a rhyme . . . hold on."

Mr. Pemberton turned to one of the bookcases and ran his finger along the spines until he found what he was looking for. He pulled out the book and paged through it.

"Here we go." He cleared his throat.

"If St. Paul's day be fair and clear,
It does betide a happy year.
But if it chance to snow or rain,
Then will be dear all kinds of grain.

"If clouds or mists do dark the sky,
Great store of birds and beasts shall die.
And if the winds do file aloft,
Then war shall vex the kingdom oft."

He closed the book with a satisfied thud. "Emily's riddle starts off with the line, 'A father's favorite rhyme will confirm the truth.' We deduced that the rest of the riddle referred to St. Paul's Cathedral and the Whispering Gallery, yes? *This* nursery rhyme—her father's favorite rhyme—confirms our deduction as definite. I mean, I know it doesn't refer to the cathedral *as such*, but it does mention St. Paul. And when you look at St. Paul's Cathedral as the answer, then everything else makes perfect sense."

"So does that mean the key is hidden at St. Paul's?" asked Jack.

"It would appear so," said Mr. Pemberton. "At least, that is my interpretation."

"But how will we find it?"

"'Speak the rhyme and the whispering shall reveal all,'" quoted Emily. "We speak the rhyme in the Whispering Gallery and see what happens."

Mr. Pemberton smiled at Emily. "Exactly. Congratulations, dear girl. You've solved the puzzle."

⊰⊱Chapter Twenty-five⊰⊱

*In which our heroes sneak inside St. Paul's Cathedral and much
whispering is done despite a nasty surprise awaiting them.*

Midnight on the third day of Emily's adventures.

St. Paul's Cathedral stood at the top of Ludgate Hill, its
dome and cross stark against the night sky. Emily thought it
looked like an upside-down goblet.

Ludgate Hill wasn't really a hill. At least, not from the
position Emily, Corrigan, Jack, and Mr. Pemberton had
taken, outside a tailor's shop in Carter Lane. The wide lane
headed in a straight, even line to the front of the cathedral,
whose stairs led up to a row of pillars that stretched across
the front of the building.

The cathedral was daunting. Not just because of its size—
although that was certainly enough to daunt anyone—but
also because of what it represented. Emily had the feeling

God would be watching them, disapproving of their entry into his place of worship.

There was a scuffling sound behind her. She turned to find Mr. Pemberton leaning on his walking stick, hopping from foot to foot.

"Sorry," he said, embarrassed. "It's all the excitement."

"Where are the others?" asked Corrigan from his usual place on Emily's shoulder.

"Oh, don't you worry," said Pemberton. "They're around. Hidden, like shadows in the night," he said melodramatically.

Corrigan snorted his irritation. Emily knew he didn't want Mr. Pemberton here. And he certainly didn't want the small army of gnomes Mr. Pemberton had roused from their sleep right after Emily deciphered the riddle. The two had argued for a full ten minutes back at the school.

"But we can help," Mr. Pemberton had argued. "We can act as lookouts, protect you should anything untoward occur."

"The only thing *untoward* will be you lot tripping over your own feet and giving us away," Corrigan had responded.

Mr. Pemberton was adamant, and he had won out in the end. Emily thought this was because Corrigan didn't want to talk to him anymore. He had simply walked off in mid-argument, leaving Mr. Pemberton to scramble around and organize his people.

And now here they were, the four of them, about to sneak into the largest cathedral in the city.

At least the fog had lifted, thought Emily, trying to look for something positive.

"Should we get on with it?" said Jack.

"A sound idea, young sir. The Devil waits for no man, as they say."

"Um . . . yes. Fine," said Emily.

They left the cover of the tailor's shop and hurried along the pavement toward St. Paul's. It towered over them as they approached, gradually blocking out the night sky. They drew to a stop at the bottom of the wide set of stairs that led up to the portico.

Emily shivered, unsettled by the silent streets. London wasn't meant to be quiet. It was meant to be filled with life, with shouting and laughter. She squinted up the stairs into the ominous shadows beneath the pillars.

"What are we waiting for?" asked Corrigan.

"We're not waiting for anything," Emily said. She turned to Mr. Pemberton, and her words froze in her mouth as she stared in shock at the gnome.

"What? Oh, my goodness. I don't have something up my nose, do I?" He hastily took out a handkerchief and dabbed at his nose. "How embarrassing. Is that better?"

"It's not that. It's . . ."

"It's your eye," said Corrigan. Mr. Pemberton's left eye was squinting, the pupil pointing off to the side.

"Oh! Do forgive me. It does that sometimes." He bent over and did something with his hands, and when he straightened up again, the eye was facing in the proper direction. "Better?"

Emily looked at Mr. Pemberton in dismay. "You have a glass eye?" she said flatly.

"Yes, lost it some years ago. Terrible accident. Luckily, a Miss . . . Oh, how vexing. What was her name? A Miss something-or-other. She fixed it for me."

"Miss LaFleur?"

"Yes, that's it! Do you know her?"

Emily locked gazes with Corrigan, seeing the same realization mirrored in his face.

"Snow?" said Jack, seeing the expression on her face. "What's wrong?"

"If LaFleur is watching, she'll report this to the Queen," Emily said to Corrigan. "We have to move quickly, before they get organized."

But even as she spoke, a line of about thirty dark figures slid out from behind the pillars up above.

But it wasn't the fey.

"Good morning, Miss Snow," said Mr. Ravenhill. He took off his top hat and smiled coldly. "You've been getting up to mischief again. Hasn't she, Mr. Blackmore?"

Blackmore staggered down the steps to stand by his master. "She has indeed, Mr. R. A right royal pain in the backside, that's what she is."

"How did they know we'd be here?" Corrigan whispered furiously.

A shrill, trumpeting sound exploded into life behind Emily. She jumped and whirled around to see Mr. Pemberton holding a small metal horn to his lips. No sooner had the notes faded than a stream of immaculately dressed gnomes filed into view from the side streets and formed a silent line behind Mr. Pemberton. Emily counted about fifty of them. Even Corrigan looked impressed.

Ravenhill chuckled. "And what are these creatures going to do? Poke us with their umbrellas?"

The scraping sound of metal on metal echoed around them. The gnomes had all pulled bronze swords from inside their walking sticks and umbrellas.

The sight of the weapons gave Ravenhill pause.

"We don't want any trouble, Miss Snow," he said. "Just come with us and your friends can go free. We're on the same side, you know."

"I'm not on your side," she shouted. "You're . . . you're *evil*." It wasn't the best insult she had ever come up with, but it was the best she could do at the time.

"Evil? Whatever gave you that idea?"

"I'll have nothing to do with you, Ravenhill. Nothing at all."

"So be it. Don't say I didn't give you a chance." He put his top hat back on. "And it's *Mr*. Ravenhill to you."

Mr. Pemberton stepped past Emily. "Sir, I urge you to stand aside, lest this end in bloodshed."

Ravenhill gazed down at the gnome, distaste plain across his features. "Oh, I think bloodshed is exactly where this is going to end." He stepped back and withdrew his own sword from inside his walking stick. He held it up to the light. "I think you'll find our iron bites harder than your bronze."

"It's the sharpness of the bite that counts, sir." Mr. Pemberton held up his sword and turned slightly so he could address the gnomes. "Gentlemen? Today is the day the Landed Gentry earn their place in history!" He smiled at Emily and Jack. "Miss Snow. Sir. It's been an honor and a pleasure." He looked over at Corrigan. "Told you you'd need us, piskie."

Before Corrigan could reply, he raised his sword high above his head and shouted, *"Charge!"*

The gnomes let out a fierce cry and surged past Emily, Jack, and Corrigan. At the same time, the members of the Order raised their own weapons and rushed down to meet them. It all seemed to happen in slow motion. Emily could see every detail as clear as if it were a frozen tableau. The angry snarls on the human faces, the set looks of determination on the gnomes, the glint of excitement in Mr. Pemberton's eyes.

Then the two sides came together with the fierce clash of metal and the solid smack of flesh meeting flesh.

Emily looked on in horror. Ravenhill was trying to fight his way in her direction, but Mr. Pemberton had gathered a small group of gnomes and blocked his way.

"Emily!" snapped Corrigan, pulling on her ear. "Get a move on."

Emily jumped and she and Jack ran along the bottom of the stairs away from the fighting. She sprinted up the steps, trying desperately to ignore the screams and shouts that were coming from down below.

She skidded to a stop in front of the doors, yanking hard on the handles. They opened quietly and smoothly and Emily and Jack ducked inside, slamming them shut behind them.

Emily heaved in great gulps of air. The silence of the cathedral was a heavy presence after the chaotic sounds of battle. She turned around to get her bearings and stumbled to a stop, her eyes wide with awe.

Never in her wildest dreams had Emily imagined such magnificence. Candlelight shone all around her, soft halos glowing gently from burnished metal. Statues on pedestals lined the passage that led into the center of the church, where .

hallways opened off from a huge circular space, its floor inlaid with a marble sun.

Corrigan hopped off her shoulder and padded across the black-and-white tiles. He looked back at her. "What are you waiting for?" he urged. "One of the priests to come and bless you?"

Emily shook herself from her daze. Corrigan was right. The longer they took, the more dangerous it was for Mr. Pemberton and his small army. She glanced at Jack. He had his back up against the door.

"You go and do your thing. I'll make sure that door stays shut."

Emily nodded, then she and Corrigan hurried along the passage and came to a stop in the center circle of the cathedral. Emily looked up to see the huge dome towering above her. She could just make out paintings on the underside of the dome, but the light was too dim to see what they were.

A railing encircled the wall about halfway between the floor and the distant ceiling. "That must be the gallery," she said.

Emily scooped up Corrigan and they searched until they found a flight of stone stairs. Emily took them two at a time, and soon found herself at a low door that opened up into the Whispering Gallery.

A thin bench followed the wall all the way around the gallery. High arched windows showed the night sky outside, and statues were carved into the wall. Corrigan leapt down to the floor.

"What now?" he asked.

Emily wasn't so sure herself. "Maybe I whisper the rhyme and you hear the answer on the other side?" she suggested. "That was how Mr. Pemberton said it worked."

"Worth a try," said Corrigan. He turned and ran around the gallery. Emily glanced over the railing and saw Jack still standing with his back against the door. He gave her a thumbs-up sign.

"Ready," called Corrigan.

Emily moved away from the balcony and took a deep, shaky breath. What if she was wrong? What if this wasn't what Wren had meant in the riddle? Then all of this would have been for nothing.

Well, one way or the other, she had to find out.

Emily leaned on the small bench and put her mouth close to the wall. "Corrigan?" she whispered. "You are an ill-mannered, annoying little piskie." Emily held her breath and waited.

A second later she heard the faintest of whispers. "And you are a stupid girl who thinks she's more clever than she really is."

Emily straightened up. She could see Corrigan standing on the bench on the other side of the gallery, grinning in her direction. At least the basic concept worked. Now to test the clue.

Emily took out the poem. She leaned in to the wall and recited it in a whispered voice.

"If St. Paul's day be fair and clear,
It does betide a happy year.
But if it chance to snow or rain,
Then will be dear all kinds of grain.

"If clouds or mists do dark the sky,
Great store of birds and beasts shall die.
And if the winds do file aloft,
Then war shall vex the kingdom oft."

After she uttered the last words, she held her breath and waited. For a long time there was nothing, then Corrigan's voice came to her around the gallery wall. "I heard the poem, but nothing's happened," he called.

Emily straightened up, her heart sinking. It hadn't worked. She looked across at Corrigan. "What do we do?"

Corrigan shrugged his bony shoulders. Emily gritted her teeth in frustration and studied the piece of paper, searching for inspiration. Had she written it down wrong? She didn't think so.

Then a thought struck her. The clue had said "a father's favorite rhyme," hadn't it? As far as she knew, her father only liked the second verse, the one that was written in the book.

Emily quickly turned back to the wall and put her mouth close to the stone.

"If clouds or mists do dark the sky,
Great store of birds and beasts shall die.
And if the winds do file aloft,
Then war shall vex the kingdom oft."

She felt an immediate change in the air. It grew tingly, like it did before a big storm. The hairs on her arms stood on end. Her teeth ached.

Then a dry, whispery voice spoke back to her.

"The first part of the key is found,
The second, though, is still around.
The place you seek is Merlin's Tower,
Repeat the rhyme and hold the power."

The voice faded as if blown away on a wind. Emily straightened up and looked for Corrigan. The piskie was hurrying around the gallery.

"Did you hear?" she said excitedly.

"I heard," Corrigan replied. He didn't seem too happy. "More riddles. Why is it always riddles? Can't they just say, 'Here you go. Go here and pick up the key.' How easy would that be? But no, they have to be all vague and mysterious. It's very annoying."

"What do you think it meant, though? 'The first part of the key is found.' We haven't found any part of the key."

No sooner had the words left Emily's mouth than they heard a dull scraping sound. Emily looked up, wondering where it had come from.

"Look at that statue," whispered Corrigan.

Emily shifted her attention to a statue a few paces away. It was a carving of a serious-looking man wearing a robe. The statue's arm was moving.

As Emily watched, a hand emerged from behind the statue's robe, holding something dark brown and crescent-shaped. The arm kept moving until it was fully extended, then the fingers started to open. Emily hurried over just as something fell from its outstretched fingers. Emily caught the object, and a moment later the arm retreated back under the cloak.

Emily looked down at the object nestling in her palm. It looked like a tree branch or root coaxed into a semicircle. There were strange runes carved into the wood.

"That's the key," said Corrigan. "At least, half of it."

Emily didn't know what to feel—excitement that they were one step closer, or disappointment that their search wasn't complete. They still had the second half of the key to find.

There was a loud booming sound down below.

"Snow?" shouted Jack. "You'd better get a move on! Someone wants to come in, and I don't think it's for Sunday service."

Emily hastily hid the key in her coat, and she and Corrigan hurried back to the stairs.

⊁ CHAPTER TWENTY-SIX ⊰
In which Emily meets the Dagda and he offers her the world.

ONE O'CLOCK IN THE MORNING
ON THE THIRD DAY OF EMILY'S ADVENTURES.

J ack had his ear to the door when she and Corrigan rejoined him. He glanced over his shoulder.

"Whoever was trying to get in has stopped. Maybe Pemberton got him."

Emily put her own ear to the door. She couldn't hear anything, but she thought this was more likely due to the thickness of the wood than anything else. She carefully pulled the door ajar and put her eye to the crack. She was right. The sounds of fighting were still there but were coming from farther down the street. She wondered if Mr. Pemberton was purposely leading the Order away from the cathedral, to give them a chance to escape.

"We should find the back way out," said Emily.

"I think we should definitely find out," said Jack.

They ran across the checkerboard tiles and found another door at the far end of the cathedral. Emily carefully pulled it open a fraction and peered outside. A small veranda lay immediately beyond the door, with four pillars holding up a sheltering roof. She leaned farther out and saw stairs to either side of the platform.

"Nothing," she whispered. "Let's go."

She stepped outside and was immediately buffeted by a cold wind. She shivered. "Do you think Mr. Pemberton's all right?"

"I'd imagine so," said Corrigan. "No matter how irritating he is, Pemberton's not stupid. If the odds get too much, he'll call a retreat."

Emily sighed. What should they do now? They had to solve yet another riddle before they could get the second part of the key. Who knew how long that would take them?

"Maybe we should go back to Mr. Pemberton's place. We can try and solve the riddle there," she said.

"I'd rather not," said Corrigan. "I've had my fill of gnomes for the night."

"Riddle?" said Jack sharply. "What are you talking about?"

"It's another riddle," said Emily. "The key is split in two. We only got one half."

Jack scowled. "Why was this Christopher Wren so obsessed with riddles?"

A large bang echoed from somewhere within the cathedral. It sounded like the front door being slammed open.

"We should go," said Jack nervously.

"But where?"

"I know where, dearie," said a voice from the darkness.

Emily's blood froze in her veins. Corrigan cursed and tried to pull out his sword, and Jack fumbled for his knife, but it was too late. A dirty sack fell over each of them. Black Annis stepped from the shadows, upending the sacks and lifting them effortlessly into the air.

Black Annis leaned in close to the sacks. "You two be good, yes? Otherwise I might have to let Jenny get ahold of young Emily here."

Emily turned around, intending to run for her life, but standing immediately behind her was Jenny Greenteeth, her black eyes shining with feverish hunger.

Emily pulled up short, looking around for another way out.

"Same goes for you, dearie," said Black Annis. "Try to escape, and I'll slice your friends open from neck to stomach."

Emily stared at the old woman in despair. Why did they have to catch up with her now? Just when she had got the first part of the key?

"You wondering how we managed to track you?" asked Black Annis. She nodded over Emily's shoulder at Jenny.

Emily looked and saw Jenny Greenteeth raising something to her thin, cracked lips. What was it? Her black tongue lashed out, catching a strand of hair and bringing it into her mouth.

"Your hair," said Black Annis. "I pinched it off you back at the Order. We tracked you with it."

Emily vaguely remembered something snatching at her hair in the thick fog.

"You can't escape us, Emily Snow. As soon as you touch water, we know where you are. But even on land, we'll catch up with you in the end. We need something personal, of course. Blood's preferable, but hair will do. How does it taste, Jenny?"

"Like fear, Miss Annis," replied Jenny. "Lovely, juicy fear, ripe for the bursting."

"Bless her," said Black Annis to Emily. "She likes the taste of fear, don't you, Jenny?"

"I do, Miss Annis. It makes me shiver."

"Right," said Black Annis. "Come along. Before that wretched sneak Ravenhill thinks to check out the back." She turned and set off down the dark street, the two sacks thrown casually over her shoulder.

Jenny Greenteeth gave Emily a shove. "Where are we

going?" Emily asked in surprise. "You're really not taking me to the Queen?"

Black Annis spat on the ground. "Never. She's a traitor to the fey. She sold her soul to get where she is today. It's the Dagda who wants to speak to you, my poppet."

Half an hour later, Black Annis led them through the massive arches at Hyde Park Corner, following the road that ran along the Serpentine. The last of the clouds had vanished from the sky, blown away by the chill winter wind. The full moon hung crisp and bright, casting a white light over everything around them. Emily saw the stone parapets of a bridge arching across the river as they walked along the path, just as Black Annis turned onto the grass, walking between sparse trees until they came to a small hill. A large oak tree grew at the base of the hill, its naked branches casting dark shadows on the grass.

"He'll be here shortly," said Annis. "And you be polite, otherwise I'll pull the skin from your face. Understand?"

Emily nodded mutely.

"Good girl," said Annis. "Come along, Jenny."

They turned and walked back along the path. Black Annis tossed the sack that contained Corrigan to Jenny, while she idly swung the bag that held Jack. Emily could hear distant conversation drifting back to her on the wind.

". . . don't see why I couldn't eat an arm. Or even a foot. She can still talk without an arm. . . ."

"Forgive them," said a voice behind her.

Emily whirled around and saw a tall figure leaning against the oak tree. He straightened and walked toward her, the shadows of the branches crawling across his features as he did so.

His face was thin, his features harsh and sharp. Like a lot of the other fey she had seen, his eyes were black. But it was his pupils that drew her attention. They were shaped like hourglasses and sat sideways in his eyes like a goat's.

The effect was unnerving. Emily took a step back. The figure stopped moving and raised his hands in the air.

"I mean you no harm," he said.

Emily thought about this, then for some reason burst into laughter. She couldn't help it. After all that had happened to her over the past days, his words sounded ludicrous. Her laughter sounded loud and strident to her ears, and she forced herself to stop.

"Do you know who I am?" he asked.

"You're the Dagda."

He smiled. "Correct. And just in case you are not aware of this by now, everything the Queen told you about me was a lie."

"And I suppose you're going to tell me that if I help you, you will take all the fey back through the gate to Faerie?"

"No," said the Dagda, much to Emily's surprise.

He gestured at the tree he had been leaning against. "This is where the gate appears. Did you know that?"

Emily turned to look at the tree. It looked just like any other of its kind. Nothing different to show it was a hidden doorway to a magical world.

"I'm not going to tell you that I'll take all the fey back through the gate. I respect you enough not to lie to you. Besides, I think we have as much right to be here as you."

"But not a right to try and kill everyone," said Emily hotly. "Not a right to try and destroy London and everyone in it."

"No," replied the fey. "That is a right I do not claim."

"Then what?" asked Emily. "What do you want of me?"

"As I said, if you give me the key, I won't take all the fey back through the gate. But what I *will* do is send Kelindria back through. Her followers will be given a choice. Join her, or remain here peacefully. Then we can return to the way things were. Kelindria has grown arrogant. She lusts after power."

Emily searched the Dagda's eyes, looking for some sign that would tell her whether he was lying. If only he was telling the truth, she would have an ally at last. Someone who could help her finish this. But what if it was another trick?

She had been lied to so many times she didn't know who to believe.

"How can I trust you?" she asked. "Everyone tells me something different, something they think I want to hear. I don't even know what the truth is anymore."

The Dagda pointed at her coat pocket. "You have the first half of the key there. I can sense it."

Emily clamped a hand over her pocket, her eyes darting around for an escape route.

"I can take it if I wanted to. You know I can. But I will leave it with you. You found it, so it is yours by right." He smiled. "Would Kelindria be so trusting?"

No, thought Emily. She would torture Emily and her brother to get hold of it.

"We want the same thing," explained the Dagda. "We want Kelindria gone and for things to return to the way they were."

"And what is it you want me to do?"

"Find the second half of the key and bring it to me. At dawn this morning, I am meeting the Queen here. If you can bring me the key, I will force her through the gate."

"Why are you meeting her?"

"I told her I wanted to put our differences aside so that we can join forces and destroy the Invisible Order. We are meeting to discuss plans to attain this goal. I will have one or two helpers hidden away. If you can bring me the key in time, I will open the gate and make sure she is sent home."

Emily allowed herself a brief flicker of hope. The Dagda seemed sincere. Could he actually be telling her the truth? Maybe they could end this after all.

A thought struck her. "Do you know where Merlin's Tower is?" she asked.

The Dagda shook his head. "I do not. But you are aware that Merlin was part of the Invisible Order? I'm sure someone at their headquarters will know."

Emily thought back to the history book Sebastian had shown her. Hadn't he said it contained the whole history of the Order? Would the answer be in there?

It was a good possibility.

"One more thing," said the Dagda. "To seal our trust, I will tell you something more."

Emily looked up into his strange eyes, and his next words chilled her to the very depth of her being.

"Your parents are alive."

Emily could only stare at the Dagda in shock.

"I do not know who took them, or why, but they live."

"Where . . . ?" she whispered, her voice caught in her throat. "Where are they?"

"I do not know. They are not in London, I know that

much. I have had my people out searching ever since I discovered the truth."

Emily tried to think through the whirling torrent raging through her mind. Her parents. Alive! After all this time . . .

"But . . . they've been gone for years."

"As I said, it is a puzzle. Although I have no idea who that person is, someone has known who you were for some time. Emily, if you give me the key, I will help you get your parents back. I promise you this." The Dagda looked up to the sky. "Now, if you want to find the second half of the key, I suggest you be on your way. There is not much time left."

Emily shook herself from her daze. "What will happen if I don't get the key in time?"

The Dagda shrugged. "I will make plans with the Queen to destroy the Invisible Order. If I cannot rid myself of one of the banes of my life, I will settle for the other."

Emily stared hard at him. "Fine," she snapped. "But you tell that Black Annis not to hurt Corrigan or Jack. If she does, the deal is off."

The Dagda smiled, a whisper of amusement. "Then I should away and warn them off. Doubtless Jenny Greenteeth is already begging to eat them. Till dawn," he said, then stepped back into the shadows and disappeared.

⊷ CHAPTER TWENTY-SEVEN ⊷

*In which Emily returns to the offices of the Invisible Order
and searches for Merlin's Tower.*

TWO O'CLOCK IN THE MORNING
ON THE THIRD DAY OF EMILY'S ADVENTURES.

Her parents. Alive.

Emily couldn't believe it, couldn't *let* herself believe it. She left Hyde Park and ran through the streets of London, her mind a swirling mess of emotions: hope, fear, anger, resentment, helplessness.

And doubt.

What if it was a lie? What if the Dagda was just saying that to get her to go along with him? She wasn't sure she could take the disappointment of losing her parents again.

But what if it was *true*? What if someone really had taken them captive? What if she could rescue them? They would be a family again. She and William would have their parents back.

No. She couldn't think like that. It was too dangerous. She used to lie awake at night imagining the return of her parents, used to dream of them all being a happy family once more. But it had never happened, and she had learned how painful it was to hope for something impossible.

But the flicker of hope wouldn't die. What if the Dagda *could* help get them back? What would she give for that to happen?

This time Emily really did shy away from such thoughts. Deep inside, she was scared of the answer, scared of what she would give up for the return of her family. No matter who else got hurt in the process.

Emily found herself back at Somerset House without much memory of the intervening journey. Her thoughts had kept returning to her parents, to memories of the past.

To dreams of the future.

She stood before the building and mentally shook herself. She had to focus on the task at hand. She couldn't spend what little time she had daydreaming about her ma and da. She'd never get them back that way.

Emily climbed in through the window she'd left open and hurried through the dimly lit corridors. She arrived at the library without incident, then quickly made her way to the door that led into the offices and rooms of the Invisible Order.

She gently pushed it open . . .

. . . then quickly jerked back as someone ran past in the corridor outside.

Emily paused, wondering if someone had found out she was back in the building. She suddenly realized it might not have been the best idea to bring the key with her while she searched for the location of Merlin's Tower.

But it was too late to do anything about it now.

Emily opened the door and looked both ways along the green-carpeted hallway. There didn't seem to be anyone else about. She slipped into the corridor and made her way toward Sebastian's office.

She had to hide twice more, once for an elderly man—ashen-faced and sweating, who was hurrying along with a huge pile of papers—and the second time for Mr. Blackmore. Emily felt her throat go dry. Was all this because of what had happened back at St. Paul's?

She made it to Sebastian's office and ducked inside, closing the door quietly behind her. The first thing she did was check on William. She smiled with relief when she saw him sleeping in the exact same place she had left him earlier. He always was a heavy sleeper, as long as the nightmares stayed away. He'd probably carry on sleeping till dawn if nothing woke him.

Her eyes shifted to the large book, still sitting on the table next to the fire. She sat down and carefully opened it, wincing at the loud creaking of the spine. She paused, made sure it hadn't disturbed William, then started paging through the book.

The earliest pages were so brittle and thin she thought they were going to crumble to dust beneath her fingers. She gently turned them over, frowning at writing she couldn't even understand. The ink was muted and faded.

There were pages devoted to ink drawings of the different kinds of fey, many of whom she had seen over the past few days. Each drawing was marked with meticulous notes.

This cataloging went on for more than a hundred pages, but it wasn't what Emily was looking for. She needed the more recent entries. She turned to the back of the book, where the paper was thick and new. The pages here were empty, waiting to be filled, so she riffled backward until she found pages with writing in them. She slowly went over the entries, finding diary entries signed by Ravenhill. She wanted to read some of them, but she didn't have the time.

Emily searched until her eyes hurt, but she couldn't find any mention of Merlin's Tower. She *had* found diary entries written by Christopher Wren, but even though she skimmed through them, she could find nothing that would help her. She finally closed the book and stared at the leather cover.

What was she supposed to do now? She had to find the second half of the key before dawn, or the Dagda wouldn't keep his side of the deal.

She was still contemplating her next move when the door opened and Sebastian hurried in. He stopped short when he saw her.

"Emily. Where have you been?"

"I . . . had some things to take care of."

Sebastian looked suspicious. "What kind of things— Actually, it doesn't matter. I don't have time to go into it. You're back now—that's all that matters." Sebastian hurried over to a wooden cabinet above his desk. He opened the cabinet and took out two pistols. He sat down opposite Emily and took bullets from a box, loading them into the gun. "I see your fast-footed friend is no longer with us."

"No. He . . ." Emily floundered, wondering what to say.

"Had some things to take care of?" said Sebastian wryly.

"Something like that," said Emily.

"Fine. Just make sure you and William don't go anywhere. You'll be safe here."

"Safe from what?" asked Emily, eyeing the gun nervously. Sebastian's hands were shaking slightly.

"We've had a tipoff. The Queen and the Dagda are meeting in Hyde Park at dawn. We're going to hide in the trees across the Serpentine and lay an ambush."

"You're . . . you're going to fight?"

"It looks like it. Ravenhill said we won't ever get a better opportunity than this."

"Ravenhill?"

"Yes, it was Ravenhill who found out."

He closed the pistols with a click.

"I thought you used iron swords and things?" Emily said.

Sebastian held up one of the bullets for her to see. "Iron and lead mixture. It will do the job much more efficiently."

Emily didn't like what she was hearing. She knew the races had fought each other through the years, but this seemed like a planned slaughter. At least with swords and knives, the fight was personal.

Sebastian registered her look. "You don't approve?" Before she could say anything, he sighed and laid the guns on the table. "Neither do I, truth to tell."

"Then don't go."

"I have to. This could be our one chance to get rid of the fey for good."

A thought suddenly struck her. "How did you solve the clue?"

Sebastian looked puzzled. "The clue? We haven't solved it. We haven't even had time to talk about it. This came up as soon as our members arrived."

Then how had Ravenhill known she would be at the cathedral? He and his men were waiting there in ambush. How was that possible, if they hadn't solved the clue? Emily thought about it for a moment, then shook her head. She didn't have enough information to answer the question, and short of asking Ravenhill herself, she doubted she'd be able to find out.

Instead, her thoughts turned to the problem at hand. She could tell Sebastian the truth. That she might have found a way to get rid of the Queen once and for all. But would that be enough? Maybe for Sebastian, but she couldn't see Ravenhill honoring any deal she made with the Dagda. He would want all of them gone, not just the Seelie. And how would that affect her chances of getting her parents back? If the Order got to the Dagda, he wouldn't be able to help her track them down.

Her best bet was to find the key and get to the Dagda before the Order did. Then what? Would she warn him? Maybe he could force the Queen through the gate and vanish before the Order even arrived. Then she would have honored her word *and* avoided any bloodshed.

"Sebastian," she said. "Do you know what Merlin's Tower is?"

Sebastian looked at her in surprise. "Where did you hear that?"

"Oh, I . . ." Emily gestured to the book lying on the table. "I saw it mentioned in there," she lied.

Sebastian frowned disapprovingly. "You shouldn't be reading that."

Emily tried to look contrite. "I know. I'm sorry."

"But to answer your question, Merlin's Tower is what Christopher Wren called the Monument. You must have seen it. Huge tower? On Fish Street Hill?"

Emily looked blank.

"Near London Bridge."

Emily suddenly knew what Sebastian was talking about. She had seen the pillar countless times over the years, but had never really given it a second glance. It was just a background part of the city, always there, invisible.

Sebastian stood up. "Only a few hours till dawn." He smiled nervously at Emily. "Hopefully I'll see you later. Wish me luck."

"Good luck," said Emily quietly.

"I want to go."

Sebastian and Emily looked over at William in surprise. He was sitting up in the chair. How long had he been listening to them talk?

"I'm sorry?" said Sebastian.

"I want to come with you. I want to fight."

"Don't be absurd," snapped Emily. "You're only nine years old."

"So?" said William hotly. "Stop treating me like a baby, Em.

I'm old enough to do things for myself. I want to fight. I want to help stop them."

"Out of the question," said Sebastian. "This isn't a game, William. People will die."

"I know that! But this is my city, as well. I have as much right as you do to defend it."

"I don't have time for this," said Sebastian. He looked at Emily. "Remember. Stay here. You'll be safe."

Sebastian took one final, distracted look around his office, then turned and strode from the room.

Emily waited, then jumped up and headed for the door. She pulled it open and looked out. The corridor was empty.

"What are you doing?" said William.

Emily turned to her brother. She gripped him by the shoulders. "Will, listen to me. Ma and Da are still alive." William's eyes widened. "Don't talk. Just listen to me. I have to do something. It's dangerous, but there's a chance it will bring them back to us. But I need you to stay here. I can't do this if I'm worrying about you all the time."

"You won't have to worry about me! I promise. Take me with you, Em. Please! Don't leave me here."

Emily saw the determination in his eyes. He wouldn't take no for an answer. She hesitated, then nodded. "Fine," she said. "Go and look for something you can use as a weapon. A letter opener or something."

William's face lit up with joy. He hurried over toward Sebastian's desk, searching for something he could use to defend himself.

Emily quickly removed the key from the door, stepped through, and pulled it shut behind her. She shoved the key in and locked it again.

William banged on the door. "Emily!" he shouted. "Don't you dare leave me here! It's not fair!"

Emily laid her head against the door, feeling absolutely wretched. "Sorry, Will," she whispered. "It's for your own good."

Chapter Twenty-eight

In which Emily ventures inside Merlin's Tower.

Four o'clock in the morning
on the third day of Emily's adventures.

Most of the buildings Emily had visited over the past three days were found within a few miles of one another. Somerset House opened straight onto the Strand, which fed into Fleet Street. She turned right before Ludgate Hill onto New Bridge Street, then left onto Upper Thames Street.

Emily hurried along the street for about half an hour, the river churning away on her right. She could smell the salty, sickening stench of fish as she hurried along the freezing streets. That meant she was close to Billingsgate Market. She wondered if Christopher Wren had purposefully kept all the locations within such close proximity. It couldn't simply be a coincidence, surely?

She passed London Bridge and turned left onto Fish

Street Hill, moving along the narrow road until it met up with Monument Yard. Here, Emily finally stopped. The Monument towered high above her. She couldn't see the top from her position but recalled there was some sort of deck where you could look out over London. The base of the pillar was an imposing block of stone. On the side she was facing, stone figures had been carved into the wall, but she couldn't quite see what they were supposed to be doing.

Emily walked around the base, looking for the way in. On the three remaining walls were huge plaques on which verses had been written in another language—Latin, she thought.

Emily found the entrance to the Monument on the fourth wall. She pushed open the unlocked door and walked forward, then paused and waited for the moonlight to brighten the shadows.

Emily didn't like it in here. She felt like she was being watched, that at any moment someone would jump out of the shadows. She took a deep, steadying breath. *Get ahold of yourself,* she thought. *You've come too far to be frightened off by an uneasy feeling.*

What had the voice said? *Repeat the rhyme and hold the power.* Well, no need to wait around for permission.

"If clouds or mists do dark the sky,
Great store of birds and beasts shall die.

287

And if the winds do file aloft,
Then war shall vex the kingdom oft."

She held her breath, listening for the slightest sound in the darkness.

Then she heard it. Stone grating on stone.

It came from somewhere to her right. Emily reached out and felt along the wall, moving her hands across the cold stone until she encountered empty air. She shuffled forward, waving her hands in front of her to make sure she didn't walk into anything, then stepped through an empty doorway. The moonlight didn't reach this far, but as she stood and waited for her eyes to adjust to the deeper darkness, she became aware of a glow up ahead.

Emily hurried forward and found a small trapdoor in the floor. The glow was shining up through the cracks in the wood. She heaved it open and found a flight of neat steps leading underground.

Emily followed the stairs into a small room dominated by a strange-looking telescope mounted on a table. The telescope was pointed straight up a hollow shaft that disappeared into the ceiling.

The light Emily had seen shining through the trapdoor was coming from a large opening in the brick wall. Emily edged forward and saw that a large section of the wall had swung inward, a secret door revealing a second set of wider, cruder stairs.

The orange light grew stronger as Emily descended, flickering against the rough walls. The stairs ended at an archway that opened up into a large room. Emily paused on the threshold, staring around in surprise.

The room seemed to be a laboratory and library mixed into one. Books lay everywhere, some opened, some closed, others in tall piles that had tipped back against the walls but still somehow managed to stay upright. Shelves hung from the ceiling, holding an assortment of vials and jars, books and scrolls.

In the middle of the room was a huge table covered with strange artifacts. Emily walked forward a few steps to get a better look. As she did so, a glass lizard turned its head to watch her progress. There was a cage filled with clockwork birds that preened and cooed to one another. Set into the actual wood of the table was a green-colored glass inlay.

Only it wasn't glass. It took Emily a second to realize that it was the twin to the dragon's eye Miss LaFleur said she had stolen from Merlin.

Emily craned to see if the eye was showing anything of interest, but its surface was totally blank.

"That's my own version of a camera obscura," said a scratchy voice.

Emily whirled around. Off to her left, hidden from view beyond the table, was what appeared to be a stone bed. An old man sat up. He yawned and stretched, various bones in his body popping and clicking as he did so. He winced. "Two hundred years of sleep. Not easy to shake off."

Emily swallowed, trying to get over her shock. The old man had long white hair that stood out at all angles, and a beard that fell to his stomach. He inspected it and shook his head ruefully.

"I tried a spell to stop its growth. Obviously didn't work, eh?"

Emily opened her mouth, but before she could say anything, the old man looked at her sharply. "Please don't ask me who I am. If you do, I shall lose any respect I may currently harbor for you."

"You're Merlin," she said.

"Correct! Well done, girl." He stood up, wincing again as his spine cracked. "How have you been, Emily Snow? It's been a long time."

Emily blinked. "I'm sorry, do we know each other?"

"Not yet, no." He waved away Emily's puzzled expression. "Don't worry. It will all make sense eventually."

Merlin hauled himself upright and hobbled over to one of the shelves on the wall. He rummaged around, then found what he was looking for and threw it across the room. Emily caught it instinctively.

It was an object wrapped in a dusty piece of cloth. Emily pulled the material away and found herself looking at the second half of the key.

Merlin waved his hand in the air. "Just . . . hold the two pieces together and they'll join. Nothing to it, really."

Emily reached inside her coat and took out the first half of the key. She brought the two half-circles together, feeling them pull on her hands as if they were magnets. She let them touch, and the roots on each one unraveled and then twined around each other, joining the two pieces together so that it looked as if they had never been apart.

"There you are," said Merlin. "Told you so."

Emily frowned. What an anticlimax. After all that she had been through to get the first piece, this seemed so . . . pedestrian. Admittedly, she was standing here talking to Merlin the Magician, but still.

"Why didn't you just put both pieces at St. Paul's?" she asked. "What was the point of making me come here?"

"Wren's idea," said Merlin. "Very . . . *careful*, that man. Congratulations on solving the riddle, by the way. I said it was too hard, but he refused to change it. Said it had to be something only you would understand."

"I nearly didn't."

Merlin shrugged. "A chance he was willing to take, if the alternative was the faeries getting their hands on it."

"Yes, but . . . what if the Queen *did* get to St. Paul's first? What if they knew where Merlin's Tower was?"

"Then we'd be finished, wouldn't we? Besides, we had to do it this way. You told us to."

Emily blinked. "I told you to? What are you talking about?"

"We hid the clues so only you could find them. Surely you must have wondered how this was possible?"

Emily nodded.

"The answer is simple. You told us to do it this way."

"What do you mean?"

"The great war. Sixteen sixty-six. The Fire King. His minions. It was a very close thing, but we had help. Your help, to be precise."

"Don't be silly," said Emily.

A change descended over Merlin. He drew himself up and glared at her. "Silly?!" he snapped. "Do not *ever* accuse me of silliness. I've been alive for thousands of years. I've seen things that would make the hardiest of men crawl into a corner and weep for days on end. When I say something, I do not lie. Just because you cannot comprehend how such a thing can be, does not make it impossible. Such thoughts are the height of arrogance."

Then, as if nothing untoward had just happened, he smiled at her.

"Of course, I can't tell you what happened—"

"Why not?" interrupted Emily.

"Because one cannot mess around with history. If I tell you what happened, then you do something differently, what then? I'll tell you, shall I? Why, it would be the end of everything."

"But . . ." Emily frowned, confused. "You just said I told you what to do so that I could get the clues. Isn't that the same thing?"

"Ah, no. Good point. You didn't delve into specifics, you see. I wouldn't let you."

"I don't understand any of this," said Emily. "How could I have been alive in sixteen sixty-six? Are you saying I've been alive since then but can't remember? That I've lost my memory?"

"No, I'm not saying that at all. But here we are drawing dangerously close to my telling you what will occur. I don't want to influence what happens, you see. Have to let history take its natural course."

He sighed and looked sympathetic. "My dear, you will find out soon enough that sixteen sixty-six is just the tip of the iceberg. How can I put this? Let's just say that this war with the fey has been fought throughout history." He paused. "And that you have been present at nearly every single important battle. You grew quite close to King Arthur, as I recall."

Emily scowled. "You're making fun of me now."

Merlin held his hands up in the air. "I wouldn't dream of it."

Emily was about to ask him something more, but he spoke before she got the chance.

"I'm afraid that is all I can say for the moment. You've woken me up, and that means the end game is approaching. The culmination of thousands of years of warfare is going to occur over the next few days. You're going to . . . Well, you are going to do whatever it is you are going to do. And I will see you again quite soon, although it might not seem that way to you." He smiled sadly at her. "And you will be a very different girl."

"Why do you have to be so cryptic?"

Merlin drew himself up again. "Madam, I am an *enchanter*. It is my *right* to be cryptic."

Emily felt totally lost. She was sure there were a hundred questions she should be asking Merlin, but right now she couldn't think of a single one. And time was moving on.

"It's not long till dawn," said Merlin, as if reading her mind. He gazed deep into her eyes. "Times are going to be hard for you, my child. But you must try and make the decisions that are true and pure. Those decisions might not necessarily be what *you* want, but such is life. We all have to make sacrifices for the greater good. You are no different. Now, off you go."

Emily reluctantly headed back to the stairs. She turned around once, but Merlin had his back to her and was partaking of some stretching exercises.

"Got to be limber for the days ahead," she heard him mutter.

Emily shook her head. Mad. The lot of them.

⊰CHAPTER TWENTY-NINE⊱
Jack and Corrigan.

Jack was freezing cold and surrounded by darkness. He could feel mud oozing through the weave of the sack, squelching between his hands and seeping into his clothes. He pushed his finger into the hole he'd managed to pick in the stitching along the seam. He wiggled it about, pulling the small gap wider. He finally got it big enough so that he could insert two fingers, then he pulled.

The stitching gave way with a loud, tearing noise. Jack froze, but neither Jenny Greenteeth nor Black Annis came to investigate. He then painstakingly pulled the rest of the stitching apart until he thought he could fit through the gap. He looked through the opening. He was surrounded by trees. Black Annis had dropped him in a large puddle.

He could see another sack close by—that must be Corrigan.

"I'm hungry, Black Annis," whined a voice he recognized as Greenteeth's. "Can't I eat them? Just a little bit? A leg, maybe? Or a juicy finger."

"No," replied Annis. "We can't harm them yet, Jenny. The Dagda said so."

"But I need *food*."

"Jenny!" snapped Annis. "Just hold on to your horses till Ravenhill gets to the meeting place. Then you can eat the entire Invisible Order for all I care."

Jack frowned. What was this? Why was Ravenhill coming here?

"Can I have Ravenhill?" asked Jenny. "I don't like him, Black Annis."

"I don't like him either, poppet, but no. He's the Queen's man now. Seems he's seen sense and switched sides. You're not allowed to touch him."

Jack felt a cold thrill run through his body. The Queen's man? Had Ravenhill betrayed them all? Betrayed the Invisible Order? It certainly sounded that way.

He had to warn Emily—

Jack paused. No, he couldn't. He had no idea where Emily *was*.

He had to get word to Sebastian. He would know what to do.

"Hss," said Black Annis. "You hear that?"

Jack froze, holding his breath. Had they heard him?

"It's someone on the path, Black Annis. Looks like a bobby. Can I have him? Please?"

Black Annis chuckled. "Go ahead, poppet. But make it quick."

Jack breathed a sigh of relief and pushed his head through the gap in the sack. There was no sign of Jenny Greenteeth. Black Annis was some distance away, moving in slow circles, dancing with an invisible partner. She wasn't paying him any attention.

Jack shrugged off the sack and stood up. He turned quickly, getting his bearings. He hesitated, wondering if he should just leave Corrigan where he was, then decided the irritating creature might still come in handy and grabbed the sack from the ground.

Then he ran as if all the bobbies in London were after him.

Jack burst out of a copse of trees and frantically looked around. There was a path just ahead, weaving through the grass. He suddenly realized where he was: Hyde Park.

Jack followed the path at a run. He thought he heard a screech of anger some way behind him, but he didn't stop. He just kept on running till he got through the gates and into the street. Only then did he glance over his shoulder for signs of pursuit.

Nothing.

He sucked in great mouthfuls of air. Then he shook the sack. "You all right in there?"

There was a moment's silence. Then a suspicious voice said, "Jack?"

Jack untied the sack and tipped it upside down, spilling Corrigan onto the pavement. The piskie scrambled to his feet and looked around, then glared at Jack. "What are you thinking, running around like that? You nearly broke my neck!"

"Why don't you show some gratitude, you little wretch! I rescued you!"

"I didn't ask you to, did I?"

Jack was tempted to simply turn around and leave the aggravating piskie to his own devices, but he had more important things to think about at the moment. He raised his hands in the air. "Enough," he said. "A truce, yes? I over-heard something back in the park. It's important."

Corrigan grudgingly nodded. "Fine. Truce. But it's only temporary, mind! Now, what's so important?"

"Ravenhill has betrayed the Invisible Order."

"Rubbish," scoffed Corrigan. "Why would he do that?"

"I've no idea. But I heard what I heard. Annis said

Ravenhill was the Queen's man now, that he had switched sides. And that Greenteeth could eat as many of the Invisible Order as she wanted when they got to the meeting place."

"Where's the meeting place?"

"She didn't say. We have to get back to Somerset House and warn them before they leave."

Corrigan said nothing.

"What, you don't want to help?" said Jack.

An uneasy look flashed across the piskie's face. "I've stayed alive this long by trying to keep to my own business, boy. Getting involved only leads to trouble."

"Don't you think you owe us? After all the trouble you've caused Emily, don't you think it's your duty to stick with this till the end?"

Corrigan thought about it, then reluctantly nodded. "Fine. I'll see this through. But for her, not you."

"Fine by me," said Jack.

Corrigan held out his hand.

Jack stared at it. "I'm not your friend, piskie. I think you're a sneak, a liar, and a backstabber. I don't want to shake your hand."

"That's good. Because I don't want to shake yours, either. I just want a lift onto your shoulders."

Jack ran all the way back to Somerset House. Part of him was hoping that Emily would be there. He remembered Black Annis said that the Dagda only wanted to talk to her. If that was the case, then maybe she had been released and had returned here to check on William. If not, he could warn Sebastian about Ravenhill, then head out to search for her.

At the wide stairs leading up to the doors, Corrigan hopped from Jack's shoulders. "I can't go in there," the piskie said. "Too much iron, remember?"

"Fine. I'll warn them, then we can find Emily and try and sort out this second clue."

"Don't dawdle," shouted Corrigan as Jack jogged up the stairs.

Jack ignored him and headed for the window Emily had left ajar. It was now wide open. Jack paused. She hadn't opened it this widely, had she? Maybe she really *was* here.

Jack slipped into Somerset House and retraced the route to Sebastian's office. The Royal Society was eerily quiet. He didn't see a single soul as he hurried through the corridors.

He hurried through the library to the door leading into the rooms of the Invisible Order. He could hear banging. And muffled shouting.

Jack hurried along the corridor. As he drew nearer, he realized the noises were coming from Sebastian's office. Puzzled,

Jack turned the key he found in the lock and opened the door, to find himself standing face-to-face with a very angry William Snow.

"Will?"

"Jack! Thank goodness. Em locked me in here. She said I couldn't go with her. That it was too dangerous."

Jack's heart sank. "She's not here?"

"Not anymore. She left about an hour ago. Jack, Em said our ma and da are still alive. That she might be able to get them back."

Jack stared at Will, surprised. How had their parents come into all this? But at least the Dagda had released her. That was something. "What about Sebastian? Is he around?"

"No! That's another reason she locked me up. The Invisible Order is going to ambush the Queen and the Dagda at Hyde Park. I heard Sebastian say so. They've all gone to fight."

Jack's heart sank. "Ravenhill, as well?"

Will nodded. "Sebastian said it was Ravenhill's idea."

He was too late. Ravenhill was leading the Invisible Order into a trap. It would be a massacre.

"Come on," he said to Will. "Ravenhill's betrayed them. We've got to warn them." He held up a hand to stop Will's questions. "I'll explain as we run," he added. "Unless you want to stay here?"

William stepped out of the office and slammed the door behind him.

"Thought so," said Jack wryly.

+≻= ≺+

They found Corrigan waiting for them outside and explained the situation.

"Maybe we should just stay out of it," said Corrigan.

"We can't!" said Jack. "Em told Will that their parents are still alive, that she had a chance to save them. It had to be the Dagda who told her that. Remember what Black Annis said? That the Dagda only wanted to talk? He must have offered her a deal."

"The key to Faerie in exchange for her parents," said Corrigan softly.

"But if she takes the key to him, she'll be caught up in this ambush," said Jack. "We have to stop it."

"I think it's too late for that," said Corrigan. He looked at William. "Didn't you say the Queen and the Dagda were meeting at dawn?"

William nodded. "That's what Sebastian said."

"Dawn's not far off," said Corrigan.

"But we have to do something!" said William.

"Calm yourself, boy." Corrigan looked thoughtful. "There may be another way. But we'll have to move quick."

⊷Chapter Thirty⊷

In which Emily comes to a sickening realization.

Emily hurried along Oxford Street, heading in the direction of Hyde Park. She had done it. She had completed the task and retrieved the key, but now that it was in her hands, she was suffering from intense feelings of doubt.

Could she really give the key to the Dagda? After all she had been through, could she simply hand it over to one of the fey? This was what the fey—all of them—had wanted all along. They had been trying to get hold of it for almost two hundred years. And now she, Emily, had it.

And she was going to give it back to them?

Maybe she should just give it to the Order. They could hide it in their vault, keep it from the fey forever. Maybe that was the safest option.

Safe for whom, though? Then the fey would keep on fighting, trying to gain control of London. It might even serve to unite them against the humans once again.

And who could say what the future held? What if they were able to trick someone else into breaking into the Invisible Order? She had fallen for the ruse easily enough. If they managed to do that, it would all be over. They would have the complete key.

Besides, if she gave the key to the Order, the Dagda wouldn't help her find her parents. That gave her pause. Was she giving the key to the Dagda because she thought it for the best, or was she doing it simply to get her mother and father back?

She *thought* she was doing it for the right reasons. If the Dagda was true to his word, he would force the Queen and her followers back through the gate. Maybe she could convince him to return the key once he had done this. That would keep the Order happy, surely? They would get rid of half the fey residing in London and get the key back, as well. That way, she could prevent any bloodshed as well as get rid of the Queen.

But how would Ravenhill feel about that? He probably *wanted* to fight.

At the thought of Ravenhill, something stirred at the back of her mind. How did Ravenhill know the Queen and the Dagda would be meeting? It wasn't as if he could have overheard them. And none of the fey would have told him about the meeting.

So how did he find out?

As she got to thinking about Ravenhill, something else puzzled her. Emily had thought the Invisible Order was waiting for them earlier at the cathedral because they'd solved the clue, but Sebastian said they hadn't even started on it.

Ravenhill was *waiting* for them. Which meant he knew where they would be before they even got there.

As soon as Emily had realized Mr. Pemberton had one of Miss LaFleur's eyes, her thoughts had immediately turned to the Queen. After all, Miss LaFleur was a member of the Seelie court and a subject of the Queen. What Miss LaFleur knew, the Queen knew. So when someone had stepped out from behind the pillar, Emily had initially thought it would be the Dark Man, the Queen's servant. But it wasn't. It was Ravenhill.

Which meant . . .

Emily stopped walking as the horrific realization sunk in.

Ravenhill had to be working for the Queen. No, he hated the fey. Why would he do the Queen's dirty work?

But what other explanation was there? Her conclusion was the only one that considered all the facts. What would the Queen gain from having Ravenhill on her side?

Once again, the answer chilled her to the bone. Sebastian had said it was Ravenhill's idea to attack the fey. But what if it wasn't? What if it was the Queen's idea? What if the whole thing was a trap, and Ravenhill was leading the Order to their deaths?

Unless . . . maybe Ravenhill was only *pretending* to work for the Queen? That was also possible. Maybe the Queen thought Ravenhill had betrayed the Order, but it was actually Ravenhill who was planning a trap for the Queen?

She looked up at the sky. The stars had faded as the new day approached. Whichever explanation was the true one, she had to warn Sebastian. If Ravenhill was acting honorably, then no harm was done. But if he really had betrayed the Order, then she might be able to stop their deaths. And where did that leave the Dagda? If Ravenhill had betrayed the Order, where did that leave him? Did he know?

Emily set off at a run. She would warn the Order *and* get her parents back. After all she had been through, it was what she deserved.

As soon as Emily came within sight of the small bridge that crossed the Serpentine, she stopped and looked around. The bridge meant she was close to the hill where the doorway was hidden, and she wanted to find a hiding place for the key before she met the Dagda again. That way she would still have a bargaining point should anyone go back on their word. She dug out a small mound of earth beneath the roots of an old oak tree and hid the key beneath earth and leaves.

Then she ran across the bridge and into the forest on the other side. She needed to find Sebastian before the Order launched its attack.

The trees closed in around her, the naked branches cutting the dark sky into a crazed jigsaw pattern. Clouds had drifted in from the sea, blotting out the dim stars. She looked around, but couldn't see anyone. "Hello?" she called softly. "Sebastian?" A cold wind sighed through the park, stirring the branches. Emily fought down a rush of fear. They were just trees, she told herself. Nothing to be afraid of. Admittedly, they were rather creepy trees, but they couldn't hurt her.

The one just ahead of her, though. She could have sworn she had seen a face—

A man stepped out from behind the trunk, leveling his gun at her chest.

Emily froze. "I . . . I'm looking for Sebastian," she said. "Please. It's urgent."

"Get out of here," he whispered furiously. "You're going to get us all killed."

Emily swallowed nervously. "Actually, I'm probably saving

your lives. I know about the Invisible Order. I know about the fey. In fact, I found the key, the one that can open the door to Faerie. The one that's been missing for two hundred years. Now, are you going to take me to Sebastian or not?"

The man hesitated, then slowly lowered his gun. "Follow me. But don't make a sound."

He hurried off through the trees. Emily followed, and it wasn't long before she emerged into a large clearing.

"Wait here," the man said, and disappeared.

Emily looked around nervously. A cold wind had sprung up. The clouds gathered more thickly above her. She shivered, not just from the chill.

"Emily?" said an incredulous voice.

Emily turned and felt a rush of relief. Sebastian was hurrying toward her.

"What are you doing here? I told you how dangerous this would be."

Emily took a deep breath. "I have the key, Sebastian," she said. "The key to get into Faerie. I found the two parts hidden by Christopher Wren and put them together, and the Dagda says that if I give it to him, he'll send the Queen back to Faerie and help me find my parents. He doesn't want to go, you see. He's happy living here."

Sebastian put up his hands. "Emily, stop. Whatever you think about the Dagda, it's not true. He's worse than the

Queen, believe me. I've heard him swear to kill every human he can and murder children with a touch of his hand. He doesn't want to live here peacefully. He wants it all for himself, just like the Queen. That's what they've been fighting about all these centuries."

Emily shook her head. "No. You're wrong. He said he would help me find my parents."

Sebastian laid his hands on her shoulders. "I'm sorry, Emily, but I know what kind of creature he is. I fear he has lied to you. He only wants the key. We have to stop them now, while we have the chance."

"No! You have to call off the attack. I think it's a trap."

"A trap? Don't be ridiculous."

"Ravenhill has betrayed you," Emily insisted. "How did Ravenhill find out the Queen and the Dagda were meeting tonight? I only found out because the Dagda brought me here and told me. Who told Ravenhill?"

A flicker of doubt crossed Sebastian's face. "He has his sources. An informant—"

"What informant? Who could possibly have known the Dagda and the Queen were meeting here? And another thing . . ." Emily went on to tell him about St. Paul's Cathedral. "Don't you see? There's absolutely no way he could have been there unless the Queen told him."

"I admit, on the face of it, it does seem suspicious,"

Sebastian said. "But no, I simply cannot fathom it. Not Ravenhill! He is the most fanatical of us all in his hatred for the fey. How would they turn him?" Sebastian thought for a moment. "Perhaps he is bluffing the Queen," he said slowly. "If what you say is true, he may be playing the double agent, getting the Queen to think he is on her side while still working for us."

"You give me too much credit, I fear," drawled a voice from behind them. Emily and Sebastian whirled around to find Ravenhill standing in the shadows, his gun leveled in their direction.

"Ravenhill?" said Sebastian. "It's not true, surely?"

Ravenhill stepped forward, emerging into the dim light. It reminded Emily of the first time she had seen him, in the alley.

"I'm afraid it is." His gaze shifted to Emily. "You know, you have been the most *colossal* pain in my neck."

"Good," she snapped.

"One can hardly fathom that so much trouble can come from such a little brat."

"You have betrayed us?" pressed Sebastian.

"I have. The Queen's people approached me yesterday with an offer I couldn't refuse. I'd like to say it was over some weighty philosophical reasoning, but the fact of it is, I decided to side myself with the winners."

"What did they offer you?"

"A Kingship."

Sebastian laughed. "A . . . a *Kingship*? Of what?"

"England. Once the fey destroy London, they accept that they will have to keep *some* of the human race alive. For the purposes of slavery, you understand. I am to be the King of all the land."

Sebastian's face twisted with hate. "The King of Slaves," he said, and spat on the ground. "It suits you."

Ravenhill gestured with his gun. "Miss Snow, if you would be so kind as to step over here. I'm sure the Queen will be most happy when I hand you over to her."

Emily hesitated.

"Come, Miss Snow. Before I shoot Sebastian."

Emily reluctantly stepped forward. Sebastian tried to hold her back, but she shook him off. Ravenhill grabbed her arm, then slowly advanced on Sebastian, his gun pointed at his chest.

"They'll turn on you, Ravenhill. In the end, you'll be left with nothing."

"That's a risk I'm willing to take," said Ravenhill. Then he brought his gun up and struck Sebastian across the head with it. Emily cried out as Sebastian crumpled to the ground.

"Just be thankful I can't risk a shot," said Ravenhill to the unconscious figure. He turned his attention to Emily. "Now if you will be so kind as to hand over the key."

"I don't have it."

"Do not lie to me. I heard what you said to Sebastian."

"I don't have it," repeated Emily. "I've hidden it away. Somewhere you'll never get it."

"Oh, is that so?" said Ravenhill. "Well, let's just see what the Dark Man has to say about that, shall we?"

❧ CHAPTER THIRTY-ONE ❧
The final temptation.

The morning mist was beginning to writhe around their legs as Ravenhill dragged Emily across the bridge and into sight of the tree where she had first met the Dagda.

The Faerie Queen and the Dagda waited on either side of the ancient oak tree that stood at the bottom of the hill, framing it between them. The Queen wore a wispy cloak, woven from strands of silver and gold. Its edges were kept above the wet grass by three unkempt human children. The Dagda was staring at something in his hands.

They both looked up as Ravenhill approached.

"What have we here?" said the Queen, clapping her hands with delight. "Emily Snow. You must tell me where Corrigan is so I can cut out his treacherous little heart."

The Dagda studied Emily calmly. "Have you come to fulfill our deal?"

"What deal is this?" asked the Queen sharply.

"None of your business," said the Dagda.

"She has the key," said Ravenhill, cutting across the Dagda's words. He gave Emily a shove, so that she stumbled forward and fell onto her knees. The Dagda looked down at her in disappointment.

"What? She has it?" The Queen cast a quick look at the Dagda, then turned back to Ravenhill. "What are you waiting for? Take it from her!"

"She says she has hidden it."

The Queen strode forward and pulled out her black dagger. But just before she brought it to Emily's face, the Dagda grabbed her arm.

"Do not be foolish," he said.

"You dare?" gasped the Queen. "The Dark Man—"

"The Dark Man has to stay hidden until the Order attack. You know that."

The Queen glared at the Dagda, intense hatred clear across her face. The Dagda merely smiled, then released her arm.

"Emily, would you come over here, please?"

Emily swallowed her fear and stood up. She hurried over to the Dagda.

"You have it?" he asked. "The full key?"

Emily hesitated, thinking of Sebastian's words. Whom could she trust? Then she realized it didn't really matter. The key was hidden, so she didn't have to tell anyone where it was if she didn't want to.

"I have it," she said.

The Dagda let out a slow breath. "Then this is for you." He opened his hand and Emily saw that he was holding an elegantly carved gold pocket watch. He released the catch and the cover slid smoothly open. But instead of the watch face Emily had been expecting, there was a small mirror. Emily hesitated, then leaned forward and looked deep into the glass.

At first, all she saw was her slightly worried reflection. Then her face faded from view and she suddenly found herself flying through gray clouds, over rocky hills and highlands covered with white and purple flowers. A distant shape appeared on the horizon, a huge castle that soared up into the air, its spires reaching impossibly high toward the clouds. Strange creatures flew around the turrets, and as she drew closer Emily saw that they were dragons, huge creatures that crisscrossed the sky above the castle.

The picture zoomed toward a window in the castle and entered a small room. The room held only a table, chair, and a bed.

Seated at this table were Emily's mother and father.

Emily gasped. It really was them. They looked a bit older, but it was definitely them. They sat at the table and held each other's hands. Then, as if sensing Emily's gaze, they both looked up.

The Dagda closed the pocket watch and held it out to her. "For you. A gift."

Emily reached out and took the watch with trembling hands. She placed it carefully inside one of her pockets.

"Now you must fulfill your part of the bargain," said the Dagda.

Emily looked up sharply. "You said you would help get them back."

"And I will, but your parents are lost in time. I do not know how this was accomplished, but it is a fact. Give me the key and we will search for them together."

Emily still didn't say anything.

"Don't you want your family back, Emily? Your mother, your father, back where they belong. No more responsibility for you. No more looking after your brother all on your own. Their fate lies in your hands, Emily. You can save them."

The urge to tell the Dagda where she had hidden the key was almost overwhelming. It would be so simple. She was being given a chance to bring her family back, the family she had long feared dead.

But at what cost? whispered a voice in her head. The Dagda had said he would send the Queen through the door with all her court, but what if something went wrong? What if the key ended up in her hands?

What if Sebastian was right? What if the Dagda really did plan on bringing his own armies through?

She wanted to trust him. But when you were promised everything your heart could possibly want, you had to ask: what was the catch? Emily squeezed her eyes shut.

"Emily," repeated the Dagda. "The key. Where is it?"

And then she heard Merlin's voice in her head, as clear as if he were standing right next to her.

You must try and make the decisions that are true and pure. Those decisions might not necessarily be what you want, but such is life. We all have to make sacrifices for the greater good. You are no different.

Emily opened her eyes and looked calmly at the imposing figure standing before her.

"I'm sorry," she said. "I can't give it to you."

He didn't say anything, but the white pupils of his eyes dilated and his eyebrows drew together in a fierce frown. He bared his teeth in a snarl of anger, and that was when Emily knew she had made the right decision.

The Dagda stepped forward and grabbed her arm. "Give it to me! Where is it?"

"I tire of this," said the Queen. "Ravenhill?"

Emily saw the Queen standing only two paces away, gazing over the park with glittering eyes. "I think it is time to give your signal, Ravenhill."

An ear-shattering crack exploded through the cold air. Emily jumped in alarm, wrenching her arm away from the Dagda. She turned and saw Ravenhill lowering the gun he had just fired into the sky.

A second later there was an answering shot from the forest. Then the members of the Order broke through the tree line, about a hundred men, all of them charging straight for their position.

Emily looked over her shoulder at the Queen and the Dagda. How were they going to stop them? It was supposed to be a trap, but Emily couldn't see what they had planned.

The Order drew closer, a silent, heaving line, their breath pluming into the air. Emily could see their faces now. She spotted Mr. Blackmore, and to her surprise he was running slightly ahead of the others, as if eager to get into battle.

And so he was the first to die.

A fey troll, a hulking slab of gray meat holding a long spear, appeared out of thin air. Blackmore ran straight into it, the point punching through his body and out his back.

Emily screamed in horror as the trap was sprung. The fey faded into view, totally surrounding the members of the

Invisible Order. They stopped running and formed into a circle. The battle was joined with screams of wrath and defiance.

Everywhere Emily looked she saw a different face, a different species, all leaping into the fray. A man who had only one of each feature and one of each limb hopped into battle swinging a bronze hammer over his head. Tiny, elflike creatures rode on the backs of crows, bombarding those below with arrows and spears so small they were all but invisible. A tall creature with a long, hairy nose held a sword in each hand, wielding them like a butcher. Another, with huge hands and huge feet, trampled into the ranks of the Order, kicking and striking those around him. Witches stepped out of the bark of trees to grab their prey as they stumbled past. Black Annis grabbed hold of people and lifted them up so that they stared into her cloaked face. Their screams of fear and horror were terrible to hear. Jenny Greenteeth simply grabbed anyone she could and tried to eat them. Emily could just make out a dark shadow crawling between the fighters. As she watched, tendrils of darkness probed outward and wrapped around a member of the Invisible Order, yanking him backward into the shadow of a tree. The Dark Man, hunting his prey.

On the outskirts, Emily saw the dark, painted faces of the Black Sidhe. They darted into the fray with their spears and fired their elf bolts from the sidelines. Keeping pace with them were tiny human shapes with the heads of rabbits, foxes, and birds. They barked and whistled as they joined in the fight, biting and scratching for all they were worth.

Everywhere Emily looked she saw the fey, Seelie and Unseelie, joining forces against their common foe.

But the Invisible Order was not giving up without a fight. Shots rang out, and the fey collapsed and died with lead-and-iron bullets eating their way through their bodies. Those who didn't have guns used iron swords, cleaving their way toward the Queen and the Dagda, trying to break through the defenses of the fey to strike down their leaders. Emily saw Sebastian at the forefront of this line, blood from Ravenhill's blow still coating his face.

And Ravenhill watched it all, an impassive look on his cold face.

Tears streamed down Emily's face. People were *dying*, and nobody cared.

"Stop!" she screamed. "Stop it now!" She turned to where the Queen and the Dagda stood, watching the slaughter. "I'll get you the key. Just stop them!"

The Dagda raised his hand and immediately the Unseelie stopped their attack and stepped back. The Queen's subjects did the same. The Invisible Order—what was left of it—looked around in dull-eyed confusion. They drew together in bloodied clumps of humanity, cries of pain and anguish the only sounds in the predawn air.

"Bring the key, Emily Snow," said the Queen. "Bring it now or we kill every single one of them."

⇥ CHAPTER THIRTY-TWO ⇤

In which Emily faces the final choice.

SIX THIRTY IN THE MORNING
ON THE THIRD DAY OF EMILY'S ADVENTURES.

Emily retrieved the key.

She stood by the oak tree where she had buried it, staring at the wooden circle in her hands. She had lost. If she didn't give them the key, they would kill all those people.

But if you do give them the key, how many more will die?

Emily walked slowly back toward the hill. At the top, she paused and looked over the field of battle below her.

The members of the Order were dragging their wounded and dead into a circle defended by those who could still wield their weapons. But the fey weren't paying them any attention. Every single one of them was looking in her direction. She could sense their anticipation, their eagerness.

Emily couldn't believe how badly she had failed. After all

that she had been through to get the key before the fey did, here she was about to simply hand it over to them.

She started walking again. The ranks of the fey formed a solid wall before her, but as she approached, they peeled off to the side, opening a clear path into their midst. As she passed the first of them, she looked over her shoulder to see the fey closing in behind her, blocking off any chance of escape. So she was not walking a path, but rather moving through the mass of terrible creatures in a small circle of clear ground.

She reached the Queen and the Dagda, both of whom had their hands outstretched.

"Give it to me," commanded the Queen. "Or they all die."

"Emily. I can still give you your parents," said the Dagda, stepping forward.

As soon as he moved, the Queen moved as well, and Emily could hear a hiss of anger and unease running through the fey behind her. She realized that whatever pact had joined them in their fight against the Invisible Order had dissolved. Both sides wanted their hands on the key. Whoever opened the door would control the way to Faerie. And that was something the King and the Queen both wanted for themselves.

Emily looked up at the sky. Dawn was arriving, but it was hidden behind thick, gray clouds. As she stared upward, something light and feathery drifted down and landed on her forehead. Then another, then another.

It was snowing.

Emily held out her hand and watched the silent snow-flakes settle on her dirty palm.

"No work today," she whispered, then smiled.

The Queen frowned. "What did you say?"

But Emily didn't get a chance to answer.

"Emily Snow!" shouted a voice.

Everyone turned to look in the direction of the voice. At first there was nothing, no indication as to who had shouted.

Then Jack and William appeared over the rise.

Emily's eyes widened in horror. What were they doing? They were going to get killed! Emily opened her mouth to scream at them, to order them back.

But then a line of fey exploded into view behind them.

Emily blinked in astonishment. Jack and William lifted swords in the air and started to run. She saw Mr. Pemberton, with Corrigan sitting on the gnome's shoulders and holding on for dear life, sprinting right behind them. And there was Merrian lumbering onto the field of battle, a huge stone ax in his hands. Behind them came the Landed Gentry and others as well, creatures Emily didn't recognize.

"Jack!" she shouted joyfully. *"William!"*

"And Corrigan!" shouted the piskie, waving his bronze sword above his head. Mr. Pemberton stumbled as Corrigan accidentally poked him in the eye, but the gnome quickly

steadied himself as he was overtaken by a horde of shouting, screaming gnomes, all of them armed with swords and
dressed in immaculate suits.

"Kill them!" shouted the Dagda. "Kill every last one of the
traitors!"

And the fey launched into their second attack of the
morning.

But no sooner had the battle been joined than the surviving members of the Order launched an attack from the
left flank, so that the Dagda and the Queen's armies were
assailed on two sides. Confusion swept through their ranks.

Ravenhill grabbed Emily's arm and wrenched her around.
Emily fought desperately, but he was too strong for her. He
yanked the key from her grasp.

He quickly handed it to the Queen, then threw Emily to
the ground and turned his pistol on the Dagda, who was just
about to launch himself at the Queen.

"I really do not advise it," Ravenhill said. "Iron rounds,
don't you know. Nasty."

But Emily paid no attention to this. She only had eyes for
the Queen.

She was doing something with the key. She untwined and
then retied some of the roots that wrapped around the circle.
Her motions were precise and practiced, as if she had done
such a thing before. When she was finished, she turned to

the oak tree and placed the key in a hollow in the trunk. It fit perfectly.

A second later a dark hole opened up in the trunk, growing in size until it became an archway opening directly into the tree itself. The outline of the arch was uneven, forming around the seams and boles of the bark. It gave the impression that the hole had grown into place over hundreds of years instead of appearing just moments before.

A sallow light burst out of the tree, bathing them in a sickly glow the color of old bone. Emily squinted through the arch and found herself looking into a massive, decaying throne room. A bulbous, oversize moon cast its jaundiced glow through shattered windows, illuminating a chamber filled with dark, withered creatures. Emily stared in horror. It was as if someone had taken the fey and transformed them into nightmarish, misshapen versions of themselves.

A movement caught Emily's eye. She focused her attention on the rear of the room, where a figure sitting on a twisted black throne slowly stood up, looking in Emily's direction.

It looked like—

No. It couldn't be. She had to be mistaken.

But the more Emily squinted into the gate the more she realized she wasn't mistaken at all.

The figure now striding through the hordes of monstrous

fey was the mirror image of Queen Kelindria. It could have been her twin.

"Em!" called a voice.

Emily glanced over her shoulder and saw Jack, William, and Corrigan running toward her. She quickly turned her attention back to the tree and saw that the creatures were stirring, turning, and following the tall, pale figure of Kelindria as she strode toward the gate.

Emily wearily pushed herself up. She couldn't let this happen. It was her fault. It was her responsibility.

Emily moved slowly toward the tree, knowing what she had to do. She turned once, smiling sadly and waving good-bye to William. His eyes widened.

"Emily! No!" he screamed.

But Emily didn't listen. All of her attention was focused on the figure on the other side of the gate. The Faerie Queen (or whoever it was), paused just beyond the doorway and pointed a shaking finger at Emily, her face a mask of hatred and fury. The finger moved slowly through the gate.

Emily ran.

She ran past Ravenhill, who tried to grab her, and past the Dagda, who was looking through the gate in shock.

And finally she ran past the Queen, the real one, who let out such a screech of anger that Emily shuddered in fear.

The finger emerging through the gate became an arm.

Emily pushed past it, still hearing the Queen's cries behind her. She reached up and wrenched the key from its place in the bark. The door flickered, darkness and shadow replacing the pale yellow moonlight.

"No!" shouted the Queen, but it was too late. Emily covered her eyes and leapt through the door. She heard Jack shouting her name from somewhere close by. The sounds of battle in Hyde Park echoed loudly for a second.

Then stopped.

She was surrounded by utter blackness.

For a horror-filled second, she wondered if she had become trapped inside the tree, but then she was falling. Light flashed by, and voices, a whirlwind of sounds and sights: the clash of steel, the whinny of horses, a shout of surprise, of fear, a deep, horrific chuckle that sent shivers up her spine, searing heat, a face made from flames, a boy in a tunic holding a sword, a man who looked somehow familiar. There were other things she didn't understand, sights that flashed by too quickly to register.

Then she landed on the grass. Emily cried out, then lay still for a moment, trying to remember how to breathe.

She finally managed to push herself to her knees. She didn't recognize her surroundings, but she could hear the sounds of water lapping close by.

She staggered to her feet, and only then realized where she was.

She was standing on the bank of the Thames looking out over London. But it wasn't a London she was familiar with. The city was smaller, less sprawling than the one she knew. The buildings rested lower to the ground, huddled close together as if in fear of something. Off to her right, London Bridge stretched across the water. Houses and buildings clustered together along its path, climbing one atop the other to make the most of available space. Crowds milled about on the bridge, and she could see people standing beside stalls and barrows.

Emily looked around numbly. A warm wind buffeted her back, and something slapped against her leg. She looked down and saw it was a piece of paper. She picked it up. *The London Gazette,* it said. Emily's eyes scrolled across the primitive typeface, then froze when she saw the date.

From Monday, Septem 3, to Monday, Octob 26, 1666.

1666!

Emily dropped the paper and stared across the Thames in numb horror. Things slowly started to fall into place. Everything the Queen had said about waiting two hundred years for revenge. Everything Merlin had said about knowing her. It was all true. She really *had* been here. She *was* here.

Emily was startled by a series of thumps on the grass behind her. She whirled around, ready to run from whatever new horror awaited.

Except it wasn't anything horrific. In fact, it was the total opposite.

Jack, William, and Corrigan lay in an untidy heap on the grass. Corrigan was hitting Jack on the head.

"Get off me! How much do you weigh?"

William pushed himself to his knees and looked around with a dazed expression on his face. Emily ran forward and grabbed her startled brother in a fierce hug. After a few moments, he tried to push away.

"Em! I can't breathe."

Emily reluctantly released William. Jack was standing behind him, his arms outstretched.

"Don't I get a hug?"

Emily hesitated, then stepped forward and hugged Jack, as well. She released him and turned to Corrigan. The piskie brandished his bronze sword at her. "Don't even think about it. I have my dignity."

Emily smiled, looking at the others in amazement. "How did you get here?"

"Couldn't let you just run through on your own," said the piskie. "I'm the only one who can keep you out of trouble." He shrugged his thin shoulders. "So I followed you in. Then these two louts followed *me*. Just made it, too, before the door closed."

"Actually," said William, "that's not quite how it happened. I think Jack and I ran through first."

"Details, details," said Corrigan dismissively.

"You said 'just before the door closed,'" said Emily. "So we did it? The Queen's army won't get through?"

"No, girl," said Corrigan gently. "You saved London." He straightened up. "But you wouldn't have been able to do it without me, eh? How many times did I save your life?"

"What are you talking about?" snapped Jack. "You've been nothing but trouble from the get-go. We'd be better off without you."

"Oh, so that's how it is, is it? I'll have you know—" Corrigan stopped as he finally took in their surroundings. "Where are we?" he asked.

"London," said Emily. "Sometime between September third and October twenty-sixth."

Corrigan frowned, still looking around. "What year?" he asked slowly.

"Sixteen sixty-six."

"Sixteen sixty-six?" said Corrigan, his voice heavy with dread.

Emily shivered, glancing at William and Jack. They were both staring at the piskie, worried looks on their faces. "What is it? Corrigan, what's wrong?"

"This is when the war begins, Emily. This is when the Fire King tries to destroy London."

Emily felt sick. She stared at the buildings on the opposite shore, trying to imagine the flames raging throughout the city. The screams of the dying.

"The Great Fire of London," she whispered.

"The second war of the races," Corrigan whispered back.

Here ends *Rise of the Darklings*, Book One of The Invisible Order. Book Two, *The Fire King*, will chronicle Emily's encounters with the Order as she tries to help Christopher Wren and Merlin the Enchanter stop the evil that is known as the Fire King.

Turn the page for a sneak peek at the sequel,

THE FIRE KING

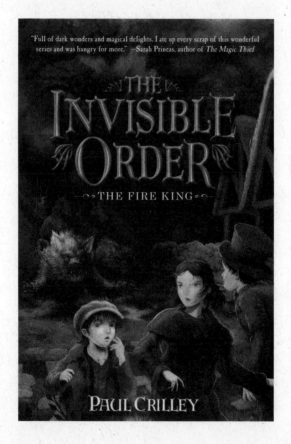

"Full of dark wonders and magical delights. I ate up every scrap of this wonderful series and was hungry for more." —Sarah Prineas, author of *The Magic Thief*

THE
INVISIBLE
ORDER
THE FIRE KING

PAUL CRILLEY

COMING FROM EGMONT USA IN SEPTEMBER 2011.

﹢﹦CHAPTER ONE﹦﹢

*London, 1666. In which Emily and Co. find themselves
in a spot of bother. A Murder of Ravens.*

Emily woke up in darkness.

She yawned, her mind going through the usual check-
list of hopes and fears that accompanied every awakening.
Would there be snow today? Would she get to the market
in time? Would she sell enough watercress to feed William
and herself?

She rolled lazily onto her back. Motes of dust glowed in
the sunlight that skewered through gaps in the wooden walls.
Emily frowned, sleepily confused. Wooden walls? Their
room in Cheapside didn't *have* wooden walls. And what on
earth was that *smell*?

Then it all came back to her in a rush of disjointed images.
The battle in Hyde Park. Grabbing the key from the Faerie

Gate just in time to stop the Faerie Queen's soldiers from invading London. And in the process, leaping through the gate and finding herself trapped here. In 1666. She quickly felt around beneath the old sacks that covered the dirt floor. The key was still there, safely hidden away.

It was only then that Emily realized how quiet it was. She sat up and looked around their hiding place—an old tanning shed on the north bank of the Thames. (Jack had suggested it. He said the smell of old animal hides would make sure no one bothered them.)

She was alone. The others had gone.

A wave of panic threatened to overwhelm her, but Emily struggled against it. *Keep calm*, she told herself. Obviously, they hadn't just deserted her. She had dozed off while they had all been talking about finding something to eat. The others must have simply slipped out to get some food.

But why had William gone? She had told him not to leave the shed. He was too young—only nine years old. The city would be far too dangerous for him.

He hadn't been happy with that. But then, he hadn't been happy with anything she had told him to do for a very long time. There had been a brief period of reconciliation after he, Corrigan, and Jack appeared through the gateway after defeating Queen Kelindria, but that hadn't lasted long, and he had quickly slipped back into his old ways of arguing with her whenever she tried to tell him what to do.

The door to the small shed opened slightly, then got stuck on the sacking that littered the ground. A mop of untidy hair appeared in the gap as Jack tried to see what was jamming the door. He shoved with his shoulder, pushing the gap wider, then slipped inside and pushed the door closed. He turned with a grin.

"I come bearing gifts," he proclaimed. His grin faltered as he took in the interior of the shed.

"Where's Will?"

"What do you mean? Isn't he with you?"

"No." Jack held up a bundle of grubby paper. "I went out to get food. Meat pastries." He looked dubiously at the paper. "At least, I *think* it's meat."

"Then where is he?"

Jack tore his gaze away from the pastries. "Probably wherever Corrigan is," he said darkly. "They seem to have taken quite a shine to each other. We need to watch that piskie, Snow. He's trouble."

Emily tended to agree. Corrigan *was* trouble, but not in the way Jack meant. He had a knack for getting into mischief, but that was about it. Yes, he had betrayed her to the Faerie Queen, but he also came back for her. He had rescued William and herself from the Queen's cells. That was what counted.

But that didn't matter to Jack. He and Corrigan had clashed from the moment they met, and that didn't look set to change anytime soon.

As to whose idea it was to sneak out of the shed while Emily slept—both Corrigan *and* William were capable of making such a rash decision.

"We should find them," she said. "Before they get into trouble."

"Agreed. But one of us should stay here. If they come back and find the shed empty, they'll just head right back into London again."

Jack was right. And as much as Emily wanted to feel as if she was doing something other than sitting around, Jack had already been into the city. She'd probably only get herself lost.

"Then you should go," she said. "But if you don't find them in an hour, come back so we can figure out what to do next."

Jack nodded and yanked the door all the way open. Hazy afternoon light spilled inside, illuminating moth-eaten pelts and three large barrels that had been shoved up against the sidewall. Outside, a dusty avenue lined with more half-ruined sheds led down to the brown waters of the Thames, the sun glinting on small waves as they lapped against the muddy riverbank.

Jack handed her the small package of pastries (Emily briefly thought about asking him where he got the money to buy them, but she wasn't sure she would like the answer, so decided against it), then hurried along the weed-choked road.

Emily watched until he disappeared behind one of the tumbledown shacks, then sat down on a smooth boulder outside the shed.

She fished around in her jacket and once again pulled out the pocket watch the Dagda, the Faerie King, had given her. The metal was covered in patterns so delicate they were hard to see unless you tilted the watch to catch the light. Emily gently rubbed her fingers across the engravings, then pressed the gold button at the top. The lid clicked open, revealing a circle of plain, dark glass. What did it mean? Had the Dagda tricked her after all? Back in Hyde Park the watch had shown Emily her ma and da, sitting in a room in an old castle, dragons circling overhead. But ever since she'd come through the Faerie Gate, all it showed was a blank face. How could she tell if the images had even been real? She'd been tricked and lied to over and over since this whole thing began. It was hard to know what the truth was anymore.

A loud caw echoed forlornly through the ramshackle buildings. Emily looked up, startled by the sound. A large raven was perched on the rotting roof of one of the sheds. But it wasn't like any raven Emily had ever seen. Instead of the normal black color, this one was totally white, with eyes that were a bright, startling blue. The bird tilted its head to the side, staring down at the package of pies in Emily's lap. It cawed again. This time, the caw sounded demanding, as if the bird was giving her an order.

Emily hesitated, then put the watch away and unwrapped the flimsy paper. She broke off a chunk of crumbly pastry and threw it onto the path. The raven let out a triumphant caw and flapped down from the roof, its pale beak stabbing violently at the food, throwing it up into the air and catching it before it touched the ground. Emily watched the bird with a mixture of curiosity and nervousness. It was the biggest raven she had ever seen. Its beak alone was about the length of her middle finger.

The bird finished the morsel of pastry. Then it tilted its head again so it could stare at her with one pale blue eye.

"No more for you," she said firmly. "Shoo." Emily tried to wave the raven away, but the bird simply followed the movements of her hands, watching expectantly for more food. When nothing was forthcoming, it hopped closer, snapping its beak rapidly together, making a *click-click click-click* noise that Emily found vaguely threatening. "Shoo," repeated Emily. "Away with you."

The bird ignored her and hopped even closer, still clicking its beak. Emily searched around for something to throw at it, but as she was doing so she saw Jack reappear at the end of the lane, followed closely by William and Corrigan.

Emily surged to her feet. The raven let out a startled cry and danced backward. It launched itself into the air and fluttered to the roof, all the while cawing its raucous displeasure. Emily ignored it and hurried toward the others. As she approached she could hear Corrigan complaining loudly from his position on Will's shoulders.

"I don't see what all the fuss is about," he snapped. "We went to look for food. What of it? What if you hadn't found anything for us? Then we'd all be starving."

"I *did* find something," replied Jack, grim-faced. "But *you* didn't."

Corrigan waved this observation away. "It was only a matter of time," he said. "We had to come back because William didn't want Emily to worry."

"Bit late for that," said Jack.

Emily met up with them halfway along the avenue. One look at Will's sullen face told her she shouldn't say anything. She knew that. But she couldn't help it. The words were out of her mouth before she had a chance to stop them.

"What were you thinking?" she snapped. "Oh, how silly of me. You *weren't* thinking, were you? That is patently obvious."

"It's not my fault if you fell asleep," responded William hotly. "Corrigan wanted to wake you up, but I said we should let you rest. I was doing you a favor!"

"Then don't! Don't do me any favors, William. Wandering

off like that was a foolish thing to do. What if something had happened? We'd have had no idea where you were."

"Nothing happ—" started Corrigan, but Emily just turned her glare on the piskie, and he quickly clamped his mouth shut.

"Anyway," said Jack uncomfortably. "We're all here now, eh? No harm done. Let's just eat our pastries, then we'll decide what to do next—"

"I can tell you what you'll be doing next," said a voice. "And it won't be eating. 'Less you can eat with a knife in your guts."

Emily whirled around. A girl who looked about the same age as Jack was leaning against one of the unused sheds. She wore a dirty shirt that might once have been white but had been washed so many times it had faded to a dull yellow. The shirt was tucked into leather breeches, which were in turn tucked into a pair of well-worn boots. Her outfit was topped off by a wide-brimmed hat with a white feather sticking jauntily from the top.

The girl was holding what looked to be a very sharp knife. She tossed it into the air, letting it turn end over end a few times before catching it again. She repeated this over and over, never once taking her eyes from the group.

After a brief moment to recover from his surprise, Jack sauntered forward, the cocky grin Emily always found so annoying flashing across his features. "Good day to you, miss.

Spring-Heeled Jack's the name," he said. "And who do I have the honor of addressing?"

The girl snorted, and for a moment she and Emily locked gazes. Emily only just stopped herself from rolling her eyes in commiseration.

"You have the honor of addressing Katerina Francesca. And most men bow when addressing me." She looked at him critically. "Although I see you are no more than a boy, so your lack of knowledge of polite etiquette is perhaps understandable."

Jack's smile slipped from his face. "Boy?" he spluttered. "You don't look any older than me!"

"Maturity doesn't come with age," said Katerina. "Something most wise people already know. But again, allowances must be made for your obvious lack of upbringing." For a moment the girl lost her haughty tone and frowned at Jack. "And what kind of a name is Spring-Heeled Jack? It's silly."

"It's not silly. It's what everyone calls me."

"Why? Don't they like you?"

Jack opened his mouth to respond, but Katerina raised a hand to stop him. "It doesn't matter. You will all come with me now."

Jack glanced over his shoulder at Emily. His look was half confused, half irritated, like he didn't know quite how to respond. Emily thought that maybe she should take a turn.

"Why should we go anywhere with you?" she asked.

Katerina smiled. "Because if you don't, you'll be killed where you stand."

"Oh, is that so?" snapped Jack. "And are you going to be the one doing this killing?"

He stepped forward, but before he had taken two steps, an army of children appeared from nowhere, stepping out of the shadows, emerging from between buildings, popping up on the broken roofs.

"Among others," said Katerina.

Actually, it wasn't quite *an army,* thought Emily, as she looked around for some means of escape. But it might as well have been. There were about thirty children, ranging from Will's age to a year or two older than Jack. Their clothing was ragged. Torn and dirty. They all had the familiar hollow-cheeked look that she was so used to seeing in London. A gang of street children.

Street children they may be, but they had blocked off all means of escape, surrounding them in a slowly constricting circle.

Jack was still standing a pace or two ahead of the others. Will tried to position himself in front of Emily, but she grabbed his arm and pushed him behind her, nearly knocking Corrigan off his shoulder in the process.

She studied the children as they approached. They were all armed, gripping knives and short swords. This surprised Emily. The swords looked like they were worth something. Why didn't they sell them for money?

"What do you want with us?" asked Emily. "We haven't harmed you."

"You're a traitor," said Katerina. "And we hunt down traitors. It's our job."

"What are you talking about?" snapped Jack. "A traitor to who?"

Katerina blinked in surprise. "To the human race, of course."

"The human . . ." Jack looked around to see if anyone else knew what Katerina was talking about. Emily simply shrugged, her eyes scanning the ranks of children for a gap through which they could run. She caught sight of movement on one of the roofs. It was the white raven, perched on a broken chimney and watching them with its unsettling blue eyes.

There was a flutter of wings, and from out of the clear sky came a second white raven. It landed on the chimney next to the first. They leaned toward each other and bumped heads as if in greeting, then turned their attention back to what was happening below them.

Strange, thought Emily absently. She'd never seen a white

raven before today, and here she was seeing two at the same time. *They must be from the same family, surely?*

"You seem pretty caught up on etiquette," said Jack to Katerina. "So why don't you explain to us exactly why you think we're traitors."

Katerina leveled her knife directly at William. "Because of him."

William's eyes widened in surprise. "Me? What have I done?"

"Stop playing the fools," snapped Katerina. "You know perfectly well who I'm talking about."

And then it struck Emily. She scanned the faces that surrounded them. The angry, fearful, hateful faces. They weren't looking at William. They were all looking at one thing, and one thing only.

Corrigan.

They were talking about Corrigan.

"You can see him?" exclaimed Emily. How was that possible? Humans couldn't see the fey unless they were given the second sight. A few, like Emily, had natural talents, but not so many as now surrounded them. It didn't make any sense.

"Why do you want to hurt him?" asked William, stepping out from behind Emily. "He's done nothing to harm you."

"Give me a chance," muttered Corrigan. "I've only just met them."

"He doesn't need to *do* anything," said Katerina. "His existence is crime enough. Our fight is against *all* the fey. And against those who associate with them," she added pointedly. "That is our charter."

Emily was about to ask about this charter when an odd sound distracted her. It was like a sheet, billowing and rippling in the wind. She looked up to where the sound was coming from and took a fearful step back.

The sound wasn't a sheet rippling in the wind. It was the sound of wings. White ravens, hundreds of them, were descending from the sky to settle on the roofs of the dilapidated structures all around them. As soon as they landed, they furled their wings and gazed at the confrontation taking place below them, their blue eyes alert.

Katerina followed Emily's gaze. As soon as the girl spotted the ravens (and as soon as the ravens had *seen* her spot them), they started snapping their beaks as the first one had done when trying to get Emily's pastry. *Click-click. Click-click. Click-click.*

Emily shivered. It was an unsettling experience, to say the least. The white ravens staring down at them while the clicking and snapping eddied through the ranks of the birds like a wave in the ocean.

"Oh, that can't bode well," said Corrigan, staring up at the birds.

Katerina whirled back to face her gang. "The enemy is upon us!" she shouted. "Ready yourselves."

The order was hardly necessary. As soon as the birds had been spotted, Katerina's gang broke away from the circle they held around Emily and the others to find positions that weren't so exposed. And while they readied themselves, the *click-click* sound rained down on them from above, getting louder and louder as more and more white ravens descended from the sky.

"I don't know what's going on here," Jack said, "but now would be the perfect time to leave, don't you think?"

Emily nodded. Jack pointed to a gap between two of the old sheds and was just about to cross the dusty lane when the clacking noise suddenly stopped. The abrupt silence seemed to echo around them, the absence of sound louder than anything that had come before.

Emily looked up at the ravens.

They had all turned to look toward the end of the avenue, where the lane turned aside and followed the muddy banks of the Thames.

Slowly, ever so slowly, Emily followed their gaze.

A dark figure was rising from the water, a figure draped in a black, sodden cloak. The figure rose to its full height and pulled the hood back to reveal the wrinkled face of an old crone, her eyes the cold, uncaring black of the deep ocean.

The murky river water dribbled from her mouth and nose as a second figure rose up from the water, her slimy, lank hair framing a skeletal, pale-green face.

Emily felt her breath catch in her throat.

Black Annis and Jenny Greenteeth.

⊱Acknowledgments⊰

First of all, many thanks to Julie Czerneda and Jana Pannicia for asking me to contribute a story to their anthology, *Under Cover of Darkness*, way back in 2005. Their invite helped crystallize a lot of research I had been doing into Victorian London and faerie lore, and *Rise of the Darklings* grew from that original short story.

Also, a huge shout-out to the amazing team over at Egmont USA. Alison, Mary, Greg, and Robert have been immensely helpful and supportive since I joined the Egmont family. But extra thanks have to go to Elizabeth Law, Regina Griffin, Ruth Katcher, and Nico Medina. Ruth and Nico, for editing and copyediting, and helping to mold the story into something a lot stronger than it originally was, and Regina and Elizabeth, whose confidence in the book has been an inspiration from the very beginning.

And finally, *mucho* thanks to my amazing agent, Ginger Clark, for somehow knowing when to show sympathy for my many writerly paranoias, and when to tell me to shut the hell up and get back to writing.